Knit One, Kill Two

Maggie Sefton

BERKLEY PRIME CRIME, NEW YORK

THE BERKLEY PUBLISHING GROUP
Published by the Penguin Group
Penguin Group (USA) Inc.
375 Hudson Street, New York, New York 10014, USA
Penguin Group (Canada), 10 Alcorn Avenue, Toronto, Ontario M4V 3B2, Canada
(a division of Pearson Penguin Canada Inc.)
Penguin Books Ltd., 80 Strand, London WC2R 0RL, England
Penguin Group Ireland, 25 St. Stephen's Green, Dublin 2, Ireland (a division of Penguin Books Ltd.)
Penguin Group (Australia), 250 Camberwell Road, Camberwell, Victoria 3124, Australia
(a division of Pearson Australia Group Pty. Ltd.)
Penguin Books India Pvt. Ltd., 11 Community Centre, Panchsheel Park, New Delhi—110 017, India
Penguin Group (NZ), Cnr. Airborne and Rosedale Roads, Albany, Auckland 1310, New Zealand
(a division of Pearson New Zealand Ltd.)
Penguin Books (South Africa) (Pty.) Ltd., 24 Sturdee Avenue, Rosebank, Johannesburg 2196,
South Africa

Penguin Books Ltd., Registered Offices: 80 Strand, London WC2R 0RL, England

This is a work of fiction. Names, characters, places, and incidents either are the product of the author's imagination or are used fictitiously, and any resemblance to actual persons, living or dead, business establishments, events, or locales is entirely coincidental.

KNIT ONE, KILL TWO

A Berkley Prime Crime Book / published by arrangement with the author

PRINTING HISTORY
Berkley Prime Crime mass-market edition / June 2005

Copyright © 2005 by Margaret Aunon.
Cover design by Rita Frangie.
Cover illustration by Chris O'Leary.
Interior text design by Stacy Irwin.

ISBN: 978-0-425-20359-0

Berkley Prime Crime Books are published by The Berkley Publishing Group,
a division of Penguin Group (USA) Inc.,
375 Hudson Street, New York, New York 10014.
The name BERKLEY PRIME CRIME and the BERKLEY PRIME CRIME design
are trademarks belonging to Penguin Group (USA) Inc.

PRINTED IN THE UNITED STATES OF AMERICA

20   19   18   17   16   15   14   13   12   11   10

Acknowledgments

A thousand thanks to Shirley Ellsworth, the inspired owner of *Lambspun of Colorado* in Fort Collins, Colorado, the knitting shop I used as a model for this series and the place I first "fell down the rabbit hole" into this fascinating wonderland of color and texture. Shirley and her staff of gifted teachers and fiber artists never ran out of patience with my questions or encouragement for my beginning efforts. Thanks also to the Tuesday night knitting group for their rowdy and wonderful brainstorming of titles for this series of novels. And special thanks to Kristi for her last-minute artwork.

Thanks also to my agent, Jessica Faust, for her unceasing encouragement and support to write this knitting mystery. And special thanks to my wonderful editor, Samantha Mandor, for helping to bring Kelly and all her friends to life on the page.

Special thanks to my four daughters, my mom, and all my dear friends who've always believed in me and supported my writing dreams. And thanks to my ninety-two-year-old aunt, Ann, whose "quilt of memories" hangs on my bedroom wall.

And a special pat on the head to my dog, Carl, who's the model for Kelly's golf-ball chasing pet Rottweiler. I must admit that fictional Carl is much better behaved than real-life Carl, with or without golf balls.

One

Kelly Flynn nosed her car onto the gravel driveway and pulled to a stop in front of the familiar little house perched beside a golf course. Everything looked the same. Aunt Helen's beige stucco, red tile–roofed cottage looked as cozy and inviting as always. Golfers were scattered about the lush greens, doggedly working to improve their games. In the background the Colorado Rocky Mountains, still snow-capped in late spring, loomed over the entire scene. It was all picture-postcard pretty, just like Kelly remembered, except for one thing. Aunt Helen was dead—murdered a week ago in her picturesque cottage.

A "burglary gone bad" the police called it. Kelly's gut still twisted at the thought. Aunt Helen would have fought back. Kelly knew she would. Even though she was thin as a stick and a foot shorter than Kelly, she was wiry and tough. And she had spirit. Spunk. She'd never go down without a fight. Not Aunt Helen. No way.

Kelly felt tears rise to her eyes again as she remembered her aunt's favorite admonition: "Never give up,

Kelly-girl. If you want something bad enough, don't you ever give up." The tears escaped, running down Kelly's cheeks, and she swiped them away with the back of her hand. She'd never even had the chance to say good-bye. At least with her dad, Kelly'd been able to tell him how much she loved him. Cancer might be an ugly way to die, but it was slower. Murder was a thief in the night, creeping in to steal away valuable loved ones. And this thief stole the only mother Kelly had ever known.

A cold, wet nose shoved against Kelly's neck, and she turned to pat the shiny black Rottweiler head resting beside her shoulder. Carl always sensed her moods. "Don't worry, boy, I haven't forgotten you. You're looking at that grass, right?" She pointed to the manicured golf course, stretching from her aunt's property all the way to the river that meandered diagonally through the scenic college town north of Denver.

Kelly let herself gaze. It had been six months since she'd returned to Fort Connor, where she spent her early childhood. Every time she returned, she wondered how she'd ever make herself leave again. The sky was bluer here, the air was cleaner, and the sun was brighter by a mile. "A mile high to be exact," as Aunt Helen used to say. What a gorgeous day. If her aunt was still alive, she and Kelly would take one of their favorite hikes along a trail in the nearby Poudre Canyon. How could it be so beautiful with Helen gone?

Carl whined to get her attention, clearly eager to explore. "Okay, boy, but you can't run on the course. The greenskeeper wouldn't appreciate your lifting a leg on every tee." Carl rolled his soft brown eyes to her in pleading mode.

"Nope. You'll just have to make do with the yard." Kelly opened the car door and slid out, grabbing a leash as she did.

Carl's ears perked up at the magic jingle, and he gave an excited yelp. That meant outside and play. Snapping the leash to his red collar, Kelly headed toward the small backyard. Tall cottonwood trees surrounded the property, shading both house and yard. Flower boxes were already planted, even though Kelly knew the frost date in northern Colorado was a yearly gamble. Somehow, Helen always won out. Her green thumb or gardener's luck could overcome even Colorado's capricious weather.

Kelly made a mental note to water the plants that evening. She wasn't about to let Helen's plants die with her. She swung the back gate open and ushered Carl inside. "It isn't the golf course, boy, but it's bigger than your yard for sure," she said, referring to her postage stamp–size townhouse yard on the outskirts of Washington, D.C. Carl didn't waste time. He took off the moment his leash was unsnapped, nose to the ground.

The sound of another car coming down the gravel driveway caught Kelly's attention, and she turned to see a red minivan drive up to the larger stucco and red tile–roofed house across the drive. A woman exited the van and entered the sprawling mirror-image of Helen's cottage.

Both houses and the assorted outbuildings nearby occupied a pie-shaped wedge of land that clung to the corner of a busy intersection. Kelly remembered when both streets were country roads cutting through fields of sugar beets and sheep farms. Now, a big box discount store swallowed the opposite corner and townhouses clustered across the street.

At least her aunt and uncle had sold their farmland to the city for a golf course and kept only the cottage and its yard. If she squinted her eyes hard enough, Kelly could block out the golfers and picture her uncle heading to the barn years ago when he was still alive.

"Kelly, is that you?" a woman's voice called.

Kelly shut the gate, knowing Carl would be occupied for hours identifying scents. She turned and recognized Mimi Shafer walking across the driveway. Mimi owned the knitting and needlework shop that now occupied what was once Aunt Helen's and Uncle Jim's farmhouse. Her aunt had been ecstatic about the arrangement, since she was an expert knitter and quilter, but Kelly had always felt vaguely resentful. She remembered when the house was filled with Aunt Helen and Uncle Jim—and memories. But Uncle Jim's long illness changed all that.

Now, Kelly felt nothing but gratitude. Mimi had been Aunt Helen's closest friend and had never left Kelly's side during yesterday's service. She gave names to faces and helped Kelly stand and sit through a liturgy that was no longer familiar.

Kelly straightened her white blouse and navy skirt. Not as tailored as her usual CPA firm attire, but sober enough for a lawyer meeting. She couldn't wait until she could change into a casual top and slacks, maybe even shorts if it stayed warm. Ever since she got back, she'd been dressed up and meeting people. Just like the office. But Colorado meant sunshine and mountains and freedom to Kelly. And that meant shorts, a T-shirt, and sneakers.

She brushed her chin-length dark-brown hair behind her ear and checked the barrette in back. Kelly'd rushed through her shower and dressing in order to fit in a morning run along the trail that ran beside the motel. She'd barely checked the mirror. After yesterday's tears, she needed to clear her head. Running always helped her think.

She waved to Mimi. "I just thought I'd let Carl use Helen's backyard today while I go to all those . . . you know, meetings. Lawyer, banker, and all that."

"That's a great idea. I'm sure he's tired of being cooped up in the motel room," Mimi said with a bright smile. Her sun-streaked brown hair feathered softly around her face. Fiftyish, slender, and pretty, she wore a powder-blue straight dress that accentuated her trim figure. But what really drew Kelly's attention was the open-weave vest she wore on top; the loosely fixed knots held the yarns together. Varying shades of blue traveled all the way to green and back again. The effect was stunning.

"Do you have time for a cup of tea or coffee?" Mimi asked, obviously hoping for a yes.

Kelly hesitated, running through her mental daytimer. That and the Greenwich Meridian time clock in her head kept Kelly on task. She depended on that clock. Back in the firm, everyone kept track of their time in tenths of an hour—six-minute intervals—billable hours. Consequently, Kelly was seldom late. "I have a few minutes. My appointment with the lawyer isn't until ten."

"Oh, darn, I was hoping we'd have more time," Mimi said, her smile momentarily missing. "I've been dying to show you the shop, but I guess it'll just have to wait until later today. Why don't we step over to the café?" She gestured toward the pathway leading around the farmhouse.

Kelly completely forgot that a bistro-style café had opened in the former kitchen and dining room of the farmhouse since her last visit. As they followed the flower beds and flagstone path, Kelly was astonished to see the café also spilled out into the shady backyard. Surrounded by high stucco walls, the entire patio was private, secluded from the outside. The whole setting was delightful and charming, Kelly had to admit.

Mimi chose a table and sat down, motioning to a nearby waitress as Kelly settled into a wrought-iron chair. "This is really quite nice. I like what they've done here," Kelly surprised herself by saying. Noticing the many tables filled with customers lingering over late breakfasts and brunch, she asked, "How's it doing? Financially, I mean. I know how hard it is for small restaurants to make it." As a beginning accountant years ago, Kelly had had several restaurants to worry about. "Shoe box clients" she used to call them, because they always kept their accounts in shoe boxes for some reason.

"Actually, quite well, according to Pete," said Mimi. "He's the young man who had the idea of turning this whole area into a restaurant. Somehow, he managed to convince the management company that owns it to invest in used equipment, and he volunteered all the labor. He put his heart and soul into this place." She shook her head. "Let's hope all that hard work hasn't been wasted . . . for both of us."

Intrigued by the cryptic remark, Kelly was about to respond when the waitress appeared. She had shoulder-length reddish-brown hair that curved around a pretty face. "Hi, Mimi," she said with a bright smile, then turned a warm gaze to Kelly.

"Kelly, this is Jennifer Stroud," Mimi introduced. "She was also a friend of Helen's."

"Kelly, I just wanted to say how shocked we were at Helen's death. She was a wonderful lady. I used to see her over at the shop almost every day, and she was always so sweet and loving. We'll all miss her a lot."

The comments caught Kelly unprepared, and she felt her eyes grow suddenly moist. She glanced down at her napkin. "Thank you. You're very kind."

Jennifer reached out and patted Kelly's arm. "Hey, that's okay. Let me bring you something. I know Mimi's order already. Earl Grey, cream. How about you?"

"Coffee, black and strong," Kelly said with a smile, which helped chase away the tears.

"Down with decaf, right?" Jennifer winked as she flipped the notepad closed. "Be right back."

"I think she was at the funeral yesterday, but I really can't remember too much," Kelly said as she watched Jennifer skirt between tables, glad for the chance to compose herself.

"Oh, yes, she was there with the other knitting shop regulars."

"Regulars?" Kelly asked, "Who are they?"

"We've got lots of knitting and needlework groups that meet regularly at the shop during the week. Some are organized, some just happen, like Jennifer's group. They're a bunch of women, many of whom are around your age, who meet after work a couple of times a week or more. Of course, anybody who shows up is welcome to sit in with any group. That's how Helen met Jennifer and the others."

Kelly could easily picture that. Helen was always knitting, and loved nothing better than to share her passion. It was a shame Kelly had proven to be such an unwilling student. Now, she was sorry she'd always feigned impatience whenever her aunt had tried to coax her into learning to knit.

"I know Aunt Helen enjoyed that," Kelly mused. "She loved meeting new people. And living across from the shop, she could make new friends almost every day. Every week when I'd call her, she'd always tell me something funny she'd heard, usually from some friend." Kelly would miss those phone calls.

"Helen had lots of friends, as you saw yesterday at the service. Everyone loved her, and we want to help you in whatever way we can, Kelly. Several people have offered to help go through the house when you're ready."

Kelly groaned inwardly. That unpleasant chore had almost slipped her mind. Whenever it had appeared, she'd shoved it away. At least having people with her would make the task easier and less painful. "I confess I've deliberately not thought about that chore," she admitted. "I guess I'm avoiding going into the house after, well, you know."

"I understand, Kelly."

"Thanks so much. I really appreciate your help. I remember how hard it was going through my dad's things, and I'd been prepared for his death."

Mimi reached out and patted Kelly's arm. "Well, you're not alone this time, Kelly. We're here to help you."

Jennifer's cheerful bustle and the inviting tray of coffee and tea arrived just when Kelly felt her eyes grow moist again. After the funeral yesterday she thought she'd cried herself dry. Apparently there was a well inside her that ran deeper than she knew.

There was no one left anymore. Her dad, three years ago. Now, Aunt Helen. Her entire family was gone.

"Here you go," Jennifer announced as she set the tea and coffee in place. "Pete even threw in one of those wicked cinnamon rolls on the house."

"Ohhh, that's cruel," Mimi groaned. "He knows I can't have the sugar."

Kelly eyed the tempting coil of golden, flaky, sweet dough slathered with a sugary cream-cheese icing that drizzled down the sides. She'd forgotten Fort Connor's community weakness for these oversized breakfast buns. The bakery that specialized in making them kept the calorie count a secret.

"It's still warm," tempted Jennifer with a grin.

Her normal willpower was either sound asleep or stunned into silence at the sight of the huge pastry. So, with no nagging voice in her head, Kelly picked up the fork. "What the heck. I'll need it for all those meetings. Lawyers are depressing."

"Absolutely," Jennifer concurred, clearly enjoying Kelly's quick capitulation. "Besides, you're tall and slender. It'll never show. On me, it'd be on my hips in five minutes."

"Oh, right," Kelly retorted with a grin. "Why don't you share it me?"

Jennifer rolled her eyes. "Don't tempt me. I was born with a sweet tooth."

"Seriously, I can't finish this monster all by myself." She sliced the bun in half and pushed one half to the side of her plate.

Jennifer glanced at the pastry. "We're not supposed to eat with customers."

Kelly sensed weakness. She took a big bite, closed her eyes, and let out a dramatic, *"Mmmmmmmmmm!"*

"That's it. Priorities." Jennifer laughed and grabbed her portion.

"Which are?" Mimi teased.

Jennifer paused after swallowing. "Right now, sugar. It's gonna be a busy day."

Kelly polished off her share and reached for the coffee, which was surprisingly rich and dark. She drank in the blissful enjoyment of the strong brew. "Yum, this is really good for the plain stuff. My compliments."

"That's Eduardo's doing. He's our cook and insists on making the coffee every morning. I think he throws in espresso or chicory or shoelaces or who knows what. But it'll wake you up, for sure."

"Bless him, and tell him I'll be back." The timer went off inside her head, and Kelly drained the cup. "Speaking of that, I have to go. Lawyers get all pinched around the edges if you're late." She scooted back her chair and brushed telltale sugar flakes off her skirt. "Oh, Mimi, I almost forgot. Could you fill a bowl with water for Carl, please? I fed him this morning, but I forgot to grab his water dish."

"No problem. I'll give him some food come dinnertime, too, so don't rush. And make sure you stop in the shop when you return. I can't wait to show you everything we've done. You haven't been in since we opened four years ago." Mimi exuded pride. "You'll be surprised, I think."

"I look forward to it. Thanks, Mimi," Kelly said as she backed away from the table. Glancing at Jennifer as she headed for the pathway, Kelly waved. "Nice meeting you, Jennifer."

"Oh, you'll see me later at the shop. With the others. Good luck with the lawyer."

Kelly hastened to her car. She'd dutifully let Mimi show off her shop, for Aunt Helen's sake, if nothing else. Kelly couldn't knit her way out of a paper bag. So all that knitting stuff would be lost on her. Her aunt had tried several times to instruct Kelly when she was growing up and even as an adult, but it never seemed to take. Kelly would fumble the needles and drop the yarn—whatever it took to appear completely incompetent. There were so many more fun things to do outside on the farm, she just couldn't sit still long enough to learn.

Besides, all those different kinds of stitches looked complicated to Kelly. Knitting here, purling there. All that yarn, needles busily working away, stitch after stitch, row after row. Looked like a lot of work to Kelly. She just didn't have that kind of patience. The only patience she'd ever had was for numbers. Numbers stayed put on paper. They didn't fall off the end of the needles.

Oh yes, Kelly thought, as she backed her car out of the parking space, numbers were far less confusing than knitting.

Lawrence Chambers tapped his gold-rimmed pen against the leather desk pad as he scanned the documents before him. Kelly used the opportunity to study the lawyer, who was the same age as her aunt. His gray hair shone silver as a stray morning sunbeam crossed the desk. Chambers had been Aunt Helen's trusted lawyer and close friend for a lifetime.

"Thanks to Helen's foresight, you should have no problem handling any expense involved with the estate," he spoke up. "You're co-signer on both bank accounts, checking and savings, as well as the safe-deposit box. It was a smart move, considering you're her only heir."

"Aunt Helen told me four years ago what her wishes were. I've always tried to oblige her in whatever way I could."

Chambers glanced up from the papers in his hand and smiled across the large walnut desk. Kelly noticed his faded blue eyes were kind.

"Helen appreciated everything you did for her. She told me so many times."

Kelly glanced away. "She was like a mom to me, Mr. Chambers. You know that. Besides, when my dad died three years ago, I promised him I'd take care of her. She was his only living relative." Guilt twinged inside. She'd never broken a promise to her dad in her whole life.

Chambers set down the papers, watching Kelly, then gestured to the wall. "That's hers, you know."

Kelly studied the framed quilted scene that had caught her eye earlier. Deep, rich browns and greens portrayed a small house nestled in the mountains, surrounded by tall evergreens. "I thought that might be her work. It's so vibrant."

"Yes, she did that from a photograph of the mountain cabin our family has had for years." He smiled. "She surprised us with it on our anniversary. That was Helen. Always doing for others. If she wasn't stitching for someone she knew, she'd be knitting for the homeless shelter."

"Yes, I know. I'm the one who used to buy the yarn online to save her money." A spark of anger flared suddenly. "It doesn't seem right, does it, Mr. Chambers. My aunt was murdered by some vagrant, exactly the sort of person she tried to help. Where's the justice in that?"

Chambers clasped his hands on top of the documents. "There is none, Kelly. This is one of those horrible, awful acts of random violence."

Kelly stared at the floor-to-ceiling walnut bookcases that lined one wall. "The officer told me this was a 'burglary gone bad.' She said this guy came into Helen's house that night, saw her purse and grabbed it. Then, supposedly Helen came out and saw him, screamed, and he strangled her. Then he ran off."

"Yes, that's exactly what the police told me. Apparently this man was a drunk and a vagrant and was always getting into trouble. He must have come into the house, grabbed her purse, and when Helen came out," his voice became strained, "he killed her for it." He sighed. "Thank goodness he was too drunk to be smart. The police saw him run away from the scene, so they caught him right away."

Kelly leaned forward in her chair and eyed Chambers. Something he'd said. "That's a little different from what the police told me. They said they'd seen this guy 'near the house,' not coming from it. Are you sure that's what they told you?"

Chambers pondered. "I'm fairly certain the detective who spoke with me said they captured the suspect fleeing the scene. Yes, that's exactly what he said. 'Fleeing the scene.' And I took that to mean he was coming from the house."

"Do you remember who you spoke with, Mr. Chambers? The woman who called me was a community relations officer and wasn't involved with the case."

"Oh, yes, I spoke with Lieutenant Morrison. He's in charge. A very experienced detective, from what I've heard. Very thorough."

Kelly opened her portfolio and wrote the name on a legal pad. "I'm sure you're right, Mr. Chambers. I mean, this guy had to be lurking around Aunt Helen's house before he came in. Looking in the windows or something." She closed the portfolio with a snap. "He must have been drunk. Why else would he have tried to steal from a woman who never carried more than twenty dollars in her purse?" A bitter note crept into her voice. It felt good to release it.

Chambers peered at Kelly over his glasses with a worried frown. "Well, uh, she may have had more in her purse—"

"Oh, no, sir," Kelly countered. "She never had more than twenty bucks and change at any one time. She always used her debit card because it kept her on a budget. And I should know, Mr. Chambers, because I drew up her budget and kept her accounts every month. She was still paying off some of Uncle Jim's medical bills, so she was very careful."

Chambers' lined face creased even more. "Didn't she tell you about the . . . the, uh, money she was borrowing?"

Kelly blinked. Surely she couldn't have heard the lawyer right. "Borrowing? Helen wasn't borrowing any money. Remember, I kept her accounts. I would know."

"I'm afraid she did. Just before she died."

Kelly stared back at him, incredulous. "*What? Where . . . I mean, who . . . how much?*"

"Twenty thousand dollars," Chambers said in a pained voice.

"Twenty thousand dollars!" Kelly sat bolt upright. "But why? And . . . and where would Helen borrow that kind of money, anyway? She was living on Jim's state pension and Social Security."

"The only place she could, Kelly. She refinanced her house. And went to one of those predatory lenders to do it." He shook his head, sadly. "I advised her against it, but she wouldn't listen. She said she needed it and would talk to me later. I assumed she was giving it to you, that you needed it for something."

"*Me?*" Kelly shot back. "I'd never ask Aunt Helen for money. I'd starve first."

Chambers sank back into his leather armchair. "Oh, my . . . oh, my," he said, clearly troubled. "I thought the money was for you, that's why I didn't worry too much when she said she needed it. After all, you're her only living relative."

Kelly stared at the diplomas that lined the wall behind Chambers' desk. This was impossible. It made no sense. Her aunt wouldn't even consider such a risky move without consulting Kelly. "This is crazy, Mr. Chambers. Aunt Helen was a sensible woman, you know that. She'd never do such a thing. Why . . . why, we just refinanced her house three years ago to pay off most of Uncle Jim's medical bills. We got a really low rate. Perfect for her. I was going to help her pay off the mortgage so she'd have it free and clear in ten years." Her hand shot out in frustration. "She wouldn't . . . she couldn't have done this stupid thing."

Chambers took off his glasses and rubbed his eyes but said nothing.

Anger flashed through Kelly, right up her spine. "Wait a minute. Do you think some sleazy con artist got his claws in Aunt Helen? Tricked her into some wretched investment scheme? I'd told her not to even talk to those weasels if they called."

"No, no, Helen was too smart for that," he dismissed the threat with a wave. "She and I frequently discussed some of the scams out there for the unwary, especially vulnerable seniors."

"When did she talk to you? When did she tell you what she was going to do?"

"About three weeks ago. She called to tell me she was refinancing the house because she needed money and asked my recommendation for a lender. Apparently she'd already been turned down by her current mortgage company and two others. There was no more equity left."

"I know, we used it all three years ago."

"Well, I asked how much she needed, thinking I'd lend it to her myself. When she told me twenty thousand dollars, I was shocked and told her so. I asked what on earth she could need that much money for, and she refused to answer. Said she'd talk to me later and hung up. I didn't even hear from her again until last Friday, the very day she was killed."

"And what did she say then?" Kelly probed.

"That's when she told me she'd found some Denver mortgage company that was only too glad to write up an above-value mortgage. She wouldn't tell me the interest rate. It must have been awful. But she did say she got the check for twenty thousand dollars. It never occurred to me she'd cash it." Chambers leaned over his desk and sank his head in both hands. "Good Lord. That's what got her killed. All that money sitting in her purse. Oh, Helen, why? *Why?*" His voice cracked this time.

Kelly pondered for a moment, giving Chambers time to

collect himself. She was still trying to make sense of everything she'd heard. Her logical mind didn't want to accept her aunt's illogical actions. It was totally out of character. Why would she put herself upside down in her mortgage at her age? Especially since she'd had to refinance only three years ago to pay off most of Uncle Jim's medical bills. And why on earth would she take all that cash home with her?

The shock of her aunt's murder had been enough to occupy Kelly's thoughts the entire two thousand-mile drive to Colorado. But now that the funeral was over and she had more time to think, Kelly began to notice details. Details that didn't belong. After all, that's what she did for a living. In her consulting role with a large accounting firm, Kelly analyzed a corporation's financial statements looking for anything that jumped out and made her buzzer go off. She'd never imagined that she'd have to turn that same concentration on uglier matters so close to home.

Waiting another moment, Kelly gently asked, "Mr. Chambers, have you spoken to the police? Did you tell them all this, I mean about the money and all?"

He lifted his red-rimmed eyes and cleared his throat. "No. I would never divulge Helen's private business. That's privileged," he sniffled.

"Then I think they need to know there was a lot more money stolen than they originally thought. I'll call this Lieutenant Morrison as soon as I leave here." Picking up her portfolio, Kelly stood and deliberately let her voice assume the official business tone she used so often. That would give Chambers something to hang on to. "Thank you, Mr. Chambers, for everything you've done and everything you've tried to do to help my aunt. I'm going over to the bank right now and check the accounts. And I'll look into this new loan as well."

Chambers straightened and rose. "That's a good idea . . . oh, wait a minute. I think I wrote down the name." He paged through the daytimer on his desk, scanning the pages. "Yes, here it is. U-Can-Do-It Mortgage in Denver." He peered at the daytimer while Kelly wrote the information in her notebook. "Ohhh, yes ... there *is* something else. Here's the note. Helen also said she was coming in soon to talk about her property. She wanted to make sure it all went to the city for gardens in case you didn't want to live in Fort Connor. But she didn't want to donate the land. It was to be sold, with you receiving all the proceeds."

Kelly stared blankly at him. Another surprise. "Gardens? Really? She never mentioned that."

"Yes, that surprised me, too." Chambers shook his head. "But, of course, she never got the chance to come in for the appointment. So you're free to sell the property if you choose."

"But that was her wish, apparently," Kelly mused out loud.

"Apparently so. She loved you very much, Kelly."

With that, Kelly knew she had to leave. If she misted up, Chambers would lose it again, and that would be embarrassing. Not so much for her, but for the older gentleman. "Thank you, again, Mr. Chambers," she said, and headed for the door.

"You're welcome, Kelly. And, I'm sure you'll find those mortgage papers in Helen's house. Take care, my dear."

Kelly waved and made a swift exit. She was sure she'd find the papers in the cottage, but the thought of going into the house where Aunt Helen was murdered still chilled her. Kelly hastened to the parking lot as she searched her cell phone's directory for the number of the Fort Connor police department.

Two

Carl was already at the fence waiting for Kelly when she pulled into the driveway. "Hey, boy," Kelly called out as she slammed the car door and headed for the yard. The sun angled over the mountains, or foothills as the locals called them, and a blazing ray of sunshine hit her right in the eyes. She always forgot how bright mile-high sunlight could be.

Kelly reached over the fence to pat Carl. He responded by placing both front paws on the fence so she could scratch his head. "I'll bet you had a better day than I did, Carl. Playing outside, chasing squirrels." At the mention of his newly discovered pastime, Carl glanced over his shoulder. "Remind me to take you to Denver and introduce you to that sleazy lender." She leaned over and let Carl lick her chin. "He was really sarcastic on the phone today. I'll bet he wouldn't be so rude sitting across from a Rottweiler." Carl obliged with a woof and Kelly laughed. The first time she'd laughed since, well, since this morning when she watched Jennifer snatch the cinnamon roll.

She turned toward the shop and checked her watch. It was after 6:00 pm. Boy, she really didn't feel like having a tour right now. She was starving and hadn't eaten since she'd grabbed some chips on the way to the bank. And after this afternoon's bleak news from the lender, she'd lost her appetite entirely.

It was back in full force now, and Kelly's stomach growled on cue. She glanced at the shop's front door. It used to be the side door for Helen's and Jim's house, with a great shady patio right in front, facing the fields and barns. Kelly remembered Helen sitting in the shade on a summer day, yarn or needlework in her lap, watching Jim out in the distance.

Kelly shook off the memories and squared her shoulders. Time to tour. Hopefully it would be short so Kelly could keep up her enthusiasm. Mimi so obviously hoped Kelly would approve of the changes she'd made to the farmhouse. Kelly was determined not to disappoint her, even though she was sure each room would be a bittersweet reminder of happier days.

She strode to the front door, noticing for the first time the colorful flowerbeds everywhere, including the shady patio, which was still as inviting as ever. A sign spelled out the shop's name in the middle of the oak door. HOUSE OF LAMBSPUN. Kelly took a deep breath and yanked open the door, stepping inside.

That's as far as she got. She couldn't take another step. The assault on her senses held her in place. Color, color, everywhere she looked. Skeins of yarns in every hue imaginable spilled out of cupboards in tidy bundles, scattered across antique tables in twisted coils, and draped languorously in billowy soft bunches along white-painted walls. Azure blues blended into turquoise and sapphire. Lime greens skipped through spring grass to rest in deep forest emerald. And the reds—oh, the reds. Kelly's favorite. Cool raspberry sherbet, melting into vermilion, heating all the way to fire-engine red.

Kelly had to catch her breath. So used to the sober decor of the accounting and corporate world, Kelly felt her senses on momentary overload, adjusting. She stepped into the tiled entryway and immediately glanced up. A skylight opened above, allowing natural light to flood what used to be a dim foyer.

She slowly ventured inside. Up ahead, she saw the dining room. The old walnut floors had been polished smooth and shone with a deep, rich luster. Stacked wooden crates lined the walls, skeins of yarns tumbling out. A round maple table was in the midst of the room, piled high with baskets and open wooden crates spilling their colorful contents.

And that was just the yarn. Knitted, woven, and stitched creations were everywhere else—sweaters, vests, blouses, gloves, hats, purses, scarves, and shawls hung from the walls, dangled from cabinet doors, were thrown over shelves, were draped across antique dressers and desks, and were folded on tabletops. It was a riot of color everywhere she looked. Kelly remembered how each room opened and flowed into the other, giving the farmhouse a special warmth. Now, colors flowed from room to room, spilling over one another in a multihued torrent, and the warmth was still there.

Kelly glanced into what used to be the open, inviting family room and saw heads bent around a table, afternoon sunshine pouring through skylights and windows that bordered the brick fireplace. Quilters and other needlecrafters chatted quietly as they worked, their stitchery spread across their laps in various stages of completion.

Customers browsed everywhere, she noticed. The women varied in age. Teenagers sorted through egg crates of yarns with glittery metallic fibers. Young women in workout clothes knelt to explore huge chests overflowing with rainbow-hued skeins. Mothers balanced toddlers on their hips as they fondled tiny sweaters the color of English oatmeal. Gray-haired matrons murmured to each other beside tidy baskets of colorful embroidery and needlework thread. And was that a man she spied in the adjoining room? He was running his hand down the smooth wooden frame of a large weaving loom. A present for him or his wife? Kelly wondered.

Everything begged to be touched. Tags proudly proclaimed wool, alpaca, silk, mohair, cashmere, Yak down. Yak down? Softness beckoned everywhere as she slowly explored the still-familiar yet delightfully different rooms. Kelly's fingers itched to touch. As she wandered from room to room, she noticed customers succumb to the same urging she had. Touch. Touch. But unlike her, they didn't hesitate—fondling scarves, vests, knitted tops, sweaters, whatever they wished.

Kelly dove right in and touched everything in sight, reveling in the sensuousness of it all. Crisp mittens and nubbly scarves felt scrunchy and springy. She checked the label. Chunky natural wool from Chile. Her hand brushed a twisted coil of burnished copper, thick as a woman's braid, doubled over and tucked end to end. Hand-painted silk, she read, and nearly dropped it when she saw the price. Fat bundles of hand-dyed mohair beckoned next— magentas, periwinkle purple, teal blue.

And what was that confection draping in billowy soft bunches on the wall? It looked like cotton candy, but it was the color of seafoam. Kelly sank her hands into the greenish-blue billows, half expecting to smell the sugar. *Surely this couldn't be wool,* she thought, and checked the label. Wool and silk, shimmering sea, it declared. How could that be? It looked so different from the other skeins that purported to be the same. She ran her hands through the seafoam confection again. Maybe it was spun by fairies in the night.

A luscious raspberry knitted top dangling from an antique cupboard caught her attention. It looked as soft as, well, as silk. She checked the tag. Eighty percent silk, twenty percent cotton. *Oh yes,* she thought, as she fondled the top, letting it caress her skin, seductively soft. She noticed the light, open weave of the stitches. The pattern alternated open and closed sections running lengthwise down to the scalloped edge. For the first time in her life, Kelly wished she could create something like that. Sure enough, right at her feet was a bin brimming over with those same silk and cotton yarns, a rainbow of spring and summer colors. Kelly could swear she heard the silk whispering to her.

She was about to sink her hands into the bin when she heard Mimi call out behind her, "Kelly! You're here. And it looks like you've started your own tour." She laughed. "How do you like it so far?"

Kelly reluctantly left the tactile temptations at her feet. "Well, I stepped inside and kind of . . . got lost, I guess." She glanced around and smiled. "I can't believe what you've done here. Everything is so different, yet familiar. I can't get over it. I mean four years ago, all I saw were boxes really. You were just getting started. I had no idea it would turn out so . . . so . . . wow." She laughed, unable to find an adequate description.

Mimi beamed. "I'm so glad you like it. We've really tried to create a special world here."

"Boy, you sure did. I almost feel like Alice."

"Alice?"

"Yeah. I walked in the door and fell down the rabbit hole."

Mimi laughed loudly, the light of recognition in her eyes. "Well, we do think of it as our own wonderland. C'mon, let me take you into our main room to meet Jennifer and friends, then I'll show you the rest of the shop."

She gestured toward Kelly's favorite room, the homey living room with its Mexican tile fireplace, barn-paneled walls, and sunlight streaming through all the windows. The comfy sofas and worn end tables were gone, squeezed into Aunt Helen's smaller cottage across the driveway. Now, in the center of the room was a huge oval antique

library table. Several young women were scattered around
the edges, knitting, of course. Kelly felt a twinge of envy.
One of them might be knitting that raspberry creation.

As she entered the room, she spied Jennifer. At least
she knew someone. "Hi, Jennifer. How are you?" she said.
Then her gaze landed on the casserole dishes in the center
of the table, and the unmistakable aroma of food reached
her nostrils. Kelly's stomach growled louder this time.
Silk may be soft, but it sure wasn't edible.

"I'm doing great, Kelly. How were the meetings?" Jennifer asked.

Kelly momentarily pulled her attention away from the
dishes. Was that pizza? Macaroni and cheese? Forget the
diet. Childhood delights beckoned. "Well, it was kind of a
tough day. You know, lawyers and all."

"Whoa. Hold it right there," Jennifer commanded, setting aside the forest-green wool in her lap. "You're hungry, aren't you? When's the last time you ate?"

"Uh . . ."

"That long. Okay, let's get you fed, then you can tell us
all about the lawyers. We had a potluck tonight and there's
plenty left." She jumped to her feet and grabbed a paper
plate and began scooping up servings of macaroni and
cheese, taco casserole, Feta cheese and tomato salad, curried chicken and rice, and a large slice of pepperoni pizza
on top.

Kelly found herself demurring in a last effort at polite-
ness. "Oh, I don't need that much."

"Don't lie. I saw you with the cinnamon roll this morning. Besides, I'm a waitress. I know hunger when I see it."
Gesturing toward the table, she said, "There's a place beside Lisa." She handed the heaping plate to Kelly.

"Go ahead, Kelly. The tour can wait." Mimi said as she
settled into a straight-backed rocker and picked up a
frothy white shawl dangling from long, skinny needles.

Kelly dutifully complied, inhaling the aromas wafting

off the plate. She sank into the chair and devoured the pizza.

The slender blonde to her left sent her a friendly smile and leaned over. "Kelly, I'm Lisa. I saw you yesterday, but I'm sure you don't remember. There were tons of people there."

Kelly managed to swallow long enough to reply. "Yes, it was a wonderful service, I thought. So many people . . ."

"Hey, don't interrupt her, Lisa," Jennifer instructed. "She's famished. Let her eat while we talk."

"I see you've already met the shiest one among us," Lisa nodded toward Jennifer. "Miss Mouth, we call her," she added with a grin.

A soft voice spoke up from the other side of the table, "Hi, Kelly. I'm Megan and I'm so glad to meet you. Helen talked about you all the time. We feel like we already know you . . . kind of."

Kelly noticed that Megan's fair skin and shoulder-length dark hair gave her face an almost porcelain quality, with classic, delicate features. Since her mouth was stuffed full of taco casserole that moment, Kelly nodded. "Boy, that's scary to hear," she said when she swallowed.

Megan smiled, revealing perfect little teeth. "No, it's good. She especially loved those trips you took with her. We must have looked at photos for weeks."

"Months," Jennifer corrected. "Boy, I could use some time lying in the sun in Provence. With some sexy Frenchman rubbing me with oil, of course."

"Olive oil, you mean," Lisa tweaked.

"Whoa," Megan protested with a laugh.

"Yesterday she begged me to help her stay on this new diet," Lisa said. "And did you see her go back for dessert tonight? Twice, yet," Lisa shook her head and gave Jennifer a wry smile. "I don't know why I try."

"Because you love fixing people," Megan tweaked.

"Hey, I tried, Lisa. Honest. But, c'mon, German chocolate cake? You know that's my favorite," Jennifer protested with a laugh that told Kelly the ribbing was all in fun.

"Every cake's your favorite."

"I'll get rid of those ten pounds, just watch."

"Not with cinnamon rolls, you won't," Lisa scolded.

"How'd you find out about that?"

Megan giggled. "Mimi let it slip."

Jennifer sent a dramatic scowl Mimi's way. "Snitch. Besides, it was only a half."

"You know, if you did one of Lisa's exercise workouts in the morning, you'd lose those pounds in a heartbeat," Megan offered, her fingers busily working a turquoise mohair-type creation that piled in her lap. "I do, and I can eat anything I want all day."

Jennifer eyed Megan sternly and paused working the needles. "Megan, you've got the metabolism of a Marine platoon on maneuvers. You could eat an entire buffet and still be your dainty, delicate, and disgustingly slender self." She went back to the dark green wool as Megan laughed. Was that a sleeve appearing in the wool, Kelly wondered?

Enjoying the friendly banter, Kelly decided to join in. "It was all my fault," she spoke up, balancing a forkful of curried chicken. "I tempted her. Practically shoved it in her mouth."

"Yeah, right," Lisa snickered.

"Of course, I plan to run an extra mile tomorrow morning," Kelly teased, winking at Jennifer.

"Traitor."

"You work out?" Lisa asked.

For the first time Kelly noticed Lisa was knitting a coral pink shade of that seductively soft silk and cotton yarn she'd seen earlier. Was that the same knitted top coming to life in her lap? "Heck, yes. Got to."

"See? Discipline," Lisa tweaked again.

"I get enough exercise running between the patio and

the kitchen every day," Jennifer countered. "Besides, it's all I can do to throw myself in the shower every morning. No way could I get up earlier to work out."

"You're perfect just the way you are," offered Mimi, needles busily working the frothy white shawl.

"See? Mother Mimi thinks I'm perfect, so there." Jennifer poked out her tongue at Lisa.

"Each one of you is unique and lovely," Mimi continued with a maternal smile. "Lisa is statuesque and willowly. Megan is delicate and dainty, but tough as nails underneath," Mimi added.

"Boy, I sure hope you've got some adjectives left, Mimi, because you've used up all the good ones on them," Jennifer teased.

Kelly almost choked on a mouthful of mac 'n cheese, trying to suppress her laughter. Even the elderly lady browsing the bookshelves in the corner glanced over her shoulder with a smile.

"And Jennifer is voluptuous and sexy," Mimi decreed with a wicked grin.

Jennifer pumped the air. "Yes! Take that, you skinny Scandinavian."

Laughter burbled around the table and spilled out into the side rooms. Kelly felt the accumulated tension of the day release at last. She poured a glass of what looked like iced tea. The taste startled her. One of those herbals, probably. She drank out of thirst.

"Where are you working out while you're here?" Lisa asked, fingers moving quickly. "I use the gym on the west side of town if you need a place."

"I try to run every day if I can, so I've been using the river trail each morning. It's not far from the motel I'm staying in. Over near the interstate." Kelly leaned back in the chair, relaxing for the first time since she arrived in town.

Lisa gave Kelly's long-legged, slender frame a quick

once-over. "You must play sports. You've got the look. Basketball?"

"Well, I used to play all of 'em back in school, but softball's my favorite. That and tennis." She brushed the wayward lock of dark hair off her forehead. "You get to be outside."

Lisa's eyes lit up. "Really? What position?"

"First base, usually."

Lisa beamed. "Boy, I sure wish you were staying around. We just lost a couple of players and really could use you. Megan and I play in a coed league in town. You'd like it, I can tell."

Kelly had to hide how much she liked the idea. But she had no time for softball. She was here to arrange her aunt's affairs, pay the bills, and get the cottage full of memories on the market. Something way down deep inside Kelly protested. She silenced it. Her job was waiting back in D.C. A very intense, demanding job with a very intense, demanding, important accounting firm. She had responsibilities. She had friends. Well, a few. She had a life. Yeah, right.

She deliberately glanced out the window toward the mountains to hide her thoughts. "Boy, I wish I could. But I can't be gone from my job that long. I told my boss I'd be taking care of my aunt's affairs and the house, and then I'd be back. A week or so. Others are handling my clients while I'm gone. I just couldn't . . ." Her voice trailed off.

"That's too bad," Megan said in her soft voice. "We're just getting to know you."

"What were you planning to do with the house, Kelly?" Mimi asked, her head bent over the shawl.

Kelly debated how to answer. This morning, she'd have responded quickly: fix up the house and put it on the market. But after talking with the Denver lender, she was no longer sure what to do. She needed to think. All of her aunt's neat financial arrangements had been thrown into disarray with the loan.

"Well, I'd planned to clean it up, then put it on the market," she offered. "But now . . ."

"Now, what?" Jennifer prodded after a moment.

Glancing around at the friendly faces and obvious interest, Kelly responded with honesty. "Things have changed. I just learned from the lawyer this morning that Aunt Helen refinanced the house only last week so she could pull out equity. Problem is, there was no equity left. I'd helped her refinance three years ago so she could pay off Uncle Jim's hospital bills. We got a great loan with low interest. And now I learn she just closed last week with some sleazy Denver lender so she could take out more money. I don't even want to tell you the interest rate."

Kelly closed her eyes and let out an exasperated sigh. "Of course, she's now upside down in her mortgage, and—"

"Upside down?" Lisa inquired.

"That means the loan is for a larger amount than the market value of the property," Jennifer explained, then glanced to Kelly. "I'm also a real estate agent. That's where I work every afternoon."

"Now it's not such an easy thing to sell the house. I'd have to bring all that extra money to closing." Kelly blew out a breath. "I've got some in savings, but my dad's death and medical bills three years ago wiped me out. There's no way I could bring that much to the table. Provided the house would sell, of course."

"Oh, it'd sell, trust me," Mimi said with authority.

"If you don't mind my asking, how much are we talking about here?" probed Jennifer.

For someone whose career meant being careful with financial information, Kelly hesitated only until two customers wandered from the room and out of earshot. Surprised at herself, Kelly felt comfortable, at ease, safe with these women. She leaned over the table and noticed the others did the same.

"Twenty thousand dollars," she whispered.

"*WHAT?*" Jennifer exclaimed. "Twenty *thousand?*"

"*Shhhhh!*" Lisa and Megan shushed loudly.

Megan's eyes were round as saucers, and Mimi's knitting had dropped, forgotten, to her lap as she stared with a worried frown.

Undeterred, Jennifer pressed. "That's crazy. Why would Helen need that much money?"

"That's precisely what concerns me. I took care of Aunt Helen's finances and advised her, and she never said a thing to me about doing this. She was a sensible woman. She'd never do something this financially irresponsible." Frustration seeped into her voice. "She had a real simple budget, and I kept her accounts every month. I mean, I knew where she spent her money. If she had some secret vice that took money, believe me, I'd know it."

"Yeah, like Helen was a secret gambler or something," Jennifer said with a snort. "Or closet addict."

"Helen? Never," Lisa agreed.

"Do you suppose she could have been one of those compulsive shoppers or something?" ventured Megan, fingers methodically working the turquoise yarn around the needles. "I mean, maybe she bought stuff out of her grocery money and gave it away. You know how she was always giving stuff away to the homeless shelter, Lisa."

Lisa nodded. "I dunno. Helen usually donated knitted mittens and scarves every year, not other stuff."

"Maybe she got hooked on one of those home shopping networks. You know, channel surfing one night," Jennifer offered. "Those things are lethal. It ought to be against the law to open the fridge door or use your credit card after midnight." Listening to everyone's laughter, she added, "I mean, I bought a set of exercise weights one night after one A.M., and I don't even exercise." She shook her head.

"Did you return them?" Kelly asked over the laughter.

"They wouldn't take 'em back. So they're in the back of the car for snowstorms."

"Well, I'm fairly certain Aunt Helen wasn't a compulsive shopper. And that's what worries me. I can't figure out why she'd need the money." Kelly dropped her voice. "Not to mention all that money was the reason she was killed. It had to be."

A somber mood settled over the table as all of them, save Kelly, concentrated on the yarns in their laps, needles working smoothly, adding row after row of stitches.

"Well, at least they've got the man who did it," Mimi offered finally.

"Tragic. If only Helen kept her door locked more. She was so trusting." Lisa shook her head.

"I heard he was drunk."

"Apparently he'd been arrested before."

"Threatened a woman in her yard near Old Town."

Kelly listened to their comments but said nothing. Finally, Mimi spoke up. "The police called me when they found Helen's door open and . . . and found her. Of course, I rushed over here. They asked me if there had been a disturbance at the shop earlier or if I'd seen anyone lurking around."

"Was there?" Kelly probed.

Mimi shook her head. "Nothing. And I'd never seen anyone hanging around here, ever. I was going to tell the policeman that but then they . . . they brought Helen out. They asked if I could come over to the medical examiner's and identify her."

"That must have been awful, Mimi," Megan ventured.

"It was." She bit her lip. "I'm sorry, Kelly, I didn't mean to—"

"That's okay, Mimi. I wish I'd been here instead." Guilt tugged inside.

"Have the police recovered any of the money?" asked Lisa.

"Nope. The detective I spoke with on the phone this

morning said the vagrant had nothing with him when caught." Kelly paused. "I could tell the detective was surprised when I told him the large amount of money that was missing, but he tried not to let on."

"I heard they found her purse in the bushes near the river."

"Purse was empty, of course."

"Of course."

"I don't understand why they haven't found some of it," Megan ventured. "Twenty thousand dollars is a lot of bills."

"Exactly what I've been thinking," Kelly mused. "I asked the detective, and he assured me they thoroughly searched the riverbank area and the golf course."

"Maybe he hid it somewhere or buried it," Mimi offered.

"The bills were probably so scattered that the police never saw them," Jennifer volunteered, a forest-green sleeve definitely taking shape now. "I mean, they could have blown across town in the breeze. Or floated downstream. Heck, they could be in Greeley by now."

"More likely one or two people found the money, and they're keeping it. They're not about to reveal themselves," Lisa offered. "There're all sorts of people who wander that trail, you know. Some homeless guys sleep out there rather than go to the mission. I helped count them in the last census."

That comment aroused Kelly's suspicions. "Yes, but if someone like that suddenly found a bunch of money, they'd spend it, maybe in a convenience store. And that would draw attention, wouldn't it?"

"Maybe," Lisa agreed. "Unless they spent it at different stores. No one would notice."

Kelly's instincts still buzzed. "Maybe I'll go back and ask the detective in charge of the investigation that question. See what he says."

"Will you go tomorrow?" asked Jennifer.

"I'll try, but first I have to tackle the house. Got to do it. Besides, that's probably where the mortgage papers are since they're not in her bank box."

"Remember, we're going to help you with that chore, Kelly," Mimi instructed in a no-nonsense voice. "Several people here at the shop want to help. Me, Rosa, and Connie—"

"And us," spoke up Lisa, nodding to the others. "I can come over first thing in the morning. I'll switch clients around. I'm a physical therapist over at the Rocky Mountain Center, so we help each other out with schedule changes all the time."

"And I can come early, too," said Megan. "I'm a consultant, so I set my own hours." She grinned.

"I'll be over on my morning break," Jennifer piped up. "The closing documents should be in one of those vinyl folders or a file. Just pull them out, and I'll take them with me tomorrow afternoon if that's okay. I'm working over at a new home site south of town. Plenty of quiet time to peruse the file and give you a rundown after work."

"Hey, thanks, I appreciate it, Jennifer. I appreciate all of you and your help. I confess I've been reluctant to go into Helen's house. I dunno . . . I'm still uneasy about everything that happened." She looked around the table and saw reassurance. It felt good. Kelly hadn't felt that in a long time.

"That's understandable, Kelly," Mimi said with a warm smile. "Don't worry, we'll be there. In fact, I've got the key so we can start early even if you're not here. I mean with the cleaning and all. We wouldn't touch anything else."

Kelly felt a tightened muscle somewhere inside her chest let go. "Thanks, Mimi. That'd be fine."

"Maybe we'll finish early, and you can go to the police after that," suggested Lisa.

"Maybe, so," Kelly mused. "I'm hoping that detective in charge is as friendly as the one on the phone."

"Well, if you ever need some help, you can ask Burt," Mimi advised. "He's a retired police investigator who comes in here every day."

Kelly blinked. "To knit?"

"Don't look so surprised. We've got guys who knit *and* weave," Megan spoke up.

"Burt spins. In fact, he's gotten so good at it I pay him to spin some of my fleeces when they come in."

"Boy, big change from police work, huh?" Kelly joked.

"Well, his daughter kind of ordered him here. He had a heart attack after his wife died last year, and Ellen just panicked," Mimi went on. "She was afraid she'd lose her dad, too, so she gave him her own prescription to add to his new exercise routine." She grinned. "Ellen knew how relaxing knitting was, so she hoped he might like that, but Burt surprised her. He took to the wheel like a natural. He learned faster than anyone I've ever taught."

"So, if you need a friendly cop, Burt'll help you out," Jennifer suggested.

"Good. I'll remember that."

"I sense there's something that's bothering you, Kelly." Lisa peered at her. "Do you want to tell us or should we just mind our own business?"

"When have we ever done that?" Jennifer quipped.

Kelly paused a minute. "I guess it's this whole thing with the money that bothers me. I mean . . . my aunt does something totally out of character and gets this huge amount of money—well, huge for her, anyway. Not only that, but she cashes the check, takes the money home, then this guy just happens to stumble in that very night to rob her." Kelly's gaze narrowed as she stared at the shelves of knitting magazines. "It's all too coincidental to suit me. That makes my buzzer go off. And now, I'm remembering her last phone calls. She wasn't her normal, happy self."

"Really?" asked Mimi.

"Yes, she was more subdued, quieter, those last couple of weeks when I spoke with her on the phone. I didn't think much of it at the time, but now I'm convinced she was worried about something."

"About what?" Jennifer probed.

"That's what I'm going to find out. Whatever it was, it made my sixty-eight-year-old aunt borrow twenty thousand dollars in a hurry."

With that, Kelly pushed back her chair to leave, while the others exchanged worried glances around the table.

Three

Balancing a coffee mug with one hand, Kelly managed to unsnap Carl's leash with the other. Not easy, considering Carl had spotted a squirrel and was straining at the other end, ready to run. She opened the cottage's back gate and watched her dog take after the squirrel. The squirrel was ready, of course, and as fleet-footed as yesterday. "He's teasing you, Carl," Kelly warned with a laugh as she headed to the front door.

Mimi and the others had already started, she noticed. Bless them. She really hadn't wanted to be the first one inside the cottage. Through the open front door, Kelly spied Mimi, cleaning cloth in hand, and Lisa plugging in the vacuum. "Hey, you really did start without me, and it's only five after eight. I'm impressed," she said.

"Shop doesn't open till ten, so I figured I could get a lot done before then," Mimi said, not looking up from the coffee table she was polishing. The scent of orange floated on the air.

Kelly didn't even try catching Lisa's attention over the

sound of the vacuum. Lisa was methodically working the carpet. Kelly stood for a moment in the doorway and looked around. The lacy white cottage curtains over the dining room window were shoved to the side, allowing bright rays of morning sunshine to pour into the rooms.

The cottage was a perfect miniature of Helen and Jim's farmhouse, including the sun room and mini–family room jutting to the side. They'd built the cottage as a home for Jim's mother years ago, and when she died, it became Helen's craft cottage. Kelly remembered the huge quilt frame that used to fill the mini–family room—yarns, fabrics, and needlework projects everywhere. Helen called it her sanctuary. When Jim was traveling across Colorado building state roads, Helen would nestle in here and pick up needles of varying sizes. Later, after Jim's death and most of the land was sold, the cottage became her home.

Would it feel different now, Kelly wondered? The cottage had always felt cozy and safe before. She entered the living room and headed toward Helen's antique desk in the corner, alert to any uneasiness. Setting her mug on the desk, Kelly stood for a moment and absorbed the sensations around her—the sunshine pouring through the windows, the dull growl of the vacuum nearby, and the delicious scent of orange floating in the air from Mimi's polishing cloth.

To her surprise, Kelly didn't feel uncomfortable at all. On the contrary, she swore she could feel a warmth around her that had nothing to do with the sunshine. Another part of her relaxed, and she started searching the papers that were spread on Helen's desk. After a thorough search, Kelly came up empty. No folder of loan papers.

Rats! They've got to be here, she thought as she headed toward the bookcases that lined one of the walls. At that moment, Mimi grabbed her polish and cloth and headed toward the sofa end tables. There, on the dining room table, Kelly spied a long black package.

Inside the black vinyl cover, Kelly found all the mort-

gage and closing documents. Flipping through some of
the pages, she shuddered. She'd forgotten how long Colorado real estate contracts had become. She'd take Jennifer up on her offer to read through and decipher the
essentials.

The vacuum shut off and Kelly heard a familiar voice
behind her. "Hey, great, you found them," Jennifer called
out as she came rushing into the cottage. "Let me take
them and put them in my car, okay? No time for a break
this morning. We're slammed. I'll see you after work at the
shop. Bye." Within fifteen seconds, Jennifer was in the cottage, grabbed the document package, and was out again—
talking the entire time. Words floated out the door in
her wake.

Kelly was impressed. "I think that was Jennifer, but
I'm not sure," she said to Lisa, who was attaching an ex-
tender arm to the vacuum cleaner.

"Yeah, she can really move when she wants to."

Just then, Kelly caught a movement outside the dining
room windows. Rubber gloves up to her elbows, window
cleaner and towels in hand, Megan was studiously polishing the glass. *Brother,* Kelly thought. *This house will be
spotless by the time they finish.*

Hating herself for the reflex action, Kelly glanced at
the carpet below and scanned for telltale bloodstains. She
saw nothing, and heaved a huge sigh of relief.

It was time to join in the communal effort. After all,
they were cleaning what was now Kelly's house. She
reached for the mound of cleaning cloths Mimi had left on
the sofa end table and was planning to start dusting bookshelves when something caught her eye. Actually, it was
the absence of something. Kelly stared at the bare living
room wall directly behind the sofa.

Where was the family quilt? The brass drapery rod and
hardware were still on the wall, but the treasured family
quilt was gone. Helen had stitched it more than thirty
years ago from various bits and pieces of fabric that held

meaning in her life. She'd included snatches of lace and crochet and needlework she'd done over the years, back to her childhood. There was even a lock of hair from their young son who died at age five. Priceless memories and bits of family history—all stitched with love. It was to be Kelly's after Helen's death. And it was gone.

"Mimi," she asked when the vacuum stopped. "Do you know where the family quilt is? Did Helen put it away in a closet or something?"

Mimi turned around and scanned the wall, her face registering surprise. "Oh, my, it's gone," she exclaimed.

"It's always hung on the wall as long as I remember. First in the farmhouse, then here when Helen moved. Why would she take it down?"

"I don't know. Maybe it's in the bedroom. Let me check." Mimi crossed the dining room, turned a corner, and peered into the bedroom. "No, it's not here, either."

Kelly stared at the drapery hardware. "Do you think she would have taken it to be cleaned or maybe preserved or something?"

Mimi shook her head. "No, Helen was an expert at caring for fabrics. She'd do it herself. Maybe she's got it stored in a box in the closet." She gestured back to the bedroom. "I can go look."

"Would you, please?" Kelly asked, trying to ignore the uneasy feeling that crept into her gut. Why would Helen do that? She loved having the quilt there. It kept her family alive, she said. Why would she take it down and store all those memories in a box?

Lisa unplugged the vacuum and scooped up the cord. "What quilt are you talking about?"

"The one Helen made thirty years ago. She called it a family tapestry. She used pieces of fabric from clothes she'd made, bits of knitting and lace and crocheting she'd done. She even had her earliest needlework pieces she'd done when she was only four years old." Kelly continued to stare accusingly at the wall, as if it could speak.

"Was that what hung from the rod up there? I've never been in here before today."

"Yes, and I can't understand why she would take it down. Helen loved that quilt . . . and so did I."

Just then, Megan slipped in the glass patio door leading to the backyard. Carl immediately appeared behind the glass, watching them inside the house. "Well, all the windows are done, and the door, but that won't last long," Megan announced. "Not with big old Carl pressing his nose against the glass." She turned around. Carl responded by barking once and plopping both front feet against the glass. She grinned. "See what I mean? He's such a sweetie, big and goofy."

Mimi returned from the bedroom. "It's not in the closets, Kelly, nor under the bed. I even looked in the dresser drawers." She frowned. "Where would she put it?"

"Put what?" Megan asked.

"The quilt Helen had on the wall. It was a family piece, Kelly says," Lisa explained.

Megan's eyes popped wide as she stared at the wall. "You're right. It's gone. I remember seeing it when she took me here to help her quilt a piece last year. It was beautiful."

"When's the last time you saw it, can you remember?" Kelly probed.

Megan shrugged. "Gosh, probably months ago. I'd only come over here when Helen needed some extra hands to finish up something. You know how she was. Always setting herself deadlines and such."

"Did she ever mention taking it down or putting it away or having it cleaned or something?" Kelly tried again. That uneasy feeling in her stomach was still there.

"No, not a word." Megan picked up Kelly's worried tone. "Where would Helen put it, Mimi?"

Mimi stared at the wall with the same look of concern. "I have no idea, unless she'd store it in the garage, but I can't see her putting that heirloom in there with dusty boxes of Jim's old books."

"Neither do I," confessed Kelly, "but I'll take a look. This is really bothering me."

"Hey, we can do that," Lisa offered, wrapping the cord around the vacuum. "I'm finished with the vacuuming, Mimi's got the dusting, Megan's cleaning the kitchen, and—"

"And it's finished, so's the bathroom," Megan declared, peeling off her rubber gloves. "This house was already clean when we walked in here this morning, Kelly, so we're done. If Mimi doesn't need me in here, I'll go search the garage with Lisa for that quilt. Surely it's around here somewhere."

"Don't tell me you're all finished," another voice spoke from the doorway.

"Connie, perfect timing," Mimi invited in the plump middle-aged woman. "Is Rosa in the shop?"

"Yes, she just came in, so I thought I'd help out over here." She wagged a pair of yellow rubber gloves as she approached.

Mimi touched Kelly's arm. "You go over to the police department and ask those questions, Kelly. I know you've been anxious. We'll look for the quilt while you're gone." Gesturing around the bright, open rooms, she added, "As you can see, we're almost finished here, so there'll be plenty of eyes searching. Don't worry. We'll look in every corner of house and garage."

"Thanks, Mimi." Kelly gestured to the others. "All of you. I can't tell you how much I appreciate it. I . . . I . . ."

"Go on. We'll handle this," Lisa pointed to the door. "Go talk to the cops. And if anybody's rude to you, write down the name and Burt'll go beat 'em up."

"Lisa," Mimi scolded with a laugh. "Ellen'll kill us if we get Burt all riled up. He's here with us to relax, remember? Go on, shoo, Kelly. We've got it."

Kelly did as she was told, grateful once again for the

outpouring of help and support Mimi and her "knitting shop regulars" had showered on her since her arrival. She wasn't used to such support. It felt good.

"I know how upset you must feel, Ms. Flynn," spoke the grey-haired matron with the familiar sad voice. Kelly remembered that voice from the many phone calls. "Families suffer so much when a tragedy like this happens. But rest assured, the investigation into your aunt's unfortunate murder is being handled with the utmost care."

Kelly glanced through the glass window of the small room she'd been ushered into when Officer Delahoy first greeted her. Outside, the main office of the police department looked no different from any business office, except that half the staff were in uniform, light-blue shirts and dark pants. Kelly wondered how many had worked on Helen's case. Glancing back to Officer Delahoy's kind brown-eyed gaze, she asked, "You said you weren't part of the investigation into my aunt's murder, right?"

Officer Delahoy smiled modestly. "No, Ms. Flynn, I wasn't. I'm a community liaison officer. I work with families who've been impacted by crimes, either directly or indirectly, like yourself. I direct them to grief counseling, therapy, whatever is needed. Did you want to see someone? I can arrange it."

"No, no," Kelly deliberately suppressed a smile. She hadn't come for counseling. She wanted answers. "No, I've got several questions about the suspect you've apprehended and—"

"Oh, well, I can answer that for you, Ms. Flynn. He's been a troublesome vagrant, an incorrigible drunk and disorderly for years. Been arrested for trespassing all over the Old Town area. He's been incarcerated more times than I can count." Her hand gave a dismissive wave. "He was seen near your aunt's house and ran when he saw police. Our officers caught him, of course," she said with a proud smile.

Kelly took a deep breath and gave Officer Delahoy her most affable smile. "Yes, Officer, thank you, I remember you telling me all that on the phone earlier. But now I have some different questions about the investigation itself. Could I speak with one of the detectives who was directly involved? Is one of them here?" She glanced through the glass again, then back to the crestfallen officer.

"Uh, well, I could check," she said, frowning a bit. Clearly Kelly's request was not a daily routine.

"Would you?" Kelly enthused. "I'd be *so* appreciative."

"Wait right here, and I'll see what I can do, okay?" Delahoy instructed as she turned to leave.

Kelly nodded and reached for the weak coffee she'd been nursing for the last half hour. Swishing the remains in the small Styrofoam cup, she downed the last of the weak brew. Ack! *How could people drink such stuff?* she wondered, and screwed up her face as she tossed the cup into the trash.

The tiny room was antiseptically clean, gray, and cold. Kelly wondered if they kept it that way on purpose. She shivered, as various scenes from movie police dramas started running through her head—interrogations, confessions, accusations—until the door opened and a tall, heavy-set man with bushy gray eyebrows entered. Kelly sat up straighter.

"Ms. Flynn? I'm Lieutenant Morrison." His deep voice seemed to resonate in the room. He sat down across from Kelly and leaned back into the metal chair, a black folder in his hand. "Officer Delahoy said you had some questions about the investigation. I was the lead investigator on the case. How can I help you?"

Kelly took a moment before she answered the imposing detective. "Thank you for giving me your time, Lieutenant Morrison," she started, flashing a charming smile. Morrison didn't return it. "My first question concerns this suspect you've arrested. Exactly why do you believe he was responsible for my aunt's murder?"

"Well, to start with, he was seen near your aunt's home by two officers and ran from them when they attempted to question him. He was intoxicated, well over the legal limit, and combative. Had to be restrained, in fact. This individual has been a particularly troublesome vagrant for a few years. Arrested for drunk and disorderly, trespassing, loitering, and public nuisance. So, we've had our eye on him." Morrison tapped the folder against his dark-blue trouser leg. "But last summer his behavior turned violent. He attacked an elderly woman who resides near Old Town. Only about a mile from your aunt's home. She walked out on her patio one summer night and saw him urinating on her rosebushes. She yelled at him, and he cussed her out."

Kelly wasn't sure, but something suspiciously like a smile tugged at Morrison's mouth. Surely not. It disappeared, and Kelly kept her rapt attention.

"Well, some old ladies would have been shocked and run inside and called us. But not this one. She cussed him back, then grabbed her broom and started to swat him. Well, he grabbed it and whacked her in the head. Knocked her down, but not out. Then he ran away, and she called us, which she should have done in the first place," Morrison said with a stern frown. "She was able to describe him well enough so that we recognized him. He denied it all, of course. Couldn't remember a thing. Liquor has fried most of his brain, no doubt. His memory, anyway. But she picked him out of a lineup."

"Wasn't he tried and sent to prison?" Kelly asked. "That sounds like assault."

Morrison's bushy eyebrows moved in agreement. "It is, but the judge decided to try intervention instead and placed the individual in an alternative treatment facility.

Rehab, you might say." He flicked imaginary lint from his trouser.

Kelly could tell Morrison did not agree with the judge's decision, so she ventured, "Doesn't sound like it took."

The detective grunted. "You might say that. Unfortunately for your aunt. This might not have happened if this guy was still doing time."

Clearly, Lieutenant Morrison believed he'd found his man. "You know, I've got some other questions about the money, Lieutenant. Why hasn't more of it been found? I mean, I was shocked to learn from the lawyer that the amount was twenty thousand dollars, and yet none of it has been recovered."

"I'm afraid not, Ms. Flynn. Only her empty purse was found, thrown into the bushes beside the trail."

"You know, that doesn't make sense," she didn't bother to hide her skepticism. "This guy runs off with twenty thousand dollars. That's a lot of money scattered beside the river. Someone should have noticed and reported it, don't you think? Some honest citizen, perhaps?"

Morrison observed her in silence for a moment before answering. Kelly got the impression he was assessing her. "They're a lot of people that use that trail, Ms. Flynn. Particularly late at night. And some of them aren't exactly what you'd called 'honest citizens.' Their first instinct if they found a bunch of money lying under the bushes would be to grab it and run like hell. In fact, that's what we think happened. One or two guys found the cash, grabbed it, and caught a bus out of town. There's a midnight bus to Denver, you know. They're long gone by now, I'm afraid."

"How would they even see the money? It was nighttime, right?"

"There was a full moon that night and a slight breeze. If those bills started blowing across someone's path, believe me, they'd notice."

Kelly deliberately stared at the wall behind him as she considered what he'd said. It made sense. Why then did something nag at her inside?

"I know this whole idea comes as a shock to you, Ms. Flynn, but we deal with individuals like this all the time. Some money comes into their lives suddenly, they grab it and disappear. Go wherever they think it's safe. Drink it up, gamble it away, usually get the rest stolen from them. It's sad, I know."

She let out an exasperated sigh. "It's all too coincidental, that's what bothers me."

"Coincidental?" Bushy eyebrows argued with each other.

"Yes. My aunt gets a loan from a sleazy lender even though we'd refinanced three years ago. Then goes to the bank and cashes the check for this huge amount of money. Huge to her, at least." Kelly lets the frustration into her voice. "And then, the very night she has all this money in her purse, a vagrant just happens to walk in and robs her. And kills her!" She shakes her head. "I don't know, Lieutenant Morrison. Helen lived in that house for the last four years, and I never heard her complain about prowlers or fear of someone even peeking in her windows, let alone robbing her. It's just all too . . . too . . ."

"Random?" Morrison supplied. "Crime often is, Ms. Flynn. I know that's no consolation, but I'm afraid it's all we've got to give you."

Kelly looked him in the eye. "Has this guy confessed yet?"

Morrison shook his head. "No. Claims he doesn't remember doing anything after he finished off the liquor. But that's exactly what he said last year after the other assault. I told you, he's fried his brain."

"Can you actually convict someone when they don't remember the crime? How does that work?"

"He'll get a fair trial, Ms. Flynn. Rest assured. Now, do you have any more questions?"

Not right now, Kelly thought to herself, but she knew when she was being dismissed. "I guess not, Lieutenant Morrison," she said as she started to stand up. Then she remembered something that had niggled in the back of her brain. "Oh yes, I was wondering if you'd discovered anything damaged or broken in the house when you, uh . . . when you found her."

Morrison flipped open the file at last and scanned it. Kelly stared covetously at the folder.

"There was an overturned chair near the dining room table, but no furnishings seemed to be damaged," he said, scanning the report. "Victim was found facedown on the living room carpet, about six feet from the table. Victim was still wearing rings and wristwatch. On the floor beside her was one broken knitting needle, another knitting needle with a single loop of purple yarn, and a bundle or skein, whatever you call it, of the same purple yarn. That's all we found near the body."

"A broken needle?" Kelly probed, her instinct buzzing. "Did you find the rest of what she was knitting? Knowing Helen, she was always knitting something."

"So we were told," he muttered as he turned the page and read. "We were curious as well, so we searched throughout the house and outside, but we never found any separate knitted item that matched the yarn."

"Now, that's strange, Lieutenant. Jewelry is left but Helen's knitting is stole?" Kelly sharpened her skeptical tone.

Morrison flipped through the pages before answering. "When a person commits a violent criminal act, sometimes they do strange things, Ms. Flynn."

"I've also discovered my aunt's heirloom quilt missing. It hung on the wall for more than thirty years, and now it's gone. We can't find it anywhere. Why would the killer steal a quilt?"

"What makes you think it was stolen?" Morrison said. "She may have given it to someone."

"She wouldn't do that."

Morrison stared at her but made no reply, his skepticism obvious. Then, he placed the folder on the table and folded his arms. "Do you have any other questions?"

"Just one. Who was it that actually discovered my aunt's body? I think Officer Delahoy mentioned an off-duty policeman."

"Yes, two of our officers had just gotten a midnight meal from a nearby drive-thru and drove over to the driveway between your aunt's and the knitting shop to park and eat. They told me that driveway afforded them a good place to watch the shopping center across the street without being seen."

"And that's when they found her."

Morrison nodded. "Yes, they noticed the front door open and lights streaming out, and knew that was unusual. You see, our officers knew your aunt's habits, and they knew that an open door wasn't normal for her. So, they went to investigate. It's a good thing they did, too, because it was while they were checking around outside in the yard that they spotted this guy crossing the golf course, heading toward the river." Morrison nodded in apparent satisfaction at his men's efficiency. "They called out to him, and he took off."

Kelly, however, picked up a detail. "Golf course? I was told he was seen near my aunt's house."

Morrison scowled. "The golf course borders your aunt's property, Ms. Flynn."

"It's a big golf course, Lieutenant, and it also borders two streets and Old Town. This guy could have been weaving his way toward the river," she challenged.

"We think not, Ms. Flynn. Why do you doubt our officer's account?"

Kelly grabbed her purse and skirted from behind the table, glad she was as tall as the detective. "I don't necessarily doubt it, Lieutenant. I'm just concerned. I'm sure you understand. I want to make sure that my aunt's killer is caught and punished. That's all."

"So do we, Ms. Flynn."

"That's very reassuring, Lieutenant," she said as she opened the door to leave. "Thank you so much for your time. I'll stay in touch."

Four

Kelly caught sight of the moving shapes the moment she pulled in front of the cottage. Someone was in the backyard with Carl. *What th—?* she thought, slamming the car door. The sound of Carl's growling reached her eyes. Oh no. What if someone jumped the fence and Carl decided to protect his newfound territory? Images of lawsuits flashed before her eyes.

Racing around the corner bushes, Kelly came to an abrupt stop. It couldn't be. No way. He was in San Francisco with his artist girlfriend. It was impossible, but the guy rolling around in the backyard with her Rottweiler bore a startling resemblance to Jeff, the Slime, her exboyfriend who'd dumped her after college.

Now that she was closer, Kelly recognized the familiar sounds of rough dog-play. Jeff used to play with Carl the exact same way—rolling on the ground, apparently unconcerned his hand was in a Rottweiler's mouth, laughing as if it were great fun. Kelly never quite captured that concept.

"Hey, mister! Who are you and what're you doing in Helen's, uh, my yard?" she yelled at the moving shapes. "Carl, stop! That's enough!"

Carl ignored her, obviously enjoying himself too much with the tussle. "Carl! Is that your name, fella?" the guy said, reaching around the dog's neck in a wrestling move. Carl responded with an excited yelp and more growling, as the guy laughed and rolled to the side. Carl darted after the rolling toy. For the first time, Kelly saw a glove in Carl's mouth.

Kelly noticed there was a big pile of dog poop not far away, and this idiot was headed right for it. What was it about rolling around with a dog on the ground that was fun? Gotta be a guy thing. "Hey, c'mon, mister!" she yelled again, heading toward the gate. "You may think it's fun now, but if he accidentally bites you, then you'll change your mind. And I can't afford a lawsuit right now."

"Whoa, Carl. Let me up," the guy protested, crawling to his knees. But Carl wasn't finished yet, and jumped from behind, sending the guy sprawling. The guy just laughed, but Kelly saw dog poop at three o'clock and closing fast.

"Carl, c'mon, let him up," she ordered in her stern attempt-at-dog-control voice. Didn't work. But this time, the guy was able to dodge Carl's lunge and scramble to his feet.

In his disappointment at game being over, Carl barked and dropped the glove, which the guy snatched. "Got it!" he crowed. "That's mine." He shoved the glove deep into his jeans pocket as he strolled toward Kelly and the gate. Carl responded by dancing in front of him, clearly hoping for more play.

"Did he grab your glove or something?" Kelly asked. "How did it get over here, anyway?"

Now that the guy was closer, she could see the resemblance to Jeff was faint. Tall and lean, this guy had brownish-blond short hair instead of carefully cut, sun-streaked blond. His face was different, too. His was a square jaw line, sharp nose, and blue eyes, not the Slime's almost too-handsome features. Although it was faint, the resemblance was close enough to stir old hurtful memories. She scowled at the guy out of aggravation at being reminded.

The guy responded with a big smile and extended his hand. Kelly hesitated for a moment then took it. His grip was firm, but then, so was hers. "I'm sorry if I scared you. My name's Steve Townsend, and Carl and I were just having a discussion over who owned the glove." He reached down and rubbed Carl's shiny black head. Carl barked twice and danced, hoping to incite more.

"Well, I could see that, but how'd the glove get over here in the first place?" Kelly kept her interrogative tone.

"Uh, yeah . . . well, I was practicing shots over at the greens," he said, pointing behind him. "And one of the guys walked by complaining real loud about losing his golf balls to some dog." He patted Carl, who obligingly stood beside him, just in case. "That caught my attention, because I'd noticed Carl in the yard when I drove by yesterday, so I volunteered to get the balls for him. That's how the big fella got my golf glove. Must have fallen out of my pocket when I climbed over the fence."

"You climbed into the yard with a Rottweiler for golf balls?" Kelly couldn't hide her shock. "You must be crazy, mister. Why would you do something like that?"

"It's Steve, and I introduced myself to him first." He smiled at Carl. "I can usually read animals pretty well. Believe me, I stay away from the unfriendly ones."

Kelly peered at the greens skeptically. "How'd those golf balls get all the way over here into the backyard?" she demanded, hands on her hips. This story sounded fishy to her. "You can't tell me those guys I see hacking away can hit a ball all the way over here."

Steve laughed. "Well, you're partly right. No way could they aim a shot over here, but some guys can't control their drives at all. And this one guy who was complaining so much has a wicked bad slice. Man, his balls go all over. I swear, he loses half the balls in the river." He jabbed his thumb in the riverbank's direction.

"You must spend a lot of time hanging around the greens if you recognize a guy's swing," Kelly barbed. She wasn't sure why she was still being combative. The guy had been nothing but friendly. "What are you, a caddy or something?"

A slow grin spread over Steve's face, and she thought she detected amusement in his eyes. "No. Years ago I spent a summer giving lessons, so I remember lots of the guys. Some improved, others didn't, like that one." The smile disappeared. "And this guy can also be a pain in the butt, so I didn't want you having any trouble right after Helen's death and all."

The sound of her aunt's name jolted Kelly and wiped the scowl away. "You knew my aunt?"

He nodded. "Yeah. She was a sweetheart. Real special." He glanced toward the cottage. "She'd invite me in for a cup of coffee and talk. I enjoyed spending time with her. She always had something good to say, you know what I mean?"

Kelly knew exactly what he meant, but the idea it would come from the mouth of this stranger was a total surprise. "How in the world did you meet her?" she probed. "Do you come over here to knit with the others or something?" Why she said that she didn't know.

This time he laughed out loud. "No, I come over whenever Mimi needs some repairs," he said, clearly enjoying her surprise. "Her son and I were best friends growing up, so she's like a second mom. I try to help her out any way I can. She's done a great job with that shop." He nodded in the direction.

His unfailing good humor and friendliness finally wore down Kelly's desire to be unpleasant. The faint resemblance was still an irritation, however. She removed the sharpness from her tone. "Yeah, I was amazed with everything she's done over there. She gave me a tour yesterday."

Steve extended his hand again. "Let's start over, okay? I'm Steve Townsend and you are Kelly, uh . . . is it Rosburg, like your aunt?"

She accepted his handshake. "Flynn. Kelly Flynn. My dad was Helen's brother. Rosburg was her married name."

"Good to meet you, Kelly Flynn. And good to meet you, too, big fella." He gave Carl a pat before he swung his long legs over the chain-link fence. "Listen, if you have any trouble from anyone over at the golf course, tell Mimi, okay? I'll be glad to run interference for you." He dug into his pocket and pulled out car keys and, with them, the wayward golf glove.

Carl started barking in anticipation. "That's enough, Carl," Kelly reprimanded.

"Might as well give it to him," Steve said, inspecting the ripped finger dangling.

"Hey, I'm sorry," Kelly said, suddenly contrite. "I'll be glad to buy you another pair."

"Nah. Not a problem. I've got lots of pairs," he said, tossing it to Carl who caught it midair. "Remember what I said about the golfers. Tell me if you have any complaints, okay?"

Her curiosity piqued. "Why do you think I might have complaints? Those were probably freak shots that landed in here."

"Well, let's just say those balls had some help getting all the way into the yard. But my lips are sealed." He pulled a golf ball from his other pocket, held it up, and winked at Carl before he walked away. "See you later, Kelly," Steve called over his shoulder.

Kelly stared after Steve for a second, aggravated all over again for some reason. Why would he see her later? And why was he calling her by her first name like he knew her? Just because he knew Mimi and Helen didn't mean he'd get to know her. Nope. That self-confident air of his put her off. It was all too familiar. The resemblance to the Slime was getting stronger.

"Carl?" Kelly dragged out the name in the did-you-do-something-you-shouldn't-have tone. Carl looked back with his "who me?" expression, glove dangling from his mouth. Remembering the ease with which Steve swung his long legs over the three-foot fence, Kelly's stare turned accusing. "Carl, did you jump over this fence? You'd better not have, or we'll both be in big trouble." She rubbed his head, and Carl dropped the glove and slurped her hand, all canine innocence. Kelly sighed loudly and glanced back at Steve's bright-red truck pull out into traffic.

"Oh, brother, this is worse than I thought," Kelly muttered, scowling at the loan documents before she drained the last of Eduardo's strong coffee. The carafe Jennifer had filled for her before leaving for the real estate office was empty. At least it lasted while Kelly sorted through Helen's bills and wrote checks that afternoon. Now, once again, it was after five and Kelly hadn't eaten since morning. The mortgage documents spread before her kept all hunger pangs away.

"I know, it's ugly. Not only would you have to bring twenty thousand dollars to the closing table, but there're penalty fees if you sell or refinance before two years." Jennifer gave a professional snort. "I've heard of this company and try to steer my clients away from lenders like this. But, bottom line, it's their money and their decision."

Kelly glanced around the cozy little bistro restaurant in what was once Helen and Jim's dining room and kitchen. Pete, the owner, was in the corner balancing out the cash register, ready to close for the day. She hunched over the table. "Jennifer, I don't have twenty thousand dollars, let alone money for penalties," she rasped. "But I have to sell the cottage. I've got to get back to Washington. My job's waiting, my townhouse," her hand shot out in frustration. "Everything's there. I've got to find a way to do this. But how?"

"I wish I could be more encouraging, Kelly," Jennifer said, her voice sympathetic. "But I've seen others try to get around these contracts, and it can't be done. Usually, they just have to wait out the two years, then sell."

"I can't do that," Kelly protested. "I have to get back to Washington and my job. I was going to call my boss tomorrow and tell him when I'd return. Now this." She dropped the documents and leaned back into the wooden chair. It creaked as she rubbed her forehead in a gesture from childhood. Thinking posture, her dad had called it.

Jennifer leaned back as well and swirled the last of her latte. "What about working from here? You know, telecommuting or whatever. For a while at least. Would your boss let you do that?"

Kelly stopped rubbing. Was that possible? She remembered when another accountant's wife had chemotherapy and he worked from home. Maybe . . . maybe she could buy some time that way. Just until she figured out this house problem. "You know, that's a good idea. I've got to have more time to solve this. I mean, Jennifer, I cannot afford a house payment AND my townhouse rent. No way." She shook her head.

"Could you find someone to sublet your place in Washington for a while?" Jennifer suggested. "I mean, just until you can find someone to rent this place."

Kelly stared in surprise. "Rent Helen's cottage?"

"It's your cottage now. And face it, that's what you'll have to do. If you can't sell it, then you can rent it. That will help with the mortgage payment, and you can get back to D.C. and your job." Jennifer smiled wryly. "Understand, I'd much prefer you could stay here with us, but my realtor-self is trying to be helpful."

Kelly frowned at the thought of renting Helen's cottage

with all the memories. Why was that different from selling? She didn't know, but it was. "How much would it
rent for, do you think?" she forced herself to ask.

"Unfortunately, not enough to cover that big, nasty
mortgage payment. But, maybe it would cover two thirds.
It isn't a huge place."

"I know, that's what I like about it. It's cozy," Kelly
mused.

Jennifer smiled. "Then I return to my original suggestion. Tell your boss you've absolutely got to telecommute
for a couple of months or so and find someone to sublet
your townhouse in D.C. I'll bet you wouldn't have as
much problem renting that place, would you?"

Kelly pondered the idea, even though it was already
resonating inside her. "You're right. There's a guy in my
office who's been living with his sister in Maryland, and
he's been dying to get a location like mine. I could give
him a call."

"Do that," Jennifer prodded. "And call your boss. Pull
out all the stops. Family and grief and all that."

Kelly caught the gleam in Jennifer's eyes. "You're
shameless, you know that?"

"I know. I work at it, that's why I'm so good."

Scooping the documents from the table, Kelly slid
them back into the portfolio. "I'll call first thing in the
morning. It's already evening back east now. More importantly, I'm starving. Want to go out for pizza?"

"Better yet, we can have it delivered here," Jennifer
suggested.

"You'll regret not ordering mine," Pete spoke up as he
approached, coffeepot in hand.

"You're right," Jennifer said with a smile. "But Eduardo's closed up the kitchen, and he'd kill me if I rum-
maged through his refrigerator."

Kelly stared covetously at the coffeepot. "Hey, Pete, let
me help you finish that off, okay?" she volunteered with a
crooked grin, extending her cup. She'd grown comfort-

able with the cafe's owner in the last two days with her frequent coffee breaks.

"Man, that is one serious caffeine habit you've got there, Kelly," Pete joked, emptying the last of the dark brew into her cup.

Kelly's stomach growled. "Yeah, I know. But it's the only real vice I've got, so I treasure it."

"We're gonna have to work on that," Jennifer teased. "While you're here, we'll help you develop others."

"Watch out for her. She's dangerous," Pete warned as he reached to dim the lights. "See you tomorrow, Jen."

"Bye," Jennifer called over her shoulder.

Kelly shoved the portfolio into her briefcase as they both rose. "Any kind of pizza is fine with me, except sardine. Here, use my card." She offered Jennifer her credit card.

"Hey, thanks. I'll call this in while you go and catch up with Mimi and the others. It's Thursday, so Megan should be here." She pointed toward the doorway leading back into the knitting shop.

The murmur of voices beckoned through the shop doorway, and Kelly was struck again by the onslaught of color as soon as she entered the room leading from the restaurant. She also noticed something else. Three small weaving looms were set up along a cabinet-lined wall. Each loom had someone hunched over the intricate contraption.

Curious, Kelly watched the beginning weavers in fascination. She'd never seem looms that small before. The last time she'd seen anything resembling the ancient arts of weaving and spinning had been on a weekend tour to Mount Vernon, George Washington's Virginia plantation. *What do you know,* she thought. *Portable looms. Wouldn't Martha be pleased.*

Mimi glanced over one student's head. "Well, how'd it go, Kelly? Have you and Jennifer finished studying the loan papers?"

"Yeah, we're finished, and it's not good news."

"Why don't you go into the main room, I'll be over in a second." Nodding to one of her assistants, she gave the student beside her an encouraging pat on the arm. "You're doing great. Rosa is the best weaving instructor in town, so you'll be picking up speed before you know it."

"I hope so," the young woman said, staring at the shuttle skeptically.

Kelly took her time wandering through the adjoining rooms, feasting on color, fondling fabrics, stroking yarns along the way. When she reached the main room, she was surprised to see Megan was the only person there. Her dark head bent over the turquoise yarn bunching in her lap, needles appearing to move at warp speed. Kelly wondered how long it would take to learn to knit that fast.

Megan glanced up and grinned as Kelly sat down, dropping the briefcase at her feet.

"Hey, Kelly, how goes the mortgage discussions?"

"Not good," Kelly said and drained the last of the last of the coffee. She hoped the pizza delivery guy drove fast. "I'd have to bring more than twenty thousand dollars to the closing table. Jennifer estimates that with penalties and fees for early sale, it could be close to thirty thousand dollars! And that's approximately twenty-seven thousand more than I have in savings."

"Whoa . . ." Megan's eyes popped wide. "So what are you going to do?"

"Well, I can't sell, obviously, not for two years, Jennifer says. That's the only way to avoid penalties."

"That's good to hear," Mimi's voice chirped, as she pulled out the chair beside Kelly and sat down.

"I'm going to call my boss tomorrow and see if he'll let me work from here for a while, a couple of months maybe. Long enough for me to figure out how I'm going to pay my mortgage on the cottage and my townhouse rent." She let out an exasperated breath. "Jennifer made a good suggestion. Maybe I can find someone to sublet my place in D.C.

until I can rent the cottage." Noticing Mimi's expression, she added, "I know, I don't want to, Mimi, but I'll have to. It's the only way I can pay the bills."

"You do whatever's necessary, Kelly," Mimi said, and gave her a reassuring pat on the arm like one of her novice weavers.

"Well, at least you'll get to stay here longer. That'll be great," Megan offered. "And you can move out of the motel and into the cottage tonight if you want to. It's spotless, and hey, Carl's already there." She grinned.

"That would be great," Kelly said, then remembered something. "Oh! Did you have a chance to look for the quilt?"

Mimi glanced down at the milk-white shawl in her lap, even her knitting slowed. "We looked everywhere, Kelly. The garage, all over the house a second time. We opened every box or container we could find. Nothing. I'm simply heartsick to think something has happened to that exquisite family piece."

The cold spot Kelly felt earlier returned to her chest. It gave a little squeeze. "Damn," she whispered. "Where could it be?"

"I'll ask everyone who comes in, Kelly, I swear I will," Mimi promised.

"It's too much to believe the drunken vagrant took the quilt *and* the money," Megan said.

Kelly was about to agree with her when Jennifer appeared, pizza box in hand. She set it on the table with a flourish. The aroma of pepperoni and cheese wafted from the cardboard box, and it wasn't even open yet. Kelly felt her hunger pangs go into hyperdrive.

"The delivery guy was backed up, so I went across the street to the pizza shop. There's enough for everyone," Jennifer announced and plopped down a large plastic bottle of soda. "I also picked up some diet drink."

Kelly hesitated long enough for Jennifer to grab a slice, then selected two gooey, cheesy slices for herself. She practically inhaled them both. Hunger retreated as the pizza disappeared. Even the knitting needles paused for a few moments as the women all talked and ate.

Now that hunger wasn't the first thing on her mind, Kelly remembered something else. "You know, I mentioned the missing quilt to the detective this morning, and he more or less dismissed it. He thinks Helen either gave it to someone or packed it away somewhere else." She let her voice convey her feelings about the ascerbic Lieutenant Morrison. "I could tell he didn't think it was important at all. And he thought I was real nosy for poking around in *his* investigation."

"You're going to keep poking, I take it," Jennifer said, pouring more soda.

"You bet. But he did tell me something I didn't know. Apparently a broken knitting needle was found next to Helen's body."

"Really?" Mimi asked. "It was broken?"

"Yes, and the other needle had only a single loop of purple-colored yarn on it. The bundle of skein or whatever was lying on the floor beside her. But there was no trace of the knitting itself, only a dangling strand of yarn and the one loop." Kelly saw their rapt attention. "Sounds like someone yanked it off the needles."

Megan's eyes got even wider. "I remember now! Helen was knitting a purple sweater. Some chunky new wool. She was halfway through the back by the time I saw her that afternoon."

"Yes, I remember, too," Mimi nodded. "She was making it for you, Kelly, if I remember correctly."

Kelly frowned. "Why would the killer steal Helen's knitting? It doesn't make sense. First, the quilt is missing, and now stolen knitting."

"Did the police notice it?" Jennifer asked.

"Yes, Lieutenant Morrison made a point of telling me they had searched around the house and outside but found nothing."

"Just like the money."

"Boy, they can't find anything."

"No way that drunk would grab Helen's purse and the quilt, then grab her knitting, too."

Kelly swished her soda in the plastic cup. "None of it makes sense. And things that don't make sense bother me." She glanced at her wristwatch. "I think I'll head back to the motel and grab a quick run before I check out. Running always helps me think. You know, sort things out." She grabbed her briefcase and rose.

"Okay, you run and think, and we'll stay here and knit and think," Jennifer said, pulling the forest-green yarn and half-finished sweater from her tote bag. "We can compare notes tomorrow."

"Do you need any help, Kelly?" Megan offered.

"No, thanks. I've got my suitcase and Carl's stuff, that's all." Smiling at them, she added, "I can't thank you enough for cleaning Helen's cottage this morning. I mean, you guys did all the work. I didn't do anything, really."

"There wasn't much to do," Mimi said, fingers swiftly working the white wool. Kelly wanted to sink her hand in it. The shawl piled in puffy billows in Mimi's lap, like mounds of white cotton. "The house was clean already."

"We simply touched it up," Megan added.

"Well, I wanted to tell you again how much I appreciate your help. Now, I can grab some dog food for Carl and settle in next door, not beside the interstate."

"Carl's staked his claim already."

Mimi chuckled. "He has the greatest time watching those squirrels. And, of course, they're not used to having a dog chasing them. They're giving him fits."

Kelly laughed and turned to leave. "Good for them. They'll keep him sharp. He's been bored silly in that little townhouse yard back home." Waving a good-bye, she headed toward the door, wondering why the phrase "back home" sounded strange when she said it.

Five

Kelly leaned against a huge cottonwood tree bordering the golf course and stretched her long legs behind her, finishing her runner's routine. This section of river trail was much prettier than the portion near the interstate. This morning she'd run through deep shade, past neighborhood parks, beside the winding river, and through tunnels beneath main thoroughfares. Her three miles had whizzed by, and she was back at the edge of the golf course before she knew it. Best of all, the weather had warmed enough for her to shed her sweats and run in shorts and a T-shirt.

Now for some of Eduardo's strong coffee before she jumped in the shower. Maybe she'd better fill a carafe. She'd need it for the phone call to her boss. Kelly edged around the golf course, heading toward the cottage, while she practiced some of the persuasive points she'd come up with last night.

Suddenly, a dark shape caught her eye. There was Carl, racing from the trees behind the cottage and onto the course. "What the . . . ?" Kelly stared and broke into a run.

Carl stopped briefly, nosed something on the ground, and headed back to the tree-lined yard. Kelly ran up behind just in time to see her dog climb over the three-foot chain-link fence and into the cottage backyard once more.

"Ah, *ha!* Gotcha!" Kelly shouted, finger pointing. "I saw that, Carl! No, no, *no!* Do not go over that fence! We'll get in big trouble if they—" She stopped mid-sentence.

A contrite Carl was lying down on the grass, head between his paws, staring at her with his I-know-I-did-something-wrong-but-I-couldn't-stop-myself expression. Right beside him was a cluster of five golf balls.

Kelly sucked in her breath. "Carl! You *did* steal those golf balls!"

Carl glanced toward his little stash of stolen treasure.

Kelly swung her legs over the fence in a swift motion—one of the benefits of being tall—and scooped up the balls. Carl jumped to his feet as if to protest ownership, then obviously thought better of it. He lay down again and stared at the flowerpots.

"You go ahead and sulk all you want. You cannot steal golf balls. Those golfers will complain about us, and we'll get in trouble," she scolded as she climbed over the fence again. "I'm going to take these balls back to the course, and don't you even think about getting them again, do you hear?"

Carl ignored her. Kelly raced to the edge of the course and threw each ball back onto the greens. She also threw a stern look toward Carl as she headed to the cottage. "I'm jumping into the shower, then talking to my boss. Don't even think about climbing over that fence," she warned, shaking her finger at her petulant Rottweiler. "I've got my eye on you, naughty boy."

Running up the back steps and into the cottage, Kelly tore off her T-shirt on the way to the shower. She'd get coffee later. Between the run and her confrontation with Carl, she had all the adrenaline she needed to plead her case to her boss.

Pete poured steaming coffee into the extra-large mug in Kelly's outstretched hand. The rich aroma of the dark brew tickled her nostrils. "Thanks, Pete. Can I run a tab? I might be here for a while."

"Works for me," Pete said, his round face crinkling into a grin. "And if you need anything to eat, let us know. We'll bring it to you right in the shop."

"Really? That's accommodating."

"It's good business." Pete winked.

Kelly took a long sip, feeling the familiar harsh-but-oh-so-good attack of a rich, strong coffee on her taste buds. Now she could handle anything—Carl and his golf ball habit, the cottage problem, whatever. She had her coffee and her boss's permission to work away from the office for "a couple of months or so." She didn't know why she'd added the "or so," but he agreed.

As she turned a corner into the shop, she spied Mimi straightening shelves. Fat spools of embroidery thread lined the shelves of two walls, floor to ceiling, in a rainbow of colors. More than a rainbow, every color imaginable, she guessed. "Wow. Look at the size of those spools," she said.

"Actually, they're called 'cones,'" Mimi said with a cheerful smile. "By the way, how'd you sleep last night? Were you comfortable at the cottage?"

"Actually, I slept surprisingly well. I forgot to set my alarm and slept longer than I have since I've been here."

"That's a good sign. Means you're settling in." She set the last cone of scarlet thread onto its shelf and gave it a pat. "How'd your phone call go with your boss? Were you able to convince him to let you stay for a while?"

"Yes, I was. Part of me was surprised, but I'm thankful

he went along with it. I promised him I'd be able to keep up my account analysis. They can send me all the files I had on my desk, and I can download everything else I need from our secure corporate website." She took another long sip. "It's definitely doable."

"That's great. If you need to use a computer, you can use ours. It'll be busy during the day, but at night it's free," Mimi offered.

Kelly was touched. "Thanks, Mimi, that's sweet, but I brought my laptop, so I'll probably be working over at the cottage."

"Well, if you get lonely, you just bring it over here and work with us around the table, okay?"

For some reason that idea didn't sound as strange as it should to Kelly, and she didn't know why. She was about to make a joke when Steve Townsend suddenly appeared in the doorway. All trace of Kelly's smile disappeared.

"Hi, Mimi," Steve said, his friendly smile in place. "I had a little time this morning, so I thought I'd come over and talk about those cabinets you want." He glanced to Kelly. "Hey, Kelly, how's it going? I heard you're moving into the cottage. You settling in?"

"For a while," Kelly allowed, still finding it hard to return his smile. Did everyone know her business around here? This shop had a heckuva grapevine.

"I guess since you two have already met, I don't have to introduce you," Mimi said as she scurried down the hallway. "Let me get my notebook, Steve, so we can talk."

"What's Carl up to?" Steve asked with a grin.

"Actually, he's been up to no good," Kelly admitted. "If he had a doghouse, he'd definitely be in it."

Steve laughed. "Let me guess. Golf balls?"

"Yep. I caught him in the act. Jumping over the fence and snatching balls from the course then climbing back into the yard." A smile finally won out as she shook her head, remembering. "If it wasn't so serious, I'd laugh, but I don't want anyone lodging a complaint about us."

"Don't worry about that. You just make sure and tell me if some loud-mouthed golfer says anything to you or gives you a hard time, okay?"

Kelly eyed him. What was with this guy? Did he have some Sir Lancelot complex or something? "That's okay, but I don't think I'll need help. I've been handling guys like that for a long time."

Steve's grin spread. "Yeah, I can tell, and you're really good at it, too."

"Damn right."

"What'd you do with the balls?"

"Threw 'em back on the course. Then I gave Carl a stern lecture."

"Oh, that'll work."

"Yeah, that's what I'm afraid of," Kelly admitted. "I'd hate to have to put him on a leash, but I may have no choice."

"Well, before you do that, let me try something," Steve suggested. "I've got some old golf balls. Let me bring them over and give 'em to Carl. That might keep him happy."

Kelly stared at him. What a great idea. She wished she'd thought of it. "You know, that's a good idea. But do you still use them? I mean, I could buy new ones."

"Heck, no. They've lost their zing. I'll be glad to contribute them to the cause."

Mimi bustled into the room at that moment, open notebook in hand. Kelly took that as her cue. "Well, you folks get to work. I'll go enjoy my coffee in the main room." She raised her mug to Mimi and Steve.

"Do that, Kelly," Mimi called to her. "I think Lisa may be there."

Kelly made her way around the mid-morning customers browsing through the rooms. Lisa was the only one settled at the library table so far, but there were the distinct sounds of a class being taught in an adjoining room. She dropped her briefcase and sat down.

"Hey, good to see you," Lisa said with a smile that said she meant it. "Did your boss okay your staying here with us?"

Kelly noticed the "with us" felt good. "Yes, bless him. So, I've got some time to sort out how I'm going to manage this two-house situation." She drank deep from her mug.

"I'm so glad, Kelly. It's going to be great having you here longer," she said, concentrating on her knitting.

Kelly eyed the luscious coral sweater that was taking shape in Lisa's lap. *It was the color of spring azaleas back in Washington,* she thought, remembering the dark green bushes that lined so many walkways in the capital city and sprang forth with vibrant corals and pinks each April.

"That sweater you're knitting is gorgeous," she said enviously. "I saw a luscious raspberry one exactly like it hanging in the other room. I'm going to buy it."

"It's gone already. I saw a woman grab it yesterday."

Kelly's heart sank. "Darn it! I wanted that sweater. I've been thinking about it ever since I saw it."

Lisa caught her eye and smiled. "You can make one yourself. We'll teach you."

The idea tickled inside Kelly's brain, but old habits—and beliefs—die hard. "Oh, no way could I do that. I can't knit a lick. Helen tried teaching me several times over the years. Couldn't do it."

"Couldn't or wouldn't?" Lisa challenged.

Busted, Kelly thought to herself. "Okay, okay," she confessed with a sheepish grin. "You got me. I purposely made mistakes so Helen would think I was totally incompetent. But it wasn't hard. To make mistakes, I mean. Trying to hold those needles and the yarn at the same time," she observed, shaking her head. "Boy, it was tricky, and I kept forgetting what to do with the needles. I kept dropping them."

"Do you style your hair with the blow dryer in the morning?"

Kelly blinked. What did that have to do with knitting? "Uh, yeah, but what—"

"Brush and blow dryer, right?"

"Yeah, what does that have to—"

"Then you can knit."

"Okay, you're gonna have to explain that one. Somehow I missed the connection."

"Simple. You hold the dryer with one hand and make one motion, while you hold the brush with the other and make another motion, right?" Lisa said. "Same as knitting. But knitting is easier."

"Good point," Kelly conceded, but unwilling to surrender yet. "It's still large movements with the dryer, though, like in sports. I can do all those things really well. It's just the fine motor activities I find hard."

"Then I'm surprised you can put your lipstick on."

Lisa was good, Kelly had to admit, and much more tenacious than Helen. She cast around for a new excuse, but didn't get the chance.

"It only takes practice, like in sports," Lisa pointed out. "You probably couldn't throw a softball well the first time either, but you learned. You can learn knitting the same way. With practice. Now, you won't start out with something like this sweater, but you can work up to it gradually. You can start with something simple, like a scarf."

"You're relentless." Kelly shook her head in admiration.

"I prefer 'determined,'" Lisa said with a grin. "Besides, I can see you really, really want to have that sweater. Face it, it's the only way you'll get it. We're not knitting it for you. But we'll teach you how."

Kelly sank back in her chair and swirled her coffee. The caffeine high had kicked in and she felt like she could leap tall mountains, or at least a skein of wool. "You don't know what you're getting into," she warned. "I can be real clumsy when I'm first learning how to do things. It even took me a while to learn to do my hair. Some girls are more, oh, I don't know, dextrous, I guess."

"Everyone feels clumsy when they first begin to knit. It feels strange, but that's normal. All it takes is doing it for a while, and the motions become more comfortable. Plus, you get an immediate reward. You see yourself creating something with every row of stitches."

That thought resonated somewhere inside Kelly. The idea was tempting. Lisa's persuasion (and the caffeine) were wearing down the years of resistance. Almost. "Well, I confess I'd really like to make that sweater."

"You can and will. Trust me."

"I may be too old to wear it by the time I do."

Lisa laughed, then added, "Do it for Helen."

Kelly grimaced, as the last of her resistance crumbled. Lisa truly was relentless. "You are shameless as well as relentless," she surrendered, hands in the air. "I give up. I'll give it my best shot, I promise. Will you be my teacher?"

"We all will, but I'll get you started. Right now, as a matter of fact." Lisa set her knitting aside quickly and stood up. "Come over here and pick out a yarn you like. Something you'd wear in a woolen scarf."

"Boy, I hope you really are patient, Lisa, because I get cranky when I can't do something. Don't take it—"

"Just come over here and pick out the yarn. Stop trying to weasel out of it."

Lisa stood beside several wooden crates that were piled artistically atop a corner table. Fat bundles of multihued yarns spilled from every crate. Charcoal shifted to lavender then violet then purple to burgundy, then abruptly to turquoise to lime with a pause on emerald. The next crate held brighter, lighter springtime colors, all traveling from muted to vibrant hues.

Kelly stood and savored it all for a long moment, trying to picture a long woolen scarf of many colors. "Decisions, decisions," she mused, reaching out to stroke the bundles. She fingered different strands of yarn until she found the colors and texture she wanted, while Lisa waited patiently.

Choosing the maroon, turquoise, and charcoal bundle, she held it out. "How about this? I like these colors."

"That'll make a beautiful scarf, and those yarns are good to work with," Lisa said as she took the bundle and read the label. "Let me grab some number-eight needles, and we'll get started." She snatched a second matching skein from the bin and headed toward the front.

"You need my credit card?" Kelly called.

"I'll tell them to put it on your tab," Lisa called over her shoulder.

First she was running a tab for her coffee, now it was knitting supplies. Kelly couldn't believe everyone was so accommodating here. Clearly, she'd been in the Big City Back East too long. She'd forgotten how to move at a slower pace. She could get used to this.

Kelly settled back into her chair and sipped her coffee as she looked through the window toward the cottage. The trees bordering the golf course blocked her vision of the greens, so Kelly couldn't tell if Carl was behaving himself or not.

"Kelly, Lisa tells me you're learning to knit. That's wonderful," Mimi said as she sped through the room, heading for the office. Steve followed in her wake and tossed Kelly a grin as he passed. She didn't return it.

"Okay, here we go," Lisa announced, pulling out the chair next to Kelly. She opened a fat bundle of yarn and shook it so that one dangling strand separated itself from the others. Lisa snapped the two long wooden needles from their plastic cover. "I bought you birch needles. I sensed you'd like wood. It's warmer and natural. I'll cast on some stitches and get you started."

Kelly watched in fascination as Lisa pulled the dangling yarn free and draped it around the fingers of her left hand, then taking a knitting needle, Lisa began an intricate maneuver of yarn and needle that resulted in several loops suddenly appearing on the needle in her right hand.

"Now, see? That's the sort of magic thing that knitters do that tells me I'll never learn," Kelly complained. "I don't even understand what you just did."

Lisa grinned. "It's called 'casting on,' and there's almost as many ways to do it as there are knitters. Don't worry about it now. You'll learn later. I just wanted to get you started with the basic, simple knit stitch. Now, watch what I do." Lisa scooted her chair closer to Kelly.

Kelly obliged and leaned over, watching Lisa's fingers intently as Lisa talked her way through the movements. "Right needle slides under the stitch on the left needle, wrap the yarn back to front, and slip the stitch from left needle to right. Under the needle, wrap the yarn, slip the stitch." Over and over Kelly watched Lisa's fingers do the maneuvers as she finished a row.

"Okay, now you try," Lisa held out the needles to Kelly.

Kelly stared at them suspiciously.

"Go on, take them. They won't bite."

"If you say so. Let's see how patient you really are."

"Quit stalling."

Kelly took a deep breath and accepted the needles, trying to hold them the way Lisa did. "Okay, now you're gonna have to talk me through this. Right needle goes here . . ." She tentatively aimed the needle's tip toward a stitch.

"Under, under."

"Under, like this?"

"Yes. Now, take the yarn and wrap it around the needles back to front."

Kelly hesitantly did as she was told. "Now what?"

"You slip the stitch off the left needle and onto the right."

Kelly stared at the stitch, then poked at it with the right needle. It didn't move. "It won't go."

"Not by itself it won't. You have to slip it off."

"What if it doesn't want to?"

Lisa snickered. "Trust me, it wants to. You just have to convince it."

"You mean argue with it? I've never argued with wool before."

Lisa laughed out loud this time. "No wonder Helen gave up on you. You're so stubborn."

"Hey, that's one of my few virtues."

"Yeah? Well, guess what? I'm the queen of stubborn. I'll outlast you."

Kelly gave in with a sigh. She believed her. Lisa gave new meaning to determined. "Okay, convince it to leave, convince it to leave." She tentatively slipped the needle beneath the stitch and pushed. "You want to leave the left needle, yes, you want to leave . . ."

Lisa laughed as the stitch finally slipped off the left needle and onto the right. "Alright! See? That's all there is to it."

Kelly stared at her. "All? *All?* That was like the labors of Hercules, for pete's sake. And that was just one stitch." She held up the beginnings of the scarf—one row of stitches, all Lisa's, and one stitch of hers. "Most scarves are four feet long. I can't argue with yarn for that long. A couple of inches, maybe, but not four feet. I'm exhausted."

"It gets easier with each row. Just sit here and relax and knit. In a couple of hours you'll be surprised how much smoother the motion will be."

Kelly feigned a look of horror. "A couple of hours! You've got to be kidding. I can't sit here and do this for two hours. I've got errands to do."

"Do them in the afternoon."

"Carl needs me."

"He's got the squirrels."

"I'll get bored."

"No, you won't. Someone is always here at the table to

talk to. Besides, it's a challenge. And I'll bet you've never resisted a challenge in your life."

Rats. Lisa spotted her weakness. Kelly was all out of excuses.

"True enough, but give me a minute, and I'll come up with something else."

Lisa shook her head, her eyes twinkling. "You are something else. But you've met your match, this time, Kelly. You're not getting out of this. You're learning to knit today if it takes all morning." She reached around Kelly's chair and snatched her briefcase. "And to make sure, I'll take your briefcase and keys to Mimi's office," she teased and sprang from the chair before Kelly could respond.

Kelly burst out laughing. "Hey, no fair!"

"What's not fair?" Jennifer asked as she approached the table and sat down. "Hey, you're knitting!" she exclaimed, pointing to the beginning effort. "Good job. Helen would be proud."

"Boy, you guys work together, don't you?" Kelly said, feeling that little tug inside at the mention of her aunt.

"You bet," Jennifer agreed, pulling the green sweater from her tote bag. "How'd you get her started?" she asked Lisa.

"Coercion, intimidation . . ."

"And guilt," Lisa added. "I used Helen."

"Good job," Jennifer nodded. "How far have you gotten?"

Kelly held up the needles. "One stitch, and it was excruciating."

"See what I mean?"

"Oh, yeah. Listen, Kelly, make it easy on yourself and do what Lisa says. She'll nag you to death otherwise."

Lisa grabbed the nearly completed coral silk sweater and dangled it between her hands. "Just keep telling yourself raspberry sweater, raspberry sweater . . ." she taunted.

Kelly had to laugh. "Okay, I'll keep trying, but I'll be

on Medicare before I finish." She stared at the needles again. "Now, where was I? Oh, yeah, arguing with the wool." She slipped the needle beneath another stitch, wound the yarn, and pushed at the stitch. "You want to leave, you want to leave."

"What the heck?" Jennifer peered at Lisa.

"Don't go there."

Accompanied by much mumbling, Kelly cajoled another stitch off the left needle and onto the right, then another, and another. But it was slow going. Great, she thought glumly, she really would be on Medicare before she finished this sweater.

Just then, voices bubbled through the doorway of the adjoining room. "Burt's class must have finished," Lisa observed.

Kelly glanced up and spotted Megan in the midst of the others filing past, all chatting eagerly and pointing to a picture-filled booklet. She grabbed the chance to cease her labors. "Hey, Megan," she called. "How was the class? What did you learn, spinning?"

"Yes, Burt's beginning class," Megan replied as she approached. She dropped her tote bag and started to pull out a chair, then stopped and stared at Kelly. A big grin spread. "Hey! You're knitting! That's great! Did Lisa teach you?"

"I'm not sure *teach* is the word. Coerce, browbeat, punish, annoy—"

"And guilt," Jennifer added. "She used Helen."

Megan laughed, settling in herself and pulling out the turquoise sweater and skinny circular needles. "Well, whatever works."

"A-hem!" Lisa prodded, pointing to Kelly's motionless hands. "Speaking of working. Get busy."

Kelly heaved an exaggerated sigh. "Slavedriver." She slowly began the maneuvers again, without mumbling this time. She decided to actually try the motions without complaining and see if they became smoother. Sometimes, yes. But sometimes, a strange knot would appear in the yarn out of nowhere. Other times, Kelly felt like she was forcing the needle through the stitches. The yarn seemed to bunch around the needle, tighter and tighter. It was like the wool had a mind of its own, and it was tired of cooperating. Now it was fighting her.

She was tempted to stop and ask for help, but stubbornness raised its head and urged her to keep going. It should get easier. Alas, it did not. She glanced around the table at the others, their hands moving deftly, creating row after row of stitches. All the while they talked and laughed and, it seemed to Kelly, barely paid attention to the yarn and needles.

"Hello, everyone," a girlish voice chirped. "I was hoping there'd be someone here after class."

Kelly looked up and stared. She couldn't help it. Bright pink-and-white lace flounced into the room as the older woman, barely five feet tall and as round and plump as a dumpling, settled into a chair beside Kelly. Her silver hair was pulled back into a neat twist and anchored with—what else—matching pink ribbon. Kelly blinked. She doubted Helen's kitchen curtains had that much lace.

"Hi, Lizzie, how are you?" Megan greeted her.

"Oh, I'm fine, dear," Lizzie said and withdrew a pastel blue baby blanket from her bag. "Burt is such a good teacher. I'm almost convinced I can spin when I listen to him. But then I go home," she sighed, "and I seem to forget what he said and get so confused."

Ah, a kindred spirit, Kelly thought. Perhaps we can sit and mumble at the wool together. Then, Kelly peered at the baby blanket. Row upon row of beautiful, even stitches, with a pattern woven into the design. Small holes outlined the shapes of flowers throughout.

Kelly examined the rows of laborious stitches she'd created. They certainly looked different from Lisa's smooth even row that started the scarf. There were holes in her piece, too. Unfortunately, they were not part of any recognizable design. Instead, they appeared at random. Boy, if this was the best she could do, it didn't matter if she finished a sweater or not. She wouldn't wear it. It'd be too ugly. Better to bury it in the garden and hope it didn't kill the flowers.

She heaved another dramatic sigh and returned to her labors, hoping that someone would notice and take pity. Maybe they'd let her stop. Admit that she was a failure at this. But the others were studiously ignoring her.

Lizzie, however, leaned over and gave her a dimpled smile. "Hello, Kelly. We met briefly at Helen's service the other day. I'm Lizzie Von Steuben. My sister, Hilda, and I were friends of Helen since . . . well, since forever, it seems. We all grew up in Fort Connor, you see." Her round face saddened. "It was such a tragic loss for us all. My condolences to you and your family. I hope you're holding up under all this stress."

Kelly was touched by Lizzie's obvious concern. "Yes, thank you, Miss, uh, Mrs. Von Steuben. Everyone has been so very kind and helpful."

Lizzie dimpled again and blushed, fluttering a hand. "Oh, it's still Miss, my dear. But you can call me Lizzie. Everyone does." Glancing at Kelly's endeavors, her eyes went round. "Ah, what, uh, exactly what are you knitting, dear?"

"She's just started on her very first scarf," Lisa piped up. "I convinced her it was a fitting tribute to Helen."

"Ah, yes," Lizzie said, intently watching Kelly's studied movements. "A scarf, very good. How's it going, dear?"

"Agonizingly," Kelly complained loudly.

Megan giggled and bent her head over her knitting but said nothing.

"Don't pay attention to her complaints, Lizzie," Lisa warned. "She's trying to play dumb and incompetent. But we're not buying it."

"I see," Lizzie observed with a smile, then glanced to

her own stitches, needles moving swiftly in the baby blue yarn. She'd glance at Kelly, then back to her own knitting. Again and again.

Kelly pushed another stitch off the needle, forcing it. Arguing was out of the question. The wool wasn't listening. "Whoever said this was relaxing was *nuts*," she declared loudly. Jennifer snickered but said nothing.

Noticing Lizzie's continued interest, Kelly waited until Lisa and Jennifer started talking again, then she leaned closer to Lizzie.

"You know, sometimes the stitches slip off easier, and other times I have to force them off," she whispered. "Why is that? I'm doing the same movements Lisa taught me."

Lizzie leaned over and whispered conspiratorially, "That's because you're strangling the wool, dear."

Six

Strangling the wool? *How'd she manage that?* Kelly wondered. She'd started out arguing with it and wound up killing it. She stared blankly at Lizzie. "How'd I do that?"

"Oh, it's easy, dear. All beginners do it," Lizzie said with an airy wave of her hand, barely missing a stitch. "Here, let me show you how to loosen the stitches." She set down her own yarn and reached for Kelly's.

Kelly clutched hers tighter. "I have to do it, or I don't learn. Show me on yours," she bargained.

"Very well, dear." Lizzie picked up her needles once again. Kelly noticed they were about the same size as hers. "Now, just watch how I loosen each stitch, just a little. Give it room to breathe."

Kelly watched Lizzie's hands slowly move through the familiar motions. But this time, Kelly noticed something different. Lizzie worked the right needle forward somewhat in a smooth motion, and sure enough, the yarn looped between the needles was looser and moved easily over the needles.

"Wow, that does make a difference," Kelly admired. "No wonder mine were so tight."

"Now, you try," Lizzie encouraged. "You'll be surprised how much easier it will be. I promise."

Somehow, Kelly believed her. Lizzie's gentle manner was encouraging. She picked up her needles and concentrated on emulating Lizzie's movements. To her amazement, the yarn cooperated. "Look at that," she said, slipping one, two, three stitches off the needle. "Thanks, Lizzie. You're a doll."

Lizzie dimpled again. "Oh, it's nothing, dear. We were all novices once."

Kelly concentrated on the new movements, watching the stitches move from left needle to the right. Before she knew it, she'd finished an entire row—and it hadn't been excruciating at all like her previous efforts. She examined the inch or so of scarf she'd created. Pretty homely. Maybe if she kept going she wouldn't notice the ugly inch once she finished. After all, this last row looked a lot better.

A loud contralto voice boomed across the room, "Lizzie, come here. You simply must see this piece." A tall, large-boned woman beckoned in the doorway to the classroom near Mimi's office.

"Yes, dear, I'm coming," Lizzie said and popped from her perch on the chair in a flutter of pink and lace.

"Hey, Hilda," Jennifer called to the woman.

"Hello, my dear. I see you have taught Helen's niece to knit. Excellent. Helen would be pleased," Hilda decreed before disappearing into the classroom again.

Kelly didn't even bother to reply this time. But Mimi did, as she bustled into the room, Steve still in her wake. "I agree, Kelly. Helen is probably smiling at you right now."

Not if she takes a good look at my first rows of knitting, Kelly thought, but kept it to herself. Thanks to Lizzie's helpful encouragement, the motions were finally becoming smoother. Another row finished, then another. Her stitches finally started to resemble knitting. Amazing.

"Oh, Lisa, I just heard from Trish," Megan spoke up. "She can't make it to the game tomorrow morning. She sprained her ankle working out yesterday. Poor thing. That'll really throw off her schedule."

"Is she training for a race or something?" Kelly asked, curious.

"Yeah, triathalon." Lisa stopped her knitting and frowned. "Darn! It's Friday night. Where are we going to find another first baseman."

"Hey, that's okay," Steve spoke from across the room where he was measuring wall space. "You're playing us tomorrow. We'd love you to show up one short."

"Yeah, I'll bet," Megan taunted. "No way, Steve."

Suddenly Lisa zeroed in on Kelly. Kelly could almost feel the red laser light dancing on her forehead. Uh oh. She knew what was coming from the smile on Lisa's face.

"Hey, Kelly, I know how you can repay me for teaching you how to knit," she teased.

"You mean I have to pay for all that abuse?" Kelly challenged, hoping to head her off. "I refuse."

"C'mon. We need a first baseman. That's your position, right?" she cajoled. "Plus you said you wanted to but you didn't have the time. Now, you do."

Kelly sorted through various excuses, but the idea was already resonating inside with an emphatic *yes.* However, she wasn't going to give in that easily. "I can't. I'm busy tomorrow morning."

"Doing what? It can wait a couple of hours."

"Knitting. You said I had to practice."

"Yeah, right, like that's gonna happen," Jennifer said with a snicker. Lisa and Megan laughed out loud.

"Why don't you ask Jennifer, instead?" Kelly ventured. This time Lisa and Megan nearly fell off their chairs laughing. Even Steve laughed as he measured. "Hey, what's so funny?" she demanded.

Jennifer grunted. "Sweating in the sun is not my idea of fun. I prefer indoor sports." She gave a sly wink.

"C'mon, Kelly," Lisa said when she stopped laughing. "You know you want to."

"Yeah, I do," Kelly admitted with a grin. "But I haven't played in so long, I'm gonna be pretty bad."

"Somehow, I doubt that," Lisa replied. "Look, meet us tomorrow at Moore Park on the west side of town. Eight o'clock sharp. We'll warm you up, won't we, Megan?"

"Oh yeah."

"See? That's why I don't like sports," Jennifer decreed. "You're always playing them at some ungodly hour of the morning." She gave a dramatic shudder.

Kelly noticed Steve approach, tape measure in one hand, notepad and pencil in the other, and assumed he was headed to measure another wall. Instead, he stopped by her chair.

"They trapped you pretty good, Kelly," he teased with his engaging grin. "First the knitting, now the softball."

Kelly was forming a retort, when Lisa piped up. "You're up to something, Steve. I can tell from your tone of voice."

Steve chuckled. "I noticed yesterday Kelly has a pretty short fuse. I was hoping if I annoyed her enough, she wouldn't show up tomorrow."

"All right, 'fess up," Jennifer prodded. "What happened yesterday, Kelly?"

Again, Kelly didn't get a chance to reply. "She chewed me out for playing with her dog," Steve said innocently.

"That's all?" Megan tweaked.

Kelly knew Steve was goading her, but just like Carl, she couldn't stop herself. "He left out the part about climbing into my backyard . . . without permission." She assumed an aggrieved air.

Jennifer drew back in mock shock, hand to her breast. Megan giggled. Lisa simply smiled.

"See?" Steve grinned. "If I try hard enough, I can make

her mad. Then maybe she won't show up. I mean, if she's any good, we don't want her playing with you guys."

Kelly had to bite the inside of her cheek to keep from opening her mouth. She started to count to a thousand but only made it to ten. "You can leave anytime now," she said archly.

"I was just about to," Steve said, clearly unfazed by her hostility. "See you folks on the field tomorrow." He gave a wave as he left.

Not two seconds passed before Jennifer spoke up, "My, oh my. That little backyard confrontation must have really fired up Steve's interest."

"Yeah, Kelly. He really likes you. I can tell," Lisa said.

"Well, that's too bad," Kelly retorted vehemently, "because I don't like him."

"Why?" Megan peered at her.

"He annoys the daylights out of me."

"*Steve?*" Jennifer asked, incredulous. "Why? You don't like good-looking guys or something?"

"He's too good-looking," Kelly shot back, more forcefully than necessary. "I don't like that. And he's too smart-mouthed and has that arrogant, easy way about him." Kelly tightened her grip on the needles, jabbing at a stitch.

The others exchanged glances before Megan ventured softly, "Methinks the lady doth protest too much." She quickly ducked her chin and concentrated on the turquoise wool.

"Ah, yeah," Lisa said. "I sense there's more to this reaction than meets the eye. Am I right?"

Kelly jabbed another stitch and yanked the yarn between the needles, scowling at the wool now. "He reminds me too much of the Slime," she confessed finally.

"The Slime?" Lisa lifted a brow.

"Got to be a guy," Jennifer decreed.

Kelly dragged that stitch off the needle and jabbed at another. The stitches had tightened once more. "Jeff was my boyfriend all through college. Love of my life, actually. I thought we were soul mates. Boy, was I wrong."

"Tell," prodded Lisa.

"Nothing to tell, except he dumped me right after graduation. Bastard. If it hadn't been for me, Jeff wouldn't have made it through business school." Yank went the yarn. The wool was fighting her now. Her grip tightened even more with the memories. "I mean, I studied with him, tutored him, practically did his homework as well as my own."

"Men are scum," Jennifer intoned. Megan giggled.

"Well, this one was. He told me he was rethinking his life and our relationship." She snorted. "Rethinking, my ass. I found out later he'd been sneaking around with another girl. Some art student."

"Really?" Megan sounded horrified.

"I told you. Scum." Unfortunately, Jennifer couldn't keep a straight face any longer.

Kelly noticed and relaxed her death grip on the needles. The wool positively sighed in relief. "So, that's why he's the Slime."

"And Steve resembles him?"

"Well, yeah, a little. Tiny bit, I guess. But it's that attitude I can't stand." Kelly scowled again. The yarn practically trembled in fear.

Lisa glanced at her watch and immediately gathered sweater, yarn, and needles into her bag. "Oops, I've gotta get to the clinic. I have clients scheduled from noon to five. See you in the morning," she said as she rushed from the room.

Jennifer checked her watch as well. "Yeah, I'd better get back to the café. Pete's real lenient with my break time, but I don't want to abuse it." She shoved the green wool back into her bag as she rose. "I'll stop in for a few minutes this afternoon late, in case anyone's here. See ya." She waved and left.

Kelly glanced at Megan. She was curious about

Megan's consulting business, since that had always been a dream of Kelly's. Leave the corporate grind behind and strike out on her own. Now, with the cottage and its huge mortgage, that dream looked farther and farther away.

"Their schedules seem to work out for them," she ventured as she continued her knitting. Now that she'd relaxed once again, the wool cooperated as well. "I'm curious. How does your schedule work, Megan? I've actually thought about consulting one of these days."

"My schedule varies every day. That's why I like it," Megan offered. "I spent four years in corporate IT and couldn't take the stress anymore. So, I checked into independent consulting and discovered that I could develop my own client list and not compete with the big guys." She eyed Kelly. "There's a lot of opportunity out there, Kelly. You should look into it during these months you've got here. You might be surprised at what you find."

Something in what Megan said resonated inside and Kelly nodded. "Maybe I will."

A burly, middle-aged man appeared from the spinning room. Kelly guessed he was Burt, since he was carrying what must be a modern-day spinning wheel. It sure didn't look like anything George and Martha had at Mount Vernon.

"Hey, Burt," Megan spoke up. "Have you met Kelly?"

"No, I haven't, and I've meant to." Burt set the wheel in the corner and approached, hand outstretched. "I'm Burt Parker, Kelly. Pleased to meet you."

Kelly took his large hand, felt the roughness, and smiled back into Burt's suntanned, lined face. It was a good face. "Nice to meet you, too, Burt. I've heard a lot about you."

"And we've heard a lot about you, too, Kelly. You were the light of Helen's life, you know."

Kelly almost choked up on that but swallowed it down. "Yeah, she was pretty special to me, too."

Burt reached out a large paw and gave Kelly's shoulder

a fatherly pat. "That's okay. Listen, I look forward to talking with you some more, Kelly, but I've gotta run right
now. See you later." He gave a friendly wave and left.

Darn, Kelly mused. She was anxious to talk to Burt,
since he was a former police investigator. Lieutenant Morrison had brushed aside several of Kelly's questions about
Helen's murder. Morrison seemed to have ready answers
for everything—finding no trace of the loan money, the
vagrant showing up right after Helen cashed the large loan
check. Only the missing purple knitting seemed to puzzle
him.

Kelly, however, didn't like coincidences. They set off
her warning buzzer. She was hoping to run all of it past
Burt and get his professional opinion. Maybe she was
worrying over nothing. If so, maybe Burt could tell her.

"**Hey,** good timing," Jennifer called out from the knitting
shop's front door. "Finished your errands?"

"Yeah," Kelly said as she exited her parked car and
headed across the driveway. "I've got my Internet service
provider, got everything fired up and ready to go, even
bought office supplies. Now, all I need are my account
files."

Jennifer pushed open the oak door. "You deserve a
break. I'm meeting friends in Old Town tonight, want to
join us?"

"I'd love to, but I've got so much e-mail waiting for
me, it's unreal." Kelly shook her head. "I'd better spend
tonight clearing it up. Ask me again next time, okay?"

"Depend on it," Jennifer said as they made their way
through the shop.

Customers always seemed to be browsing, Kelly noticed, no matter what time of day. She glanced toward the
counter in the far room and hoped they were buying as
well. Mimi scurried through the room then, pencil behind
one ear, notebook in her hand.

"Hey, Mimi, how're those cabinets coming?" Jennifer asked as she paused in front of a whole wall of yarns. Fat yarns and skinny yarns tumbled out of the artistically arranged wooden crates, tempting Kelly with their texture and colors.

"Steve's going to pick out some I can choose from tomorrow. I'm hoping he'll be able to get them installed next week. Of course, that depends on his schedule." Mimi said all this as she passed through the room and out again.

"I guess he's a pretty busy handyman," Kelly ventured, squeezing several pudgy skeins.

"Who?" Jennifer asked, squeezing some herself as she moved among the crates.

"This Steve guy."

Jennifer stopped and turned to Kelly with a laugh. "Steve? Trust me, the only person he does handyman jobs for is Mimi. And that's because he and her son were friends growing up." She grinned. "Steve's actually a builder. Pretty successful, too. He's been involved in some big projects off the interstate lately."

"Oh," Kelly said, clearly surprised. "Then why is he always hanging around here and the golf course next door?"

"Installing cabinets and playing golf, probably." Jennifer gave her an enigmatic smile before she returned to the yarn. "Take a look at these yarns and picture a winter scarf," she said, holding up a fat multicolored bundle.

"I'm already knitting a scarf," Kelly countered.

"Yes, and a beautiful one it will be when it's finished. But right now I sense you need a boost of confidence that only comes with finishing something. Something really pretty." She fingered the colorful strands. "These wools knit up fast because they're big and bulky and you use large needles. You can knit one up in a weekend. See?" She pointed to a chunky wool scarf of mottled cream and chocolate that hung beside the crates.

"Wow," Kelly breathed, fingering the soft fibers, the huge stitches. "That's the same wool?"

"Yep. And all you use is the knit stitch. You already know that. So, which one do you like?"

The idea of completing something fast was as appealing as the yarns. She grabbed the fat bundle from Jennifer's hand. "This'll be beautiful."

"I agree," Jennifer said and grabbed a matching bundle. "You'll need two. Go grab a chair while I get the needles and put these on your tab." She raced off.

Kelly was surprised to see Burt sitting at the table, several books spread open before him. "Hi, Burt. Preparing for your spinning class?"

Burt smiled. "Yeah, I try to give everyone lots of references so they can learn from the experts, too." He went back to scribbling on a pad.

Kelly glanced around and saw that they were alone in the room and decided to grab the quiet moment. She settled into the chair nearest Burt and leaned over the table. "Burt, do you mind if I ask you a couple of questions?" she asked in a soft voice.

Burt looked up. "Sure, Kelly. Have you started to spin, too? I heard you're learning to knit."

"Ah, not exactly," Kelly had to laugh at the image. "No, I have some questions about some of the, uh . . . the details surrounding Helen's death. Several things are bothering me, and, well, I just wanted to run some of them past you if I could. Mimi told me you were a retired police investigator."

The relaxed expression on Burt's face faded and another one appeared. He settled back into his chair. "Sure, Kelly. But the person you should be asking is the lead investigator. Lieutenant Vern Morrison. He's in charge."

"I've already spoken with him, and he's, well, he's not all that forthcoming," Kelly said, gesturing. "I get the feeling that I'm almost bothering him."

"Did he answer your questions?"

"Yes, but his answers left me with more questions."

Burt peered at her for a moment. "Why don't you give me an example. I'm not sure I know what you mean."

"Okay. I told him that I thought it was just too coincidental that this dangerous vagrant happened to show up at Helen's house right after she'd cashed a check for twenty thousand dollars."

Burt's eyes widened. "Twenty thousand dollars?"

Encouraged that she'd actually gotten a reaction from a police investigator, even a retired one, Kelly explained. "Helen's lawyer told me the other day that she'd recently refinanced the cottage so she could withdraw a large amount of money. She cashed the loan company check that afternoon, and that evening she was killed." Kelly shook her head. "Coincidences like that make me suspicious. But Morrison simply stared at me and said nothing. Like it wasn't important." She sat back and watched Burt.

He examined the calluses on his right hand for a few seconds. "I'm sure he was thinking the same thing, Kelly, only he didn't show it. Morrison is a good cop. Close-mouthed, yes. But he doesn't miss much."

"Well, I'm afraid he may be missing something here. I don't believe that drunk just happened to stumble into Helen's house that night." Kelly's hand jerked out in irritation. "The lawyer called it a 'senseless act of random violence.' I don't buy that."

"I'm afraid it does happen, Kelly," Burt offered, his face revealing traces of the tragic scenes he'd witnessed.

Kelly made a disgusted sound. "Why is there no trace of that money? Helen got twenty thousand dollars in cash, and yet there wasn't one bill found floating on the river or in the bushes." Kelly scowled. "Morrison said there were all sorts of people who could have found the money and grabbed it, then gotten out of town before the police ever searched."

"Well, that is true. It would be easy for some trouble-maker to make off with the money. Grab it, run down the trail past the river, then hop over to the bus station, and get out of town."

Kelly sighed. Darn it. She was hearing the same scenario from Burt that Morrison gave her. Was she the only one who saw things differently?

"But what I'm curious about, Kelly, is why Helen would need twenty thousand dollars. What was happening?"

A huge sigh of relief shot through Kelly. At last. Someone had picked up on her primary concern. "Now, that's the biggest puzzle of all, Burt," she confessed. "I took care of Helen's affairs, and she never indicated anything was wrong. It was totally out of character for her, and I'm clueless as to why she'd do it." She watched Burt process her answer as well as her concern.

"That's interesting, Kelly," he said after a moment. "I can understand why you're concerned."

"Oh, goodness me, Burt, are you still here?" Lizzie chirped as she fluttered into the room.

Kelly concealed her disappointment at being interrupted. At least Burt had validated one of her concerns. She wished he'd say something more. "Have you been here all day, Lizzie?" she asked.

"Well, I've been in and out," Lizzie said as she settled at the end of the table. "Hilda is teaching one of the advanced knitting classes. I wanted to watch. And help, of course." She dug into her bag and removed the beautiful blue blanket.

"Okay," Jennifer announced as she bustled into the room. "Here are the needles and yarn. I've got enough time to cast on some stitches and get you started." She plopped into the chair beside Kelly.

"Well, you ladies have a good evening," Burt instructed as he stood and gathered his books and notepad. "I'll see you folks next week." Before leaving, however, he patted Kelly on the shoulder again. "Nice talking to you, Kelly. I'm sure we'll have another chance to chat."

"I hope so, Burt. Nice meeting you," she said as he waved goodbye. Turning her attention back to Jennifer, she saw her casting on loopy, loose multicolored stitches onto the biggest needles Kelly had ever seen in her life. She blinked. "Whoa! Those look like something out of a cartoon. Are they really needles?"

"Sure are, and you use them with these great chunky yarns. That's why the scarf knits up so fast. Watch." Jennifer proceeded to slowly do the knit stitch and suddenly big stitches appeared in a chunky row.

"Well, I'll be darned," Kelly observed.

"Here. You can take over. I've got to go home and get ready for tonight." She handed over the huge needles and ball of yarn. "Enjoy." She grabbed her tote bag as if to leave.

"Hey, don't leave yet," Kelly pleaded. "I want to make sure I can do this."

Kelly stared at the needles, then fondled the beautiful soft yarn. Yummy. This could be fun. Did she simply jump in?

"Start knitting like you've been doing," Jennifer coaxed. "Same motions."

"Okay," Kelly said, still dubious. She pushed the big clumsy needle beneath a stitch, wrapped the springy yarn over the needles, and slipped the stitch. It certainly did look strange. Not neat and tidy and even like her stitches were starting to look like in the smaller yarn.

"Keep going. Finish the row."

Kelly did as instructed and stared at the row. It still looked strange. Colorful, but strange.

"Now do another."

She did and was amazed how far apart these rows were from each other. She held up her efforts. "You sure it's supposed to look like this?"

"Absolutely," Jennifer reassured. "Just keep knitting row after row and trust in the process. I guarantee that you'll love it after ten rows. I'll stay till then." She checked her watch.

"If you say so." Kelly went back to her stitches. After a couple more rows, Kelly found she was liking the way the part chunky, part skinny yarn looked. The stitches were all different. Springy and soft, soft, soft.

"Kelly, dear," Lizzie spoke up after a moment. "I've been wondering if you've heard from Helen's cousin since you've been here? I spotted her at the service. But she's such a shy person, she didn't stay like everyone else. Has she given you a call?"

Kelly stared at the colorful wool in her lap, but this time she didn't see it. *Cousin?* What *cousin,* she wondered. *Helen never mentioned any other living relatives. Neither did her dad.*

She peered at Lizzie. "I wasn't aware Helen had any other living relatives. She always told me she was the last one left in her family."

Lizzie paused her knitting and pondered for a second. "Well, perhaps she's a distant cousin or something. I think she used to live in Wyoming. At least that's what Helen said when I asked her a couple of years ago."

Knitting forgotten in her lap, Kelly continued to probe. "Does she still live in Wyoming? What else did Helen say?"

"Well, that's about all," Lizzie replied. "Helen seemed reluctant to talk about her for some reason, so I didn't press it. I do remember asking if her cousin would like to be contacted by the Altar Guild. I was serving as chairwoman that year, you see. But Helen was quite adamant about saying no. She said her cousin was terribly, terribly shy. That's why she never stayed after church and introduced herself, apparently." Lizzie gave a little sigh as if it was hard to believe that anyone would not enjoy the company of others.

"What's her name?" Jennifer prodded. Kelly noticed she no longer looked anxious to leave.

"Ummm, let me see, I think she said it was Martha. Yes, that's it. Martha. I'm afraid Helen neglected to tell me the last name." Lizzie smiled. "Maybe she was afraid the Altar Guild would come calling."

Martha. Martha. She had a distant relative named Martha. "Thank you for telling me, Lizzie," Kelly said. "I had no idea there was another family member in the area."

"Helen never mentioned another soul in the three years I knew her," Jennifer volunteered.

Kelly's mind started racing. Obviously this Martha was someone Helen felt close to or she wouldn't have been so protective of her. Shy cousin Martha. Kelly had to find her. But how without a last name? Then, an idea tickled.

"Lizzie, does that church—"

"St. Mark's, you mean?"

"Yes, St. Mark's, does it have a directory of members or something like that? Maybe I can go through the entire directory checking out all the Martha's until I find her."

"Oh, that won't be necessary, dear," Lizzie said with a wave of her hand. "I'm fairly certain you can find her at the weekday mass. I think she comes nearly every day. I notice her every Monday when I go to Guild meetings."

Kelly couldn't believe what a gold mine of information Lizzie turned out to be. "There's only one problem, Lizzie. I don't know what she looks like. Can you describe her a little, so I can recognize her?"

Again, the airy little wave. "Oh, I can do better than that, dear. Why don't you come to church with Hilda and me this Sunday, and I'll point her out to you. I'm fairly certain she comes to Sunday service as well. And if you can't speak with her in all the crowd, then you surely could on a weekday."

Jennifer turned her head and gave Kelly a sly grin and a wink. "Boy, she trapped you on that one," she whispered.

She did, indeed. Kelly had to admire Lizzie's style. But that didn't stop her from trying to get out of it. She hadn't been to church in years, since before her dad died. Holidays and Helen's service didn't count.

"Jennifer, I think it would be ever so lovely if you could join us, too," Lizzie continued with her dimpled smile. "Hilda and I would simply love to have your company."

Kelly couldn't resist. She turned to Jennifer with a wicked grin of her own. "Yes, Jennifer, I'd just love to have you join us. Please do."

Jennifer waved away the double assault. "Ladies, thanks so much, but you'll enjoy the service much more without me. I haven't been to church in so long, I'm sure the walls would shake. You wouldn't want to lose all that stained glass, now would you?"

"Don't be silly, dear. It'll be fine, and Hilda and I will take you both to the Jefferson Hotel for their special Sunday brunch afterward. We like to treat ourselves every Sunday. They have those cinnamon rolls you like so much, dear." She eyed Jennifer, the invitation dangling.

"Lizzie, you truly are wicked," Jennifer gave in with a sigh. "You know I can resist anything except those."

"Wonderful!" Lizzie enthused. "Now, I suggest we come early for the nine o'clock service. That way we can make sure we don't miss Martha." Lizzie's knitting picked up speed.

Kelly caught Jennifer's eye. "Give me your address and phone number and I'll pick you up Sunday morning. I'll even bring coffee."

"Please. Lots of it," Jennifer said with a resigned shake of her head as she withdrew a business card from her bag.

Seven

Kelly bent over, hands above her knees, and squinted at the batter hunched over home plate. The sky was that brilliant Colorado blue she remembered so well, and the mile-high sunlight was brutal. She adjusted her *USS Kitty Hawk* baseball cap. Its brim was frayed, but it was her good luck charm. It was also her dad's. She couldn't play without it.

Her right knee was skinned from her slide into second base in the last inning. There was dirt and grit imbedded in her left knee from an earlier slide. Her knees stung, her back ached from first basemen's crouch, and her right shoulder was sore from throwing—and she couldn't be happier.

The batter swung at Lisa's curve ball and missed. Kelly's foot reached out for first base instinctively. Why had she deprived herself of this simple pleasure these last few years? She loved playing ball. She'd played it her whole life. In fact, softball had been the one thing she could depend on when her dad took a new job and they had to move again. Every time she'd come to a new school, that's how she found friends.

The batter swung and cut the air. Strike two. Lisa's got some stuff, Kelly had to admit. She glanced over her shoulder at the varied group on the field. Coed leagues were always a melting pot of twenty- and thirty-somethings. It reminded her of the accounting firm's team she used to play on before . . . well, before her dad got sick. She'd let a lot of things go when Dad got sick.

Yeah, like your life, a voice nagged inside.

Over in left field, Megan was swaying side to side, her fielder's glove at the ready and her face smeared with enough sunscreen to shut down a solar array. Kelly grinned. What a contradiction Megan was. Shy, geeky tech writer, hardware-software guru, and, according to Lisa, a passionate fashion designer at heart. Kelly was surprised that Megan played softball. Kelly would never have imagined quiet, dainty Megan running down a ball. But there she was, playing her heart out and getting dirty.

"Hey . . . batter-batter-batter-batter-batter!" yelled a grinning middle-aged guy from the bleachers. Memories surfaced as Kelly recalled hearing the familiar parental chant, called out to children still learning the game.

A woman's movement caught her eye, and Kelly stifled a laugh. There was Jennifer, hiding her hangover behind sunglasses and a hat that would have done Scarlett proud, sipping a double espresso latte.

"Too many tequila shooters last night," was all she muttered as she passed Kelly on the way to the bleachers. The fact that Jennifer was even here at ten o'clock on a Saturday morning was amazing.

The batter swung again, and this time she connected, then headed down the baseline as the ball landed fair. Old instincts took over then, muscles long trained into movements that were second nature. Kelly didn't even have to think. Lisa snatched the ball in a nanosecond and whipped it to Kelly. It hit her glove with a satisfying *whap.* Oh, yeah. Kelly reached out to tag the girl as she slid into base. *Gotcha,* she said inside.

"Way to go, Lisa!" she called out as she threw the ball back to the pitching mound. Lisa snagged it with her graceful long-armed movement. Kelly rubbed her right shoulder. Even sore, it felt good. In fact, she felt good—until she spied the next batter.

Steve Townsend strolled to the plate with the easy assurance of someone who knows he can hit anything the pitcher sends across. Not a problem. Kelly frowned at him out of habit. Of course, he'd probably hit it out of the park. Everyone said he was a baseball star in high school and college. It was too much to hope for that he'd play down a notch.

She was right. Steve connected on Lisa's first pitch, a low-dropping slider that seemed to hang over the plate, just waiting for Steve to hit it. He obliged. Kelly winced at the satisfying *smack* of ball meeting bat—the reverberation that carries on the wind when wood meets force and sends it back again. She watched the ball sail over everyone's head and far into the outfield.

A homer, of course, she thought glumly and debated whether she should trip the smug bastard as he rounded her base.

Kelly pulled in front of Jennifer's condo and grabbed her cell phone. When she'd called five minutes ago to let Jennifer know she was on the way, Jennifer said she was straggling out of the shower. Punching in the numbers, Kelly was surprised to see Jennifer coming down the concrete steps.

"Wow, that was fast," Kelly commented as Jennifer climbed into the car. "I'm impressed. I thought you'd still be getting dressed."

"Old memories returned. I could swear I heard Sister

Josephine's voice nagging me to hurry up or I'd be late for mass." Jennifer looked around. "Where's that coffee?"

"Right here." Kelly reached in the back and brought out the tall cup with familiar green logo. "Drink up."

Jennifer complied without a word.

"I guess you went to parochial school, then?" Kelly asked as she headed through the early morning Sunday traffic.

"Yeah, until eighth grade. You can imagine how happy the nuns were to see me go."

Kelly laughed. "I'll bet you gave them fits."

"I did my best. How about you?"

"I went to public schools, everywhere we lived. My dad was a district manager for a large automotive chain, so we moved around a lot."

"Boy, I sure would have liked moving around as a kid," Jennifer said between sips. "I was bored out of my skull back in the Midwest."

"Where?"

"Indianapolis."

Memories triggered. "We lived in Fort Wayne for about a year, before we went to Detroit, then on to Newark, New Jersey, for two years, then finally settled in northern Virginia for my last three years of high school."

"I thought you grew up here."

"I did, but when I was ten my dad got promoted and we went on the road. Actually we went to Saint Louis for a year before Indiana."

"Boy, you really did move around. Was it hard making friends? In school and all?"

"Yeah, it was always kind of scary at first. But playing ball helped. Maybe that's why I love it so much. That's how I made friends in every new school." She shook her head at the flood of memories coming back as she drove. "It was still hard though," she said wistfully. "Sometimes I'd make up all these fantastic stories about why my dad and I had to move around so much."

She turned onto a large avenue, bordered on both sides by older gracious homes, but Kelly didn't even notice. "One of my favorites was that my dad was this notorious and untouchable card shark who roamed about the country making his living in shadowy back rooms of fancy casinos. I'd sit next to him and pour his whiskey, and count cards, of course."

"Of course."

"Then afterward, we'd sneak away in the early morning light. In a red convertible, too." Kelly laughed. Where had that memory come from? "I'd daydream out the window of our old yellow Plymouth station wagon. Dad called it beige, but it looked dog-barf yellow to me."

Jennifer raised her hand. "Had one of those." She up-ended her cup then pointed. "Saint Mark's is up ahead."

"Oh my gosh, is that Lizzie out front?" Kelly said as she slowed the car, spying pink-and-white fabric fluttering in the spring breeze.

"Sure is." Jennifer waved through the window, then pointed to the right. "You can park in this lot on Sunday."

Kelly pulled in and grabbed the first space she spotted. "Boy, she really likes pink, doesn't she?" Kelly said with a chuckle as they both headed through the lot and across the street.

"Oh, yeah."

Lizzie stood on the church steps waiting, a huge grin on her face. "Good morning, girls! You're bright and early, too," she announced.

"Don't remind me how early it is, Lizzie. I'm barely awake now," Jennifer teased. "I hope the priests are as boring as I remember, so I can go back to sleep. We are sitting in the back, I hope?"

Lizzie's musical little laugh ran up the scale as she settled herself between the two of them. "Jennifer, you're such a caution. Yes, we are sitting in the back. In fact, I've got our places already saved. Come along." And she encircled her arms around theirs and guided them through the open doorway and into St. Mark's.

They paused at the entrance to the sanctuary, and Kelly's gaze swept over the graceful vaulted ceiling, the tall marble columns, and walls of stained glass—window after window. Poignant memories surfaced. The last time she'd been here with Helen was Christmas Eve mass.

Jennifer deliberately walked over to the sconce of holy water and peered into it. "Well, I don't see any ripples, so the walls aren't shaking. Yet. The Heavenly Powers must not know I'm here."

"Come, dears," Lizzie indicated the last pew in the center.

Kelly settled between Lizzie and Jennifer and noticed that they could watch both entrances from this vantage point. Good job, Lizzie.

Lizzie straightened her pink flounces and whispered. "I've already explained to Hilda why we're sitting back here. Now, I suggest we start our prayers. That way no one will notice our surveillance." She pulled out the cushioned kneelers and settled herself.

"Okay," Kelly went along and gingerly knelt. Both knees complained, still sore from yesterday's game. Glancing over her shoulder, she noticed Jennifer had already cuddled into a cozy position against the side of the pew, arms folded, eyes closed. "I take it you're praying," Kelly whispered.

"Repenting is more like it," she replied without opening her eyes.

Kelly leaned her arms on the pew in front and watched the church slowly fill with people. Pastel spring colors were everywhere, and Lizzie was not the only lover of pink. The overcast sky must have cleared, because Kelly noticed brilliant colors splashed across a side wall. Sun painting through stained glass.

Since she'd been going to the shop, Kelly seemed to notice colors more, vibrant colors everywhere she went.

How come everything looked different to her now? she wondered.

Her knees sent a painful message, and Kelly eased herself off the kneeler and onto the seat. Clasping her hands, she still kept her reverent pose. Lizzie was actually saying prayers, Kelly observed, a pearl rosary dangling between her fingers.

Kelly didn't pray anymore. It didn't work. She'd prayed a lot when her dad was first diagnosed with cancer and all through his treatment. All those prayers, and none of them worked. He died anyway.

Lizzie's voice broke through Kelly's painful memories. "Don't make a stir, dear, but I believe I see her. She just passed us. The woman in the navy blue dress." Lizzie nodded toward the left aisle.

Kelly focused on the parishioners in the aisle. A slight, gray-haired woman in a navy blue dress slowly walked toward the front of the sanctuary. Choosing a side pew, she settled in and immediately sank to her knees, head lowered, hands clasped. Kelly wished she could have seen her features. From the back she looked like half the older women in church.

As if reading her mind, Lizzie spoke up. "We'll get a better look at her when she leaves, dear. She'll pass right by us again. I suggest you wait for a weekday service to introduce yourself. Not so many people around, you see. She appears easily startled."

Kelly suppressed a smile. Lizzie was turning out to be quite the stake-out queen. But she'd made a good point. The church was filled with people. They'd be standing in the aisles by nine o'clock when the service began. If this Martha was as easily startled as Lizzie suggested, she might panic when Kelly introduced herself. If she chose to run rather than talk, she could disappear into the crowd of departing parishioners. Not the ideal way to begin a relationship, Kelly decided.

"Thanks, Lizzie, that's a good suggestion," Kelly
leaned over and whispered.

Kelly flicked the tiny speck off her dark blue skirt and re-
crossed her legs for the fourth time in the last thirty minutes. She leaned back into the empty pew and observed
the nearly empty church. Only a handful of people sat in
the front two pews for Monday morning mass. Kelly had
shown up early and chosen a spot mid-church for her vantage point. She figured when she introduced herself,
Martha would be too far from the door to make a run for
it. Meanwhile, Kelly did her best to appear absorbed in
prayer so the priest wouldn't include her in the proceed-
ings.

Her planning paid off. Martha arrived alone, five minutes before the service began. All Kelly had to do was
wait for the service to end. While the priest's voice rose
and fell in the familiar ritual, Kelly pondered the best way
to greet Martha. She wanted to appear friendly and nonthreatening, but she wasn't sure what that looked like.

Instead, her mind kept bringing back scenes from the
night before when she'd joined Lisa, Megan and the rest
of their team for dinner and drinks in a cozy Old Town
café. Kelly hadn't laughed that much in a long time. It felt
good. It also felt good to hear everyone ask her to continue to play with them.

"Please, Kelly," the shortstop, Sherrie, pleaded across
the table. "You're awesome, girl. We need you."

The effusive praise and encouragement had stroked
something deep down inside that Kelly hadn't felt in a
very long time. That felt better than good. She was really
glad she'd gotten her boss's commitment for a couple of
months "or so." The "or so" might be stretched.

The sudden movement of the prayerful few in the front
captured her attention, as they stood and held out their
hands for the blessing that ended each service. Kelly

straightened her businesslike attire and grabbed her shoulder bag. Most of the attendees were older, but not all, she noticed as they headed down the aisle.

Martha was near the end of the group, so Kelly rose, genuflected, and crossed herself out of habit. Then she stood quietly, waiting for Martha to approach, hoping no one else would strike up a conversation with her.

As Martha drew closer, head bent, hands still clasped as if in prayer, Kelly tried to study her features but couldn't get a good look. Finally, the older woman was only a few feet from the pew, and Kelly stepped into the aisle to face her.

"Martha?" she asked in a soft voice which she hoped was nonthreatening.

The older woman stopped abruptly, her head jerking up in obvious surprise. She stared back into Kelly's face, her eyes wide with concern, as if she wasn't used to being spoken to by strangers. Kelly stared into huge blue eyes, made even bluer by Martha's white face. Kelly sincerely hoped Martha didn't have a heart condition, because she looked scared to death.

"Yes?" she answered barely above a whisper.

"Martha, I'm sorry if I startled you, but I wanted to introduce myself. I'm Helen Rosburg's niece, Kelly Flynn, from Washington, D.C."

The startled blue gaze changed. Fear changed to wary observation. "Ahhh, yes. Kelly." She nodded. "I can see the resemblance now."

Relieved and a bit surprised at Martha's acknowledgment, Kelly continued. "Someone from the knitting shop had seen you at Helen's service last week and mentioned you attended this church. So I thought I'd come by and meet you." She attempted a bright smile. "I was surprised to learn Helen had any other relatives in the area. She always said she was the last one in the family."

Martha's pale face had regained some color and a tiny smile as well. "Well, that's almost true. I'm one of her distant cousins from Wyoming, so we never saw you folks down here that often. My father had a sheep ranch way up near Lander. I didn't even move here until a few years ago."

Kelly noticed Martha seemed to cradle her left arm with her right. *Perhaps she has a handicap,* Kelly thought. *That could be why Helen was so protective of her.* All manner of questions bubbled up inside Kelly now about this extended family she never knew. "Martha, I'd really like to find a time to chat with you about the family and Aunt Helen, if I could?" she ventured. "Is there a time I could come and visit you? Do you live here in Fort Connor?"

Martha glanced toward the stained-glass windows, morning sun beginning to heat up the glass and send colorful shards of light across the pews. Kelly could feel her hesitation, but when Martha turned back, she said, "Yes, of course. Why don't you come by this afternoon about two?"

Delighted Martha was so obliging, Kelly beamed. "That would be wonderful! I'll look forward to it. Where do you live?"

"I'm in a small house in Landport, just north of town. On Maple Drive—"

A woman's voice interrupted, calling from the back of the church. "Martha, are you coming, dear?"

Martha waved to the other woman. "I'll be right there, Myrtle," then turned back to Kelly. "My house is a small white frame, two-eleven Maple. I'll expect you at two, Kelly."

With that, Martha hastened down the aisle to join her friend, leaving Kelly grateful for the invitation and a bit startled at Martha's speedy departure. "Good-bye, thank you," Kelly called as the two women left the church.

Eight

Kelly glanced at her watch as she closed her car door. If the mail had brought her office files, she'd have a couple of hours to get them set up before her visit with Martha. She was headed toward the mailbox until she heard the sound of an increasingly familiar voice in her backyard. Sure enough, there was Steve playing with *her* dog. Didn't this guy have a dog at home?

"Here you go, boy. All yours," Steve called and threw several golf balls into the yard. Carl responded with an excited bark and raced off to catch them as Steve approached Kelly. "Maybe these old balls will keep him off the course."

Kelly had already forgotten. "Yeah, thanks. Let's hope it works."

"Let's hope," Steve said with a grin as he reached into his jeans pocket and withdrew a golf ball. "I rescued these a minute ago. Carl had six of them."

Kelly winced. "Darn it! I was hoping—"

"What? That he'd heed your lecture?"

Kelly scowled at him, which seemed to amuse Steve to no end. He actually grinned wider. Brother, this guy annoyed her on purpose. What was with him, anyway? She took a deep breath. "Noooo, I was hoping he'd get bored and stop, I guess."

"Why would he? It's a fun game. He steals balls. You fuss at him. Do you scowl at him the same way? I mean, like you are right now?" Steve laughed. "Face it, Kelly. You're fun to tease."

Of course, that only made Kelly scowl more, which made Steve laugh even more. "Don't you have something better to do than stand here and be annoying?" She challenged.

"Matter of fact, yes. I'm going to throw these balls back onto the course so the golfers can find them, then go take Mimi to see some cabinets," Steve said as he turned to leave, then stopped. "Uh oh. Too late. I think Carl's busted."

To Kelly's dismay she spied three male golfers striding off the edge of the greens and headed right toward them. One man, in plaid slacks, pointed at them with his golf club. When he drew closer, Kelly could see he didn't look happy.

"Hey! Are those my golf balls? Dammit! I've been looking for them," he yelled as he strode up.

"No, Mr. Houston, those are some old balls of mine," Steve answered congenially, pointing toward the balls scattered about the yard. "I was about to place yours on the greens now. The dog's new to the neighborhood, and I'm sure the balls were just too tempting. He'll settle down."

"Settle down, my ass!" Houston yelled, clearly furious. "I've been losing balls all week because of him."

Kelly noticed his two middle-aged golfing companions hung back from the fray a few feet and stared at the ground. The balding man shook his head and grinned at his taller, better-dressed companion.

"It's your lousy slice, Frank, that's been losing the balls," Baldie taunted. "The dog's just doing what comes naturally. Chasing balls." Then he and his natty friend snickered in unison.

Watching Houston's face flush even redder, Kelly spoke up. "Mister, I apologize for my dog—"

Houston cut her off, jabbing his club toward Carl. "That mangy hound has no business stealing my golf balls just because they roll over here. I'm going to report him!"

Watching the club's movement, Carl burst into a ferocious, snarling bark, glaring right at Houston. Houston jumped back.

"See? He's vicious! Look at him!" he yelled, which only made Carl bark more.

"Carl, easy!" Kelly commanded, hand raised, as she stepped between Houston and her dog.

"For God's sake, Frank, put the club down!" Well-Dressed yelled. "You're deliberately provoking him."

"Yeah, Frank," Baldie interjected. "You're on *his* turf now. If you wanta discuss territorial imperative with a Rottweiler, go ahead. We'll pick up the pieces."

Oh, great, Kelly worried. They've already put Carl into the killer Rottie category.

"Carl has never attacked anyone before, I assure you," she swore, hoping to convince them.

"He's vicious, I tell you! Vicious, and I'm gonna report him—"

"Look, Mr. Houston," Steve interrupted, stepping forward. "I can vouch for the dog myself. He's not vicious, are you, Carl?" Steve placed one hand on the fence and gestured to Carl. Carl obliged instantly by standing up, paws on fence, so Steve could rub his head. Steve patted Carl with one hand and reached into his pocket with the other, withdrawing the stolen golf balls. "Here you go," he offered them to Houston. "Now, I've got a much better way to solve this. Why don't—"

"Look at that!" Houston exclaimed, staring at the balls.

"Tooth marks on my new Titleists! I just bought these."
His companions snickered behind their golf gloves.

"I've got a better way to solve this, Mr. Houston,"
Steve offered. "Let me help with that slice of yours. See if
we can reduce the angle a little. You're almost on the
green now—"

"By about fifty yards," Baldie said with a derisive
snort.

"And with a little tweaking, we can get you straightened out, I'm positive," Steve continued, barely missing a
beat.

"You giving free lessons, Steve?" Well-Dressed inquired with a smile. "If so, sign me up."

"On special occasions, Alan," Steve replied.

"What's so special about this?"

Steve shrugged. "I like the dog and don't want to see
him get a bad rep."

Kelly watched this exchange with fascination. The
older men were paying careful attention to Steve, as if his
offer of golf lessons was a big deal. Even Houston had
calmed down. Brother, Steve must be one heckuva golf
instructor.

"You serious about those lessons?" Houston peered at
Steve.

"Absolutely."

"What if it takes more than one lesson?" he bargained
with an oily smile.

"Then it takes more than one."

"Jeez, Frank, don't push it," Baldie jabbed. "Take the
lessons and leave the dog alone."

Houston scowled at Carl, who returned the favor.
"Okay, I'll take you up on the offer. When can we start?"

"I'll check my schedule and give you a call," Steve
said. "Got a card?" Houston searched his pocket and
obliged.

Kelly felt the ball of tension in her stomach start to re-
cede, until she heard a woman's voice call out.

"Hallloo! Excuse me? Are you gentlemen searching for golf balls, I hope?"

Oh no, Kelly thought as she watched a very pretty blonde, attired completely in pink shirt, shorts, and tennis shoes walk up, dangling a golf club side to side.

"I seem to have lost mine," she declared. "It's so embarrassing. I've just started lessons, and I'm absolutely awful! I declare, I'll never master this game. I don't know how I hit one all the way over here."

"Frank, why don't you check those," Baldie ordered, pointing to Houston's toothmarked balls. "Maybe one of them is hers."

"Oh, no," she shook her golden head. "Mine are specially marked, and they're pink. That's so I can't lose them."

"Good idea, ma'am," Steve said with a lazy smile. Well-Dressed hid his laughter behind a sudden cough.

"I'll be sure to look for it, ma'am," Kelly offered. "I'm afraid my dog has been tempted by the flying balls and—" She paused, watching Carl suddenly bound over to the corner of the yard and nose behind the flowerpots, then trot back to the fence.

"What the—?" she said, staring at the object in Carl's mouth. "Carl, what have you got?" She held out her hand. Carl obediently dropped a pink golf ball into her palm.

"Oh, my!" Pinkie exclaimed. "He found my ball. What a nice doggie." And she reached out to pat Carl on the head. Carl slurped her hand while everyone except Frank Houston laughed out loud.

Kelly walked up the narrow sidewalk leading to Martha's front porch. The concrete was cracked and broken in places, she noticed, and the little frame house was badly in need of paint. However, the gardens were immaculately tidy and filled with blooming plants. Splashy bright tulips—red, yellow, purple—reached for the sun. She glanced about the older neighborhood streets. Kelly hadn't been in Landport for years, usually passing straight through on the way into the canyons. As a small, northern bedroom community for Fort Connor, the pace was slower and appealed to many who wanted out of the traffic and ever-increasing development to the south.

As Kelly started up the creaky wooden steps, she heard the squeak of a screen door opening. Martha appeared in the doorway, in a pale-blue cotton housedress and bedroom slippers.

"Hello, Kelly, come in. I've made us a pot of tea," she greeted and held the screen door wide.

"Thanks, Martha, that's sweet of you," Kelly said as she entered. Then she held out a slim rectangular box. "I brought these. They're from that fancy chocolate shop in Old Town."

"Oh, aren't you sweet, Kelly. Thank you." Martha's thin face brightened with a smile. "You settle into a comfy chair, and I'll bring our tea." She placed the chocolates on the dining room table as she walked past.

Kelly glanced about the sparsely furnished living room and dining room and noticed a familiar chair beside the floor lamp. She headed straight for it and sat down, immediately sinking another two inches lower. She remembered this chair. It was Uncle Jim's and was one of Kelly's favorite spots to read when she was a child. She ran her fingers over the worn upholstery with fond recollection of enjoyable hours spent there.

Helen must have given it to Martha years ago, she mused, scrutinizing the other furniture as well. By the time Martha emerged with a small tea tray in one hand, Kelly had identified three chairs and two end tables that once resided at her aunt's. She wondered if Helen had provided all the furniture. Didn't Martha have furniture of her own? Kelly also couldn't help noticing the definite absence of a common item in most elderly women's homes: knickknacks.

There were none on the fireplace mantle or on the shelves. Lacy crocheted doilies adorned the backs of chairs and shelves instead. As for framed pictures, there was only one hanging on the wall. It looked to be an enlarged photo of Helen and Jim. Every older home of this vintage that Kelly had visited over the years had its walls covered with family portraits and modern photos. Memories recaptured. Where were Martha's family photos? Where were Martha's memories?

Martha crossed the living room, teacup in hand. "Here you go, my dear." She offered the cup to Kelly. "I've put some cream and sugar in it already. Is that all right?"

Not really, but Kelly would bite her tongue before saying so. "That's fine, Martha," she lied as she accepted the cup. "Come, sit. Stop fussing about me."

Martha took her cup and settled into a high-backed maple rocking chair. Kelly noticed she steadied the saucer against her left hand while she held the cup with her right and wondered how she'd injured her arm. But then, Kelly had so many questions she didn't know where to begin. Meanwhile, Martha rocked quietly and sipped her tea, studying Kelly.

"I can see you've got a lot of questions, Kelly," Martha spoke up. "Foremost, you're probably wondering why Helen never told you about me."

"Ahhh, yes," Kelly said, relieved Martha initiated the subject. "I have to admit I'm curious. Helen always said she was the only one left in Colorado."

A smile sparked briefly on Martha's thin face, then was gone. "Well, I guess that's technically true. I lived my whole life in Wyoming."

Kelly gestured toward the empty walls. "I was actually hoping you had some photos or family albums. It would be wonderful to see some of these relatives. Do you have any photos at all?"

A cloud passed across Martha's face. "Yes, I had many albums and pictures, Kelly. A lifetime's worth. But they're

all back in Wyoming. Back in what was once my home."
She sipped her tea.

"What happened? Did you lose your home?" Kelly
asked, intrigued by the cryptic reply.

Martha set her empty teacup on an end table and folded
her hands in her lap before she settled a somber gaze on
Kelly. "No, I walked away from it. Ran, actually. In the
middle of the night. I literally took the clothes on my back
and my purse, that's all. You see, my husband's drinking
had increased over the years, and he started hitting me.
Just a slap at first, but it got worse each time. I won't go
into the details, they're still too painful. But one night,
four years ago, he broke my arm, then he passed out on
the sofa, drunk. That night, I knew I had to escape, or he
might kill me the next time. I ran five miles down the road
to the closest neighbor and begged them to drive me to
Cheyenne. There, I called Helen. She'd always said to call
if I ever needed her. Bless her soul, she drove up to get me
that very night."

Kelly sat mute, stunned by what she heard.

Martha continued. "Helen took me to the hospital in
Fort Connor, then helped me find this place, and even paid
the rent until I got my Social Security checks again. She
asked her lawyer, Mr. Chambers, to help me. You see, I
was deathly afraid of my husband discovering where I
was. So, Mr. Chambers handled everything, dear man."
She rocked silently, staring ahead.

Kelly sat in silence, questions bombarding her inside.
"Martha, I'm so sorry," she said finally. "Trust me, I will
never divulge your whereabouts to a living soul, I swear."

Martha's thin face relaxed visibly. "Thank you, Kelly.
You're truly as caring as Helen always said you were. But
we no longer have to worry. I read in the Wyoming papers
last January that my husband had died. Drinking, of
course. He ran his truck off the road and crashed into
some boulders one night. He died instantly, the paper
said." Her voice trailed off wistfully. "It was so very sad

and such a waste. He really was a good man at heart. It was the drink that did it."

Kelly held her tongue and decided to turn the conversation toward the future, not the past. "Has Mr. Chambers checked into your inheritance rights, Martha? You and your husband were still married, right?"

A smile played with the corners of Martha's mouth. "Ever the accountant, aren't you, Kelly? Helen depended on your cool head and sharp mind. Yes, Mr. Chambers is looking into the estate for me. Again, for free. I can never repay that man."

"Are your children in Wyoming?"

Martha's smile vanished. "In a matter of speaking. Our only child, our son, Ronald, died when he was only seventeen. He was driving too fast on one of the country roads. He's buried there on our land." Her voice faded away.

Kelly sat and sipped the sugary tea, choosing her words. She hadn't expected to hear a story such as this. "Martha, I will be happy to help you in any way I can," she said finally. "When Mr. Chambers finishes with the estate settlement, I'll do your taxes, if you'd like."

"Oh, would you? That would be so helpful. I confess I've never had a head for business. Ralph always handled that, including our taxes."

Kelly paused, forming her next question. The possibility that Helen had intended the loan money for Martha had been niggling in her mind ever since she'd learned of Martha's existence. Maybe she could work into it.

"How is your health, Martha?" she ventured. "I mean, does your arm give you any trouble? I notice you favor it."

In affirmation, Martha stroked her left arm gently. "It twinges when the weather changes. And of course, I no longer have the same use of it that I used to. But I've adjusted. I've even learned how to open jars." She lifted her chin a bit, Kelly noticed.

"So, your health is good, then," she continued to probe. "I mean, your heart and everything?"

Martha almost looked amused. "Yes, indeed, it is. I know I look frail, and the arm adds to that, but inside I'm strong as an ox, Kelly. I used to work sunup to sundown on the farm years ago. Kept me healthy, I guess. Why do you ask?"

Kelly let out a sigh. "Well, to be honest, I was wondering if you held the answer to something that's puzzling me. You see, I learned last week that Helen had refinanced the mortgage on her cottage and withdrawn a large amount of money. She never told me she planned to do that. So I was trying to figure out why she'd need the money and not tell me." Kelly stared through the tall living room window, not really seeing the trees outside. "When I heard about you and met you briefly in church, I confess, I thought perhaps she'd intended the money for you. And maybe you needed it for . . . for something." She gestured in an attempt to explain. "Maybe you needed an operation or surgery . . . I don't know."

"Money? H-how much m-money?" Martha whispered, her face completely drained of color.

Kelly glanced back at the sound of concern and set her tea cup on the table immediately. It was a good thing Martha had said she was healthy, because she looked as if she was about to pass out that minute. "Martha, are you alright?"

"Yes, yes," she said, dismissing the question with a wave of her hand. "Tell me about this money again. When did Helen withdraw it?"

That cold feeling returned to Kelly's gut. Clearly, Martha knew nothing about Helen's large withdrawal. The neat and tidy answer to the money puzzle had been eliminated, leaving Kelly once again with her nagging doubts. "Helen never told you she was taking out another mortgage and withdrawing cash?" she probed.

"Never. When did this occur?"

"Chambers said she called him the very day of her death and told him she'd just received the check from the loan company. He also said he never dreamed she'd cash it that afternoon."

"That was the day she was murdered?" Martha looked truly horrified now.

"Yes. That's the thing that bothers me the most. The very day she cashes a check for twenty thousand dollars, someone just happens to break into her house and kills her." Kelly deliberately let the lingering resentment seep into her voice.

Martha sat bolt upright in the rocking chair. "*Twenty thousand dollars!*" she exclaimed, eyes as round as saucers.

"That was my reaction, too," Kelly declared. "Frankly, I was hoping you were the answer. Now, I'm left with all my nagging doubts about her death."

"What do you mean, Kelly?" Martha asked, concern evident on her face. "The police have the wretched man responsible for her death. He's in jail, I thought."

"The man in jail is a vagrant the police saw running away from the vicinity that night. They're convinced he's the killer because he has a history of drunken violence." She screwed up her face. "He has no recollection, of course. And on top of that, all the money is missing. Not a single bill was found at the house or near the river. And that doesn't make sense to me, Martha. The police have all sorts of theories for how the money disappeared, but—"

At that, Martha sprang from her rocker and began to pace the worn oak floor. "Oh, dear . . . oh, dear . . . oh, dear . . ." she muttered as she walked, fingers plucking at her left arm.

"What is it, Martha? What's the matter?"

"I had this feeling, a bad feeling," Martha said, so softly Kelly wasn't sure if she was talking to her or not.

"What feeling, Martha? Please tell me," Kelly coaxed. "It might be important."

Martha made one more turn about the small room before stopping in front of Kelly's chair. "Helen was worried about something, and she wouldn't tell me what. But I knew something was wrong. When I questioned her, all she said was, 'Our sins come back to haunt us, don't they?' "

Kelly sank back into the familiar cushioned chair. Sins? Aunt Helen? Surely not. That made no sense. "What did she mean, Martha? Do you have any idea?"

Martha's brief glance answered Kelly's question. "Yes, I'm afraid I do," she said as she returned to her rocker. She rocked quietly for a full minute before speaking. "I'm sure she meant her youthful indiscretion years ago."

With great effort, Kelly kept her jaw from dropping and waited for Martha to continue.

Martha observed Kelly's rapt attention. "Years ago, when Helen was still in high school, she had a . . . well, she conceived a child. This was nineteen fifty-five, so things were very different than they are now. Oh, my, yes. Her parents were stricken, of course, especially when she refused to name the father." Martha's voice got softer as she stared toward the windows. "Her father and mine were brothers, and even though our families didn't see each other often, we stayed in touch. Helen and I were only a year apart. Her father insisted she come to our farm in Wyoming to spend the rest of her pregnancy and have the baby. He also insisted she put the baby up for adoption, or she couldn't return home."

Kelly sat in shocked silence, stunned by what she heard.

"Naturally, Helen and I grew very close during those months. My mother and I both were with her at the birth. And when she gave up the baby." She paused.

"That must have been so hard," Kelly whispered, feeling an anguished tug inside.

"It was," Martha replied. "But we placed him with a local agency, the Sisters of Charity, and they assured us he'd have a wonderful home. A healthy baby boy. Blond and blue-eyed."

"When was he born?" Kelly asked.

"December eleventh, nineteen fifty-five. I remember it was snowing the night he was born. Helen stayed with us through Christmas, then returned to Fort Connor after New Year's. That next year was much happier for her. She met Jim Rosburg that spring, and they were married in late fall." Martha's expression softened. "They had a good marriage."

"Did Helen ever get curious about the child? Or try to look for him in later years?"

Martha shook her head. "Not to my knowledge. Helen and I never spoke of that particular bit of shared history again."

"But you think her comment last month referred to that?" Kelly pried.

"I'm afraid so," she said, rubbing her arm. "I had this bad feeling come over me when she said it. And I asked her straight out if she meant the child, but she wouldn't answer. Of course, that worried me even more."

"Do you think the child learned of her identity and contacted her?"

Martha shook her head. "I don't know if it was the child or perhaps the father who had come back to 'haunt' her, as she said. I wish I knew."

So did Kelly. Hundreds of questions were buzzing inside now, but Kelly had no answers. "And she never revealed the name of the father?"

"Never."

"Did she ever say anything about him?"

Martha sighed. "Only that he 'couldn't marry her.' That's all she ever said."

Hmmmm, Kelly thought. *Couldn't or wouldn't?* she wondered. And who was he? Maybe Helen kept the birth certificate or something. Something with the father's name on it. Kelly had yet to really search the desk or dressers in the cottage. Perhaps Helen left a clue to this man's identity.

Had the baby's father reentered her life? Had the child found out his true mother and contacted her? Which was it?

Kelly pulled herself out of the comfy chair. "Martha, I cannot thank you enough for trusting me with all this. I'm going back to the cottage to start searching right now. Helen may have saved some memento or something from the past that might tell me more."

"Do you really think her death is connected to all of that in the past?" Martha asked, face puckering with concern again.

"I don't know, Martha. But like you, I've got a bad feeling about all of this. Something's not right about the police version of Helen's death, and I intend to find out what it is."

Nine

Kelly snapped on the miniature Victorian desk lamp, and a golden circle of light spilled across Helen's maple desk and onto the floor. Dusk had settled, and she didn't even notice. If it hadn't been for Carl barking for supper in the yard, she wouldn't have known it was dark outside. Her stomach growled, and she checked her watch. No wonder she was hungry. At least Carl was smart enough to know dinnertime when it arrived.

She'd been so absorbed in searching that she'd lost all track of time. Checking her stainless steel mug came up empty. Just like her search. She'd gone through every drawer in Helen's house—desk, bedroom dressers, dining room cabinets, china closet, kitchen drawers, even the tool drawers in the garage. Nothing. Kelly had even checked the undersides of each drawer and cabinet in case Helen had hidden a document in the cracks. There was no paper, no picture, no record of any kind that indicated this child existed.

Kelly stood up and indulged in a long stretch. Food

would help. She always ran dry of ideas on an empty stomach. On the way to the kitchen, she noticed that the knitting shop was already closed and dark. It seemed like only a few minutes ago that she'd called Mimi and asked about the boxes in the garage. Now, it was nearly night.

Mimi had confirmed that the boxes contained only books. No papers or folders of any kind. *Darn,* Kelly thought, *every place turned up nothing.* Helen must have eliminated every trace of that event in her life.

Kelly surveyed the fridge's meager contents and chose a peach yogurt. She really needed to buy groceries. At least there was some coffee left, and she drained the last of the pot into her mug. Snagging a spoon, she wandered back into the cozy living room and sat in the middle of the old oriental rug to enjoy what passed for dinner. Was there any place she hadn't looked, she wondered?

She surveyed the room and consumed the yogurt in two minutes flat. Her glance traveled over the bookshelves, drifted away, then abruptly returned. She'd noticed on the lower shelf some varying size volumes, not the neat and tidy rows of novels and handyman and history books. Curious, she settled beside the bookcase and removed one. It was an atlas. Just to be sure, she riffled the pages, then replaced it and withdrew the black leather volume beside it. The leather felt smooth and warm to the touch. On the front was an American flag inlay and the name of Helen's high school and the date—1955.

Helen's high school yearbook. Kelly felt a little buzz inside, and it wasn't connected to caffeine. Helen was eighteen when she gave birth, that meant she was seventeen when she became pregnant and still in high school. The baby was born in December, after her graduation. *Maybe the father was a fellow student,* Kelly thought as she turned the pages.

Black-and-white photos of young women in white blouses and impossibly full skirts, crinolines peeking from beneath. Clean-shaven young men with crew cuts.

Every page, it seemed, had a signature. That didn't surprise Kelly, knowing her aunt's vivacious nature. Helen probably had lots of friends. Loopy, swirling script recorded best wishes. And spare, cramped signatures wrote across photos.

There was Lawrence Chambers, she noticed. Younger-looking but somber even then. He stared out with wide eyes. "To Helen—the brightest girl in class!" he wrote beside his picture. Kelly paged through the class snapshots and into the activities section of the yearbook. Greetings and best wishes adorned nearly every page.

Kelly was about to riffle through the last pages, when she spotted another signature. This one wasn't childish scribble or loopy swirls, but bold, heavy strokes of a black ink pen. "Yours, always. Curt," the jagged script read. Above was a photo of a lean and lanky young cowboy holding a horse's reins and staring right into the camera, as if daring the photographer to capture his image. Kelly leaned over the photo, fascinated by the young cowboy. All trace of boyhood was gone from his face. Only the slightly cocky lift to his chin hinted at youth. Something about the photo made Kelly's antennae buzz. Maybe she'd hit pay dirt after all.

She scanned the credits for his name. Curtis Stackhouse. Flipping to the back, she scanned the index and found two more photos. One a blurry shot of Curtis on the football squad and the formal graduation "mug shot." Kelly noticed that the dare-you look in Stackhouse's eye was evident even there.

Kelly stood up and headed for the dining room and her laptop computer. Thank goodness her office files hadn't arrived yet. That way she wouldn't feel guilty spending the rest of the evening tracking Curtis Stackhouse on the Web.

• • •

"Hey, good morning," Rosa called out when Kelly made the turn from the restaurant doorway into the knitting shop.

"It's a great morning, Rosa," Kelly declared as she made her way around a weaving loom. "Are those all knitting magazines?" she asked when she noticed Rosa's armload.

"Well, some are. Others are pattern magazines, and weaving magazines, and spinning magazines, and designer magazines." She smiled over her shoulder. "You name it, we've got it."

"I'll have to check those later," Kelly promised and headed for the main room, balancing briefcase, knitting tote bag, and coffee mug. She almost got there, but the changing display in the middle room captured her first.

The fat multicolored bundles of chunky yarn she chose for her new scarf were now replaced by solid pastels—pink, lime, coral, tangerine—all just as pudgy and soft and begging to be touched. Kelly freed up one hand and started squeezing the plump bundles, unable to resist. New skeins in different colors had been added to the other displays as well. Naturally, she had to examine those, indulging the irresistible desire to sink her fingers into the softness.

Another new display on the center table caught her attention next. It was a little girl's coat in a rich burgundy. She leaned over the table and fingered the fabric. It resembled an old-fashioned bathrobe and felt even softer. What was it, she wondered?

"It's French chenille," Rosa spoke up beside her. "It comes on one of those big cones, see?" She pointed to the corner, and sure enough, there was a huge cone of burgundy chenille.

"It feels like an old-fashioned bathrobe," Kelly joked. "But softer."

"Oh, yeah. It's yummy soft and knits up like a dream. You should see how fast this little coat knits up."

Kelly stared in awe. It had tiny sleeves and a collar and buttons. "Easy for you to say. I'm just learning. No way could I do that."

Rosa tossed her long dark braid behind her back and laughed. "You'll be surprised how quickly you'll learn. I made one of those for my little girl in January. She turned five, and it was absolutely adorable on her. Meanwhile, you could start with something really easy, like those trendy washcloths."

"Washcloths?"

"Yes, for the bath. They're all the rage. People are knitting those up like crazy. They sell for $30 in the boutique shops."

Kelly's mouth almost dropped open. She was about to comment when Megan came through the foyer and into the shop. Like Kelly, she had a mug in one hand and her tote bag in the other.

"Hey, Kelly. You missed all the excitement yesterday afternoon. The police came over with some yarn they found by the riverbank. They wanted Mimi to identify it to see if it was Helen's."

"What?!" Kelly exclaimed as she followed Megan to the library table where she deposited her things and sat down. "Darn! I wish I'd been here. Was it that Lieutenant Morrison?"

"No, it was a regular uniformed officer," Megan replied as she settled into a chair. "I only got a glimpse of the wool. He had it in a plastic bag. But Mimi could tell you more, after all, he was talking to . . . oh, there you are, Mimi. Tell Kelly what happened yesterday with the purple wool."

Mimi appeared from the office area. "Hi, Kelly," she greeted and started straightening books on the shelves, glancing briefly over her shoulder. "One of the police officers investigating the case came by with a plastic bag with charred pieces of purple wool inside. He wanted to know if it was the same wool Helen was using for the sweater."

"Was it?"

"It appeared to be the same." Mimi continued to move among the shelves, patting books into place. "There was a small section of sweater that hadn't been charred, and I could tell from that."

Kelly frowned. "And he said they found it near the riverbank recently?"

"Yes. I believe he told me they found it yesterday. And they wanted me to identify it before they sent it to the criminal investigative lab in Denver."

"I wonder why they didn't find it the first time they searched the riverbank," Kelly mused out loud, swirling her coffee. "Lieutenant Morrison swore they searched every inch of that trail by the river. And now, a week later, a piece of Helen's sweater shows up."

"Burned, too," Megan contributed, head bent over the turquoise sweater she was completing. Two sleeves had appeared.

"Why would he burn it?" Kelly speculated as she reached into her tote bag and brought out the colorful chunky wool scarf she'd started two days ago. Hopefully, she'd remember what she was doing. "That makes no sense. Here's this drunken vagrant with a purse full of money and he takes time to burn a half-finished sweater."

"I agree, it makes no sense," Megan concurred. "I mean, according to the police he tried to hide the money near the riverbank. If so, then why would he start a fire and draw attention there?" She shook her head.

"Why, indeed?" Mimi spoke softly as she approached.

Kelly glanced into Mimi's worried face. "There are too many things about Helen's death that don't make sense to me, Mimi. I don't like it."

Mimi reached out and patted Kelly's shoulder. "I know you don't, dear. I don't, either. Why don't we knit on it."

"Knit on it?" Kelly repeated with a smile. "What do you mean?"

"Well, whenever I need to think things over, I sit down and knit quietly for a while. It calms my mind, so my thoughts become more ordered or something. Anyway, that's how I work through problems." She smiled then headed toward her office.

"Works for me, too, Mimi," Megan piped up. "Even software code unravels as I knit."

Kelly picked up the oversized needles and half-finished scarf. "Okay, if you say so. Now, let's see, where was I?" She slowly attempted a knit stitch and it cooperated perfectly. Good, she hadn't forgotten and continued the stitches. After a few rows of colorful chunky stitches, Kelly did notice herself relaxing, just a little. She glanced up at Megan, who was intently working an edge. Strange. She didn't feel the desire to talk. It was kind of peaceful just sitting there, knitting in the comfortable room with the morning sun pouring through the windows. It really was peaceful . . . until a man's voice shattered the quiet.

"Well, hello there, Ms. Flynn. The girl at the counter told me I could find you here."

Kelly jerked around and saw a man who looked vaguely familiar. "Yes, I'm Kelly Flynn. And you are . . . ?"

The well-dressed man flashed Kelly a big smile and strode forward. "You probably don't recall, but I was in the threesome that came looking for golf balls the other day. But I wasn't the one acting like a horse's behind." A wicked smile claimed his face.

It was a nice face, Kelly noticed. Tanned, ruddy complexion, topped off with wavy graying hair. Recognition sparked inside. He was one of the golfers, the well-dressed one, and he was even better dressed now. Kelly could tell a hand-tailored suit when she saw one.

"Oh, yes, I remember now." She peered at him, suddenly worried. "Carl didn't steal your golf balls, did he?"

The man threw back his head and laughed out loud for

a second. "No, Ms. Flynn, he didn't. Mainly because I don't have a slice like Frank's. So Carl shouldn't see any of my golf balls. I wanted to introduce myself to you professionally." He reached inside his jacket and withdrew a card, handing it to Kelly. "I'm Alan Gretsky. I'm a real estate broker with Metropolitan Realty. We're the biggest in the area now."

Kelly relaxed as she read the card. Thank goodness. He was a realtor. Realtors she could deal with a lot better than irate golfers. "Ahh, thank you, Mr. Gretsky. I'll keep your card."

"Well, Ms. Flynn, I was hoping we could schedule a few minutes to talk. I'm sure you've noticed all the new retail development that's come to this area recently."

"It's hard to miss, Mr. Gretsky," Kelly relaxed against her chair, bracing for the pitch she could feel coming.

"All that new building has made your property even more valuable, Ms. Flynn," Gretsky said, shoving one hand into his pocket in a relaxed pose. "I spoke to your aunt about selling her place last year, but she wasn't interested. And, believe me, I totally understood her position, Ms. Flynn." He placed his other hand on his heart in apparent empathy. "At her age, moving would be a very traumatic experience. But you, I understand, already reside in another state, am I right?"

He'd done his homework. Kelly nodded. "Yes, I do, Mr. Gretsky. I live in Washington, D.C."

"So, selling this property wouldn't be out of the question, would it?" He cocked his head with studied casualness.

Kelly decided to cut to the chase, so Gretsky would leave and she could get back to her knitting. "Normally, that would be true. However, I learned my aunt recently refinanced and the mortgage terms include very heavy penalties if the property is sold within two years. So, I'm afraid I'll be renting the property instead of selling, Mr. Gretsky. But I'll be sure to keep your card for the future."

Gretsky's disappointment was clearly evident. "I'm, well, I'm sorry to hear that, Ms. Flynn. There are some clients of mine who were most interested in this location." He shook his head and frowned. "Listen, let me check into some things, and I'll get back to you, all right?"

Not really, Kelly thought, but replied, "If you wish, Mr. Gretsky, but I'm afraid it's a waste of your time."

"Maybe not," he said as he turned to leave. "Maybe there's a way to work things out. Meanwhile, you have a good day now." He flashed another bright smile and a wave as he left.

Kelly exhaled a loud sigh as she returned to her knitting. "You gotta love salesmen. If there's a breath left in a corpse, they'll revive it to get a sale."

Megan giggled. "Well, at least he wasn't too pushy."

"Give him time. I sense he won't give up."

After a few quiet minutes, Megan asked, "Have you looked into the consulting ideas yet?"

"No, not yet. I've been so involved in . . . in . . ." Kelly hesitated. How much should she reveal of Helen's past? Would she be disloyal to Helen's memory if she told her friends? Helen was dead. Murdered. And Kelly sensed the real killer was not the man in jail. Perhaps Megan and the others could help in her search for answers.

"You don't have to explain, Kelly. You've been up to your neck in trying to sort through Helen's things and get yourself settled since you got here. Don't worry. You'll have plenty of time to check into the possibilities. Then maybe you won't need Mr. Smiley's services after all." Megan looked up with a wicked grin.

"Yeah, maybe you're right. Meanwhile, there're some other things I need—"

"Hey, there! Missed you yesterday," Jennifer declared as she breezed in and plopped into a chair beside Kelly. She pulled out the nearly finished emerald green sweater. "I'm on break so let's do some quick catch-up. I assumed

Megan has already told you about the wool found by the river, right?"

"Yes, I did, and Kelly is just as suspicious as we were that it hadn't been found before."

"Okay then," Jennifer's needles began moving quickly. "What I want to know now is how was your meeting with Helen's cousin, yesterday? Was she as timid as she looked?"

Kelly watched Jennifer's needles and wondered if they could keep up with Jennifer's quick tongue. "Actually, yes. She clearly doesn't do well with strangers, but once I told her I was Helen's niece, she relaxed. Sort of."

"Helen has a cousin?" Megan asked in surprise. "I never knew."

"Neither did I. So you can imagine my surprise when Lizzie told me last Friday. Helen never mentioned her."

"Lizzie was kind enough to show us this cousin for a price," Jennifer added.

Megan laughed. "Let me guess. She invited you to church."

"Yep. And brunch afterward at the Jefferson Hotel. Believe me, only the thought of those cinnamon rolls got me through the sermon." Jennifer gave an aggrieved sigh.

"Thanks to Lizzie, I was able to recognize Martha at the Monday morning service. There weren't many people around, so she didn't run away when I approached her. In fact, she invited me to her house in Landport yesterday afternoon for a visit."

"Really? That's great. Did she know anything about why Helen needed money?" Jennifer probed.

"Not a thing. In fact, when I told her, she was visibly upset." Kelly saw their rapt expressions and leaned forward, lowering her voice, even though no one else was near. "She told me Helen had been bothered recently by something or someone from her past."

"Someone from her past had been bothering Helen?" Megan whispered, eyes wide.

"What kind of someone?" Jennifer pried. "A good someone or a not-so-good someone?"

"That's what bothers Martha, and me, too. Especially now that she's told me the rest." She purposefully paused. Both Jennifer and Megan leaned forward simultaneously, obviously waiting.

"Well?" Jennifer demanded. "You can't tease us with this Helen-has-a-past tidbit, then drop us. You know we'll pry it out of you eventually."

"You have to promise me you will absolutely keep it to yourselves, no one else. Except Lisa. I'll tell Mimi and Burt this afternoon. Okay? I feel disloyal enough as it is."

"Disloyal? Why?" Jennifer challenged. "Helen's been murdered. Maybe this someone knows something that can trap the killer. Heck, maybe he *is* the killer. Or she."

"That's what I told myself," Kelly admitted. "Okay, here goes. Martha confided that Helen had an illegitimate child right after high school. Her father sent her to Wyoming to live with Martha's family until the baby was born and placed for adoption. Helen and Martha became real close during that time, because they were both the same age. Anyway, Helen's father said she couldn't come home unless she gave up the baby. So, she did as she was ordered and afterward, returned to Fort Connor. According to Martha, Helen met Uncle Jim that next spring and married him in the fall."

"Wow," Megan breathed softly, even her knitting needles slowed.

"Do you think your Uncle Jim was the father?" Jennifer offered. "Maybe they couldn't marry until they were eighteen or something like that."

Kelly shook her head. "No. I remember Uncle Jim telling me he'd just come into town after getting out of the army, and he bought this piece of land for a sheep farm. Then he met Helen on a blind date. One of his army buddies introduced them." She went back to her own knitting as she continued. "Martha said Helen never mentioned the baby again. Or anything about that episode in her life, until last month. Helen came over and looked really worried, according to Martha. She asked Helen what was wrong, and all Helen would say was 'our sins come back to haunt us, don't they?'"

"Uh oh."

"Sounds like the kid found out who his mother was and showed up," Jennifer said. "I've heard of that happening."

"Or the father came back into her life, maybe," Megan suggested.

"Yeah, I figured it had to be one or the other. Or both. Who knows? So I spent all yesterday afternoon going through every drawer and storage cabinet in the cottage, searching for some clues to this child's identity. Or the father's."

"Did you find anything?"

"Nothing about the child. No documents, birth records, nothing. But I did find something interesting in her senior yearbook."

"Ahhh, yes, those god-awful records of our socially challenged years. I burned mine."

Kelly had to smile. "Well, I'm glad Helen didn't. Because I saw a great photo and personal inscription from this hunky cowboy, and I'm going to see what I can find out about him. Seems he still lives in the area. He's a rancher, from what I found on the Web."

Megan grinned. "Let me guess. You googled him."

"Sure did. None of us can hide anymore. A simple Web search can track us down," Kelly joked.

"Forget the Web. I want to see the photo," Jennifer demanded. "A hunky cowboy from Helen's past. Sounds promising." She glanced at her watch, then shoved her knitting into the tote bag. "Gotta get back to work. Talk to you folks later. And I expect to see that photo."

"Will do," Kelly promised as Jennifer sped away.

"Wow . . ." Megan said again. "This is all so surprising. I mean, it doesn't change my feelings about Helen at all. If anything, it deepens my respect for her that she'd make that kind of sacrifice."

"That's how I feel," Kelly said, relieved to see her faith in her friends was justified.

Rosa leaned around the doorway to the classroom area. "Megan, did you want to see the new designer magazines before I put them on display?" she asked.

Megan nearly leaped from her chair. "You bet," she exclaimed and dropped her knitting on the table as she sped from the room. "Be back in a minute, Kelly," she called.

Kelly continued knitting in silence, adding row after colorful row to her scarf, surprised how peaceful it felt. Soon, she'd finish this first skein and have to start the second. Now, how did Jennifer say to join those ends, she searched her memory?

"Well, good morning, Kelly, I was hoping to see you here," Burt's deep voice cut through the quiet.

"Hi, Burt," Kelly said with a warm smile. "You here to teach a class?"

"Naw, I'm here for my morning constitutional," he joked. "Mimi probably told you I come every morning to spin some of her fleeces. Hafta confess I enjoy the spinning a heckuva lot more than that exercise regimen the doc's got me on."

"I bet. Hey, can you do it out here? I'd love to watch. I've heard those classes going on in the background, but I haven't had a chance to watch yet."

"Sure thing. Actually, this spot by the windows is my favorite. All the sunlight sure feels good," he said as he grasped the spinning wheel in the opposite corner and carried it closer to the windows. "There, now," he said, settling the interesting-looking contraption next to a rocker.

"Boy, it sure doesn't look like Martha Washington's spinning wheel at Mount Vernon," Kelly observed as she watched Burt open a bottom cupboard and pull out a large plastic bag. "Is that what you spin?"

Burt settled into the rocker and grabbed two handfuls

of the creamy white fibers in the bag. "Yes, this is a fleece. Straight from the sheep. Cleaned and carded, of course."

Searching her memory for Mount Vernon trivia, she found one. "Carding, that's done on those square things with teeth?"

Burt grinned. "Yep, you have to remove all the unwanted particles and stuff before you can spin it." All the time he spoke, his fingers were pulling the puffy white cloud of fibers apart. "What I'm doing now is to get the fibers separated into what's called *roving* so they're easier to spin. Now, just watch," he instructed.

Kelly was already watching, fascinated by the intricate movements. Burt's fingers wound the roving around a slender spool, then held it taut as his feet started the wheel turning. Slowly the fibers started twisting into a strand of yarn, which fed onto the wheel and wound onto a wooden bobbin.

"Wow," she said after watching the rhythmic motions for a few moments. "Look at how much you've done already," pointing to the bobbin filling with yarn.

"Yeah, and look how much is still in the bag," Burt joked.

Kelly settled back with her knitting, listening to the soft hum of the wheel, and sorted through the competing questions in her head. Which to ask first?

"I guess you heard that the police brought some wool over here for Mimi to identify," she ventured. "Apparently Helen was knitting a purple sweater when she was killed. And the killer stole it. Broke a knitting needle, too. Lieutenant Morrison told me they found the needles and remaining skein of yarn lying beside her body."

She watched Burt for a reaction, but didn't see any. He continued to concentrate on his spinning for a moment before he spoke. "What else did Morrison say?"

"Nothing. Other than they never found the sweater when they were searching the house or vicinity. I asked him straight out why would the killer steal a half-finished sweater? Morrison simply stared back and said he didn't know." Kelly shook her head. "He also told me they made an exhaustive search of the riverbank area at the time. But now, only yesterday, they find some pieces of Helen's wool, burned no less." She deliberately infused the last words with skepticism, hoping to incite a comment.

Burt continued to spin without a word, so Kelly decided to simply pour out her concerns. She was tired of keeping it inside. "You know, Burt, that makes no sense at all. If this drunk really was the killer, why would he take time to steal Helen's knitting? I mean, he'd already grabbed her purse full of money, right?"

"That's a good question," Burt replied, minding the wool.

Encouraged by the positive response, Kelly kept on. "Something else is missing from the cottage, Burt. Helen's heirloom quilt is no longer on the wall where it's always been. Mimi and the others searched every nook and cranny in the house and garage and never found it. I told Lieutenant Morrison, and he simply said Helen probably gave it to someone." She gave a dismissive sound. "But Helen would never do that, Burt. She made the quilt and meant it for me. It's a personal record of her family. No way would she give it away."

"Hmmmm," was all Burt said.

"And there's no way I'll believe that drunken vagrant stole it. After all, he's got Helen's purse in one hand and her knitting in the other. I mean, according to Lieutenant Morrison, that's what happened."

Burt smiled. "Boy, I'll bet Morrison's ears are really burning about now."

"Well, they should be," Kelly gave an indignant sniff. "It's so illogical, it's ludicrous. This guy is drunk and staggering, yet he's able to do all these intriguing complex maneuvers. I don't buy it, Burt."

"What do you believe happened?" Burt asked after a minute.

Kelly took a deep breath and plunged in. "I don't think that vagrant killed Helen. I think someone else did. And that someone else planted the burned wool near the river because that's where the vagrant slept. Making him look more guilty. But I think someone else murdered Helen for the money. Someone either found out about the money or asked her to get it for them. Why else would she take out that loan? And why would she keep it secret from me?"

The wheel finally stopped turning as Burt met Kelly's gaze. "Do you have any idea who that someone might be, Kelly?" he asked, voice somber.

"Not yet, Burt, but I'm going to find out," Kelly swore. "Helen's cousin told me yesterday that several weeks ago, Helen had been contacted by someone from her past, and she was very upset about it. She wouldn't tell her cousin who it was. I think this person contacted Helen and wanted money."

"Then why kill her?" Burt countered. "She had the money right there."

Kelly glanced toward the sunshine. "I don't know, Burt. Maybe something went wrong. Or maybe, it wasn't enough money. Something happened, and Helen wound up dead. The money was stolen. And the quilt, too."

Burt frowned. "The quilt doesn't make sense. Neither does the knitted sweater. Money, yes. Those things, no."

"I know, I know," Kelly gestured impatiently. "There are too many loose ends. That's what drives me crazy."

Burt started the wheel again, his fingers returning to their rhythmic movements as the bobbin filled. "I'll make a couple of phone calls. On the quiet. Don't want to step on any toes, but I still have my contacts in the department. I'll let you know what I find out, okay?"

An immense burden seemed to lift from her shoulders. At last, her suspicions were taken seriously. "Thank you, Burt, I cannot tell you how much I appreciate your help."

"Don't get your hopes up, I'm only going to ask a few questions."

Kelly was about to thank him again, when she spotted a familiar white truck with red and blue stripes come down the driveway. Her office files had arrived at last.

Ten

Mimi toyed with the teaspoon. She'd stirred her cup of Earl Grey tea so much, Kelly was sure it was cold as a stone by now. "This is so very disturbing, Kelly," she said after a moment. "In a way, it was almost comforting to believe that Helen's death was a random act of violence. But now . . ."

"I know," Kelly picked up the thought. "Now, there's a real possibility that the killer knew her, and that's a very scary thought."

"Frightening," Mimi agreed and shivered. "I cannot imagine who this person from her past might be, can you?"

Kelly glanced around the empty café. Pete didn't mind if Mimi's staff entered after closing. Sometimes it was the only private spot available. She leaned back into the wooden chair and swirled the dregs of her coffee. She'd deliberately waited until nearly closing to speak with Mimi, not only to avoid the afternoon customer rush, but also so she could make progress on her office accounts.

Responsibilities had landed with the delivery of her corporate client files. Kelly was amazed how foreign these accounts looked to her after nearly three weeks away from them. Her mind had drifted so far from corporate accounting issues, she wondered at first if she could lasso it back. That image made her laugh. Coming back home to the West was affecting her in more ways than she knew.

"I'm guessing either the child found out his birth mother's identity and approached Helen, or the father re-entered her life. I searched every place I could in the cottage but found nothing about the child. However, I may have found a clue about the father in Helen's high school yearbook."

"Really? What was it?"

"There's a very personal inscription on one of the photos. It's not much, but it's something." Kelly drained the last drops, grounds and all, and screwed up her face at the bitter taste. "His name's Curtis Stackhouse, and he's a rancher in northern Colorado apparently. Unfortunately, I couldn't find much personal information on the Web. I've found notations of land sales, he's listed as a livestock breeder, both sheep and steers. There's a photo of him judging sheep at a state fair years ago. Calves, too. He's a member of various organizations but they didn't list addresses or phone numbers. And he's not listed in the phone directory at all. In fact, there're no Stackhouses listed."

"Hmmm, Stackhouse," Mimi pondered, staring off into the darkened café. "I don't recall that name. But Steve would probably know."

"Steve? Why would he know?"

Mimi smiled. "Steve's family has been in Fort Connor for generations. I think his great-grandfather farmed here in the 1880s or some such. His father used to be one of the biggest ranchers and landowners in northern Colorado. Over the years, of course, he's sold most of it, but his father knew just about every ranching family that ever lived here. And Steve has probably met most of them growing up. His mom and dad used to throw big barbeques every summer." Mimi's expression grew wistful. "I remember going to those parties. There was music and great food outside in the summertime. Oh my, they were nice."

Kelly deliberately said nothing, not wanting to disturb Mimi's memory. She wondered how she could pump Steve for information without revealing Helen's past. Immersed in her thoughts, she was startled at the sound of Rosa's voice.

"Connie's on the phone. She doesn't think she can help Megan with the trip to the wool festival tomorrow. She's home sick with stomach flu. Do you want to talk with her?" Rosa asked as she leaned around the archway into the café.

"Ohhh, no!" Mimi exclaimed. "Poor girl. Let me talk with her," she said and left to grab the white portable in Rosa's hand. "Don't leave yet, Kelly."

Kelly grabbed her empty mug, wishing Pete left some coffee, and headed back into the bright lights of the shop. Checking her watch, she realized Carl was probably visualizing roast squirrel for dinner. It was dusk outside already. If she left now, she could run by the shopping center and buy groceries. She didn't think she could face peach yogurt again.

Rosa was going through the familiar closing routine. Kelly grabbed her tote bag and was about to leave when Mimi called out, "Wait, Kelly. I need to ask you a favor."

"Sure, what is it?" Kelly answered as Mimi hastened toward her.

"I was counting on Connie to help out Megan tomorrow morning. We're taking a group of our senior knitters to a wool festival up near Rocky Mountain National Park. We've got five ladies signed up, and Megan will need help driving them over and back. Would you be able to go with them tomorrow?" she asked. "It would take the whole morning and early afternoon, probably. I know that's asking a lot, Kelly. After all, you just got your files and you're working—"

Kelly held up her hand. "I'll be happy to help out, Mimi. No problem. I can work ahead tonight, so I can take off tomorrow morning," she said with a reassuring smile. "Besides, it'll be good to get up in the mountains."

Mimi beamed. "Ohhh, thank you, Kelly. That's so sweet. You'll enjoy the festival, too. There are sheep and alpaca and llamas and demonstrations and vendors. Goodness, if it has to do with wool, it's there."

"Sounds like fun," Kelly said, heading toward the door. "I'm going to the grocery store already, so I'll gas up the car for tomorrow."

"Oh, don't worry about that. We won't need your car. Steve's taking his truck. As a matter of fact, you can ask him about that rancher while you're riding into the mountains."

That caught Kelly by surprise. "Steve? Why's he going?"

"He volunteered to pick up this loom that I ordered." Mimi said over her shoulder as she headed toward her office. Rosa was already turning off lights. "The craftsman will be at the festival, and I simply don't have a vehicle big enough to carry that thing. Thanks, again, Kelly. See you in the morning. Nine o'clock would be great." She turned a corner and was gone.

Kelly frowned after her. Sneaky, Mimi. Very sneaky.

"I'll let you ladies out here," Steve said and aimed the truck to the side of a huge exhibition building, away from the packed parking areas. "That way you won't have to walk far. The entrance is right around the corner." He pointed toward the crowd of people milling around the front.

Kelly was amazed at how many people were already at

the festival, and it was only mid-morning. She couldn't remember being at these fairgrounds before. Maybe they were new, she thought, as she read the signs hanging over several of the barns spread out in a horseshoe. Sheep. Alpaca. Llamas.

"Oh, thank you, Steve, dear. You're such a gentleman," Lizzie said. "Isn't he, Kelly?"

"Oh, indeed, he is, Lizzie," Kelly agreed, trying not to smile as she shouldered open the passenger door of Steve's big red truck. Glad she'd worn sneakers and jeans, Kelly easily hopped to the ground and offered her hand to Lizzie. Even with the built-in step below the running board, the petite little knitter would need help making it to the ground.

Now that she was back in the West, Kelly reacquainted herself quickly with the oversized vehicles that filled city streets and county roads as well as interstates—the Serious Trucks, or as her dad used to say, "trucks with attitude." Kelly wondered if every owner needed a whole cavalry worth of horsepower and towing capacity, especially when she saw most of them parked outside grocery stores, garden centers, and fast food restaurants—sparkling clean with nary a speck of dirt of them. She checked out the huge tires on Steve's truck. They were caked with mud.

She wasn't surprised. Thanks to Lizzie, Kelly had heard about Steve's latest building project, his next development planned north of town, how he started his business, his college career, all the academic as well as athletic honors, why he chose getting his hands dirty building houses after obtaining his architect's degree rather than working in an office, his family's connections to Fort Connor, and on and on. Kelly was truly impressed at Lizzie's grilling techniques. She'd put any corporate interviewer to shame. Kelly half-expected Lizzie to ask Steve his bank balance.

To Steve's credit, he'd tried several times on the hour-long ride into the mountains to change the conversation. Kelly would pick up his lead and Lizzie would cooperate for a few minutes. Or until one of them stopped for a breath. Then, straight as any marksman who's found his target, she'd return to probing Steve.

Steve would catch Kelly's eye overtop Lizzie's immaculately coiffed silver-gray hair and grin, then politely, good-naturedly answer her questions.

"Grab hold, and I'll help you down, Lizzie," Kelly offered.

Lizzie scooted herself to the edge of the seat, which was difficult because she was wearing yards of rose pink cotton, gathered fetchingly with, what else, but white lace. "Oh my," she declared, eyes wide. "It's so far down."

"Don't worry, Lizzie. Let me help you." Steve stepped up and in one smooth movement had picked up Lizzie and deposited her safely on the ground.

"Ohhhh, thank you, you're *so* considerate," Lizzie chirped, hand fluttering at her breast. "Isn't he, dear?"

"To a fault," Kelly concurred obediently, watching Steve turn to hide his grin.

The unmistakable whine of bagpipes sounded suddenly, and Kelly was about to ask who they were, when Megan strode up.

"I've found them, ladies," she called over her shoulder to the little gaggle following in her wake. "I almost lost you guys when you went right past the parking lot."

"It'll be easier for me to load the loom here. The builder said I could use his space," Steve explained.

"Ladies! I hear bagpipes. Hurry up, or we'll miss them," Lizzie called to Megan's charges.

"Okay," Megan glanced at the ladies, then Kelly. "Let's get them all inside together, pick a meeting place, then let them scatter."

"Sounds like you've done this before," Steve said with a chuckle.

"Oh, yeah." Megan nodded, waving her charges forward. Lizzie was already heading toward the entrance. "Steve, I'll call you on your cell when we're ready to round 'em up and leave. Will you be here the whole time?"

"Yeah, I've gotta track down this guy and load the loom and secure it for the ride back." He glanced around. "Don't worry. I'll amuse myself. I already recognize some people I know, plus I'll check out the vendors. Good luck, you two," he added before he strode off.

"Anything I should know? I've never chaperoned seniors or knitters before," Kelly teased as they fell in behind the ladies.

"Yeah, matter of fact," Megan said, pulling the entrance tickets from her jeans pocket. "Keep an eye on Lizzie, okay? She's prone to mischief sometimes—"

The rest of her sentence was drowned out by the bagpipers' nasal hum and whine. As the little group rounded the corner, there were the pipers—bagpipes wailing and plaids fluttering in the mountain spring breeze—cutting a swath through the crowds. Kelly felt her blood stir as it always did at the sound of the pipes. Her dad used to say it was "the Irish" stirring in her. The pipers, twelve in all, headed toward the livestock barns, while spectators paused at food stands and llama lectures to watch. Kelly noticed a young boy bringing up the rear with a placard proclaiming the upcoming Battle of the Bagpipes that weekend.

"Okay, ladies, here're your tickets," Megan waved the packet in the air. "Let's get inside and find a meeting place, then you ladies are on your own." The ladies flocked around, accepting their tickets and obediently handing them to the door attendant.

All except one, Kelly noticed. Lizzie stood, staring after the departing pipers as if mesmerized, the pipes fading into the distance. "Come on, Lizzie," Kelly encouraged, taking her arm and guiding her to the door. "Let's go inside and see the wonderful world of wool."

"Very well, dear," Lizzie acquiesced with an audible sigh. "Those pipers were magnificent, weren't they? Such strapping men, too. Don't you think? I especially noticed the tallest one in the back with the gray beard. My, my, he was a handsome devil."

"Uh, yes, I suppose they were," Kelly agreed, a little surprised at Lizzie's turn of thought.

"I wonder if they're real Scotsmen. What do you think?"

"Ahhh, gee, Lizzie, I really don't know," Kelly admitted, shepherding her through the doorway and into the cavernous hall.

"I've always wondered what a Scotsman wears beneath his kilt," Lizzie said, as causally as if she were describing a new yarn. "Do you know, dear?"

Kelly barely heard her, her attention was already captivated by the myriad variety of vendors' booths and stalls that stretched almost as far as she could see. "Uhhh, no, Lizzie, not really," she replied, absently.

Megan's voice cut through Kelly's fascination long enough to imprint where and when they were all to meet for the return trip. Sorting that tidbit away, Kelly felt the pull of the colors and textures all calling out to her at once—come and touch. She gave an offhand wave to Lizzie as she merged with the clusters of people moving between booths. "See you later, Lizzie. Enjoy yourself."

"Oh, I will, dear. Don't worry about me."

With that, Kelly dove into the colorful sea surrounding her, floating from stall to stall—fingering lace so delicate she was sure it was cobwebs, not thread at all, knitted sweaters and shawls in every color and texture imaginable, and weaving like she'd never seen before. Nubbly and patterned. Fabric so fine and soft, she was sure it was woven by fairies. Kelly was amazed at the designs. Some were worn, others were hung as art. And, indeed it was. Dazzling colors and designs that tempted you to touch as well as admire.

Kelly immersed herself in the sensation of it all, drifting happily through the busy aisles, stroking fabrics and squeezing twisted coils of wool and mohair and alpaca in every hue, brazen and demure. The silk vendors' stalls held her captive as she caressed the sinfully soft selections. Hand-painted or blended with fibers less regal, Kelly swore it whispered her name, just as it did in the shop every time she passed. Perhaps she'd become good enough to knit that sweater after all. Maybe. She was nearly finished with the chunky scarf.

It was only when she caught sight of a food vendor's hot dogs and her stomach growled did Kelly notice the time. Whoa. She'd been wandering for over two hours. Only an hour and a half left to sightsee. Indulging the sudden craving for a hot dog with all the trimmings, Kelly also grabbed a soda and left the exhibition hall. She really owed it to herself to visit the animals that provided the luxurious fibers for all those glorious creations.

Walking toward the livestock barns, Kelly glanced at the mountains and took in her breath. She hadn't been up here to the national park in years. She'd forgotten how gorgeous it was. The views of the Rockies were stunning, as sun glinted off the glacier-tipped peaks.

She lingered at the llama lecture, as a man explained the varied abilities the stately animals possessed. The llama stood patiently, clearly used to being ogled and examined, while the handler pointed out the animal's qualities to a cluster of listeners.

From there she wandered toward the barn with the alpacas, similar to llamas but a bit smaller. There, the breeders were holding forth as eager owners-to-be gathered around and asked questions. Kelly noticed all the blue and red ribbons adorning the stalls. Here, the alpacas watched *her* and came up to the fence as if posing for a photo. Kelly was convinced they looked disappointed she didn't have a camera.

She also couldn't help noticing the heightened level of

care and nurturing lavished on these interesting animals. Most stalls had carpets covering the dirt. And the owners were quick to clean up any of nature's occurrences, lest their expensive animals step in anything. Perusing a newspaper article on the growing alpaca business with the title, "Have You Hugged Your Investment Today?" she could see why the owners were so solicitous. Each animal was worth tens of thousands of dollars.

Kelly was pondering why until she spotted the spinners with their wheels. There, she sank her hands into a loose skein of one hundred percent alpaca wool and understood at last. Soft, soft, luxuriously soft. Unbelievably soft. Creams, grays, browns, combinations of all, even a stunning tweed.

She began to notice the intricate patterns on the animals' bodies and saw that the spun wool often varied in color as well. Before leaving the barn, Kelly glanced over her shoulder once more and could have sworn she spied an alpaca smirking at her, as if to say, "Told you."

Draining the last of her soda, Kelly tossed the can into a handy trash barrel and headed toward the sheep barn. Here, the familiar sound of bleating filled the air, and she realized another alpaca bonus. They were quiet.

Lambs prodded into an unruly judging line protested each maneuver. Some were as docile as their reputation. Others were unrepentant troublemakers and made Kelly laugh out loud with their antics.

"He's having none of this," Steve observed as he drew beside her.

Kelly chuckled. "You know, it's been ages since I've been around farm animals. I'd forgotten how much fun it was."

"It's fun to watch, all right. But if you have to clean up after them, that's another story." Steve shoved his hands in his back pockets. "Helen told me they had sheep in the early days, until it cost them more to raise than they fetched at market."

Kelly closed her eyes to recall. "You know, I can still remember the sheep. It was when I was real little. Then they sold them off." She shook her head. "It just didn't pay in those days. If Uncle Jim hadn't had his job with the state highway department, they never would have made it. Finally, he started boarding peoples' horses, and that helped a lot. At least it allowed them to keep the farm."

"Let's go over there," Steve said, pointing across the barn. "That's the best of breed awards."

They skirted around the younger animals, and Kelly spotted the huge adult sheep. Wow. She'd forgotten how big the woolly creatures could get. A huge black ram strutted past them, head high, clearly lord of the realm. Kelly had to agree. He was magnificent.

As she and Steve strolled slowly around the fenced judging area, Kelly noticed three men standing and talking. Two were dressed in corporate attire—suits, ties, and shiny shoes—definitely out of place in a barn where one could, and frequently did, step in something. The other man, taller than his companions, was dressed appropriately in Colorado Cowboy Modern—jeans, boots, denim shirt, and a Stetson. Something about the man was familiar, and Kelly found herself staring. Fortunately, the man was actively listening to his companions and didn't notice her.

"I thought we'd spy Lizzie here," Steve spoke up. "She was headed down toward the livestock barns a little while ago."

"Lizzie was heading to the livestock barns?" Kelly repeated, surprised for some reason. Dainty little Lizzie didn't strike her as a budding alpaca breeder. Of course, she could have been after the wool.

Steve shrugged. "Well, that's where I assumed she was going. She was actually talking to one of the Scottish bagpipers when I saw her, but they were close to the barns, so I figured—"

Kelly grabbed his arm. "Wha-what did you say?"

"I said she was talking to one of the bagpipers." Steve peered at her. "Anything wrong?"

The memory of Lizzie's curiosity about the Scotsman's undergarments suddenly flashed through Kelly's mind, along with Megan's earlier warning: "Keep an eye on Lizzie. She's prone to mischief."

"Oh my gosh," breathed Kelly. "We'd better find her. *Now!*" She turned and raced from the barn.

"Why? Hey, where're—?" Steve called out then hastened after her. "What's the matter?" he demanded when he caught up.

"Megan warned me to keep an eye on Lizzie before we split," Kelly explained while they threaded their way through masses of people. The crowds had increased since morning. "She said Lizzie could get into mischief. I didn't know what she meant until now."

"What kind of mischief is she talking about? I mean, she's nearly seventy, isn't she?"

"That may be, but Lizzie was transfixed by the bagpipers earlier, particularly one of them she described as 'a handsome devil.'" Hearing Steve's laughter, Kelly shot him a look. "It's not funny."

"Yeah, it is."

"Not when her last question to me when we entered the hall was, 'What do Scotsmen wear beneath their kilts?'" Kelly noticed heads turning on that one, and the crowd seemed to part around her. She felt Steve's hand on her arm.

"Wait a minute," he said between spurts of laughter. "You can't seriously think that sweet little old lady would . . ." He gestured aimlessly.

"I don't know, but I don't want to find out, either. Megan will kill me when she finds out," Kelly declared.

"Kill you when I find out what?" Megan asked, drawing beside them. She took a big bite of a chili dog.

Kelly decided she'd better wait until Megan swallowed or they'd have to stop the Lizzie search and administer the

Heimlich maneuver on Megan. "Uhhh, we're just looking for Lizzie. Steve saw her around the barns. We don't want her to get lost."

Megan gulped. "Lizzie? Where is she? What's she doing?" She peered around the crowds.

"Well, you said to keep an eye on her." Kelly angled toward the sheep barn once more, craning her neck to see around the crowds. "Where did you see her, Steve?"

"Actually, she was right beside the barn when—" He stopped and pointed. "Wait a minute, isn't that her right over there?"

Kelly followed the line of sight and caught a glimpse of an unmistakable pink cotton skirt fluttering in the spring breeze. People were still blocking her view, but it had to be Lizzie, she thought with a sigh of relief. "Oh, good, there she is," she said and hastened to shepherd the wayward little knitter back into the fold. Until Steve reached out and caught her arm.

"Wait, hold on," Steve said as he peered above the crowds. "Uh oh . . ."

"What? What's the matter?" Megan demanded, weaving side to side, trying to see around people. "What's she doing?"

Steve started to laugh. "You . . . you don't wanta know," he managed before he bent over double, laughing.

Kelly's heart skipped a beat, and she shouldered her way between two husky men so she could see what Steve was talking about. When she did, she came to an abrupt halt and stared, mouth open.

There was Lizzie, all right, but she wasn't alone. She was still talking with the tall, handsome-devil Scotsman. Talking and looking. The Scotsman stood, hands on hips, while Lizzie demurely held up his plaid kilt, observed for a few seconds, then lowered it once again.

Kelly saw a slight movement to her left. Megan's chili dog dropped to the dirt. She stared horrified, face beet-red. Steve, meanwhile, was still bent over with silent laughter, hands on his knees. Obviously, it would be up to her to handle the situation, Kelly decided, and snapped out of shock mode. She cleared her throat and yelled, "*Lizzie!* We need you back with the others *now!*"

Lizzie turned and waved, smiling brightly. "Coming, dears," she chirped as if nothing unusual had just occurred.

"Oh . . . my . . . God . . ." Megan whispered. "I don't believe she did that."

"Believe it. Now I know what you mean by mischief," Kelly said, shaking her head.

Meanwhile, Lizzie was bidding farewell to the grinning bagpiper, who kissed her hand before she rejoined them. That seemed to delight her no end. "What an adorable and obliging gentleman," she cooed, when she rejoined them.

Kelly grabbed Lizzie's elbow and steered her back toward the exhibition hall. "That's an understatement," she muttered to Megan, who still had a slightly glazed look.

Steve had finally stopped laughing, out loud at least. "Folks, I've got the loom all loaded and tied down, so whenever you want or need to head back into town, let me know."

"Ohhh, thank you, dear," Lizzie said. "But I haven't even seen the wool exhibits yet."

Kelly shot Steve an I-don't-believe-she-said-that look, and he turned his head to hide more laughter.

When they approached the hall entrance, Megan stepped up and encircled Lizzie's arm possessively. "Now, Lizzie, you're going to stay with me while we see the exhibits, okay? No disappearing allowed, understand?" She leveled a stern gaze at Lizzie.

Clearly unflappable and unfazed, Lizzie beamed. "Of course, dear. We'll see everything together. Oh, do you think we might have a spot of lunch, first? I'm simply famished."

"Let's meet the others first. Then we'll all go together,"

Megan agreed, then turned to Steve. "Listen, Peggy is staying here with a weaver she knows, so I'll be able to take everyone back with me, Steve. You and Kelly can go on back into town. Kelly, I know you've just gotten your accounts, so you're probably swamped."

"You sure you won't need any more help?" Kelly gestured, adding pointedly, "I mean, can you handle everything?"

Megan nodded in schoolmarm fashion. "Oh, yes. We're meeting the others in ten minutes. I'll have some help then. Don't worry. We're fine now. Ready, Lizzie?"

"Oh my, yes," she enthused. "I'm so excited."

Megan refrained from comment, instead guiding Lizzie through the entrance.

Kelly stood, hands on hips, and shook her head, watching the little round knitter wave good-bye before she disappeared inside the hall. "But, I haven't seen the wool exhibits, dear," she said, in a breathless imitation of Lizzie.

"I think she's seen enough," Steve said with a laugh.

It was contagious, and Kelly joined in, laughing at the bizarre scene they'd just witnessed. No one at the shop would believe it. Or maybe they would. After all, they've known Lizzie longer. How on earth would she explain it to Mimi?

"My truck is parked on the other side of the building," Steve said, looking over the crowd. "We can stop for some coffee on the way out if you want to leave now."

Kelly's taste buds tingled in anticipation. She was about to reply when a man's voice caught her attention, and she turned around. There were the men she'd noticed from the sheep barn, standing only a few feet behind them. City Suit was introducing a fourth man to Colorado Cowboy. Something he'd said caught her attention, what was it?

"What are—" Steve started then paused, when she held

up her hand. She focused on the group, blatantly eavesdropping.

"Jeff," City Suit said to the newcomer. "I want you to meet Curt Stackhouse. He's been good enough to guide us through this land deal."

Kelly drew in a deep breath, observing Colorado Cowboy as he smiled and shook hands all around. Of course, she thought. That's why he looked familiar earlier. He's got the same smile. The same face. Older, of course.

"Do you know them?" Steve asked in a low voice.

"Well, not really, but . . ." she hesitated, wondering how she would explain. More importantly, now that she found Stackhouse, how would she introduce herself, let alone ask him questions?

"Well, you're sure acting funny," Steve observed.

Suddenly Kelly got a wild idea. She'd need Steve's cooperation, though. It was crazy, but it was the only chance she had. Now that she'd found Stackhouse, she wasn't about to lose him until she knew where he lived. "Uh, Steve, would you be willing to . . . to . . . uh, take a ride with me?" she ventured.

"We're already planning to take a ride back into town, remember?" he joked.

"I mean another ride. Before we go home."

"I guess that depends on where."

She exhaled a breath. "I don't know yet. Wherever that tall guy in the Stetson is going. Once he splits from the city guys, I mean." She gestured behind her.

Steve peered first at the men then at her. "And why do you want to follow him?"

"Well . . . it's a long story," she confessed, glancing over her shoulder to make sure they were still there. "Let's just say I need to know where this guy lives, so I can talk with him. Ask him some questions."

"Why don't you talk with him now? He's right behind you." Steve was observing her very carefully.

"Uhhh, it's kinda hard to explain—"

"Try."

"Too many people around. It . . . it has to do with Helen," she admitted finally.

"With Helen or with what happened?" he probed.

Kelly met his level gaze. "He's a link to her past. And I'm hoping he knows something or someone. I'll . . . I'll explain later."

Steve stared at the men again for a long moment. "It'll be tricky. We don't know where he's parked or what he's driving."

Kelly pondered that for a minute. "Well, I could follow him while you get the truck, but we'd have to meet . . ."

"I know. Give me your cell phone," he said, hand outstretched.

Kelly dug into her pocket and withdrew the phone. Steve took it, punched in numbers, then returned it. "That's my cell number. You follow this guy while I get the truck. I'll park along the side of the road over there and wait." He pointed past the gates. "Call me when you've seen him getting into his vehicle, then come out to the road where I can pick you up, okay?"

Great idea, Kelly had to admit. "Okay, got it." She nodded, then teased. "You sound like you've done this before."

"Just don't lose him," Steve advised, turning back into the crowd. "This better be good, Kelly," he called over his shoulder.

Eleven

"**Mimi** thought you might know this guy or his family," Kelly said, observing the new spring grass that stood a foot tall beside the winding road. "She said your father knew all the ranchers in the area."

"Stackhouse, Curtis Stackhouse," Steve repeated as he guided the truck around a curve. "That name is vaguely familiar, so I must have heard of him or met him once. Heck, it could have been years ago or last month. I meet a lot of landowners in my business. Some are ranchers, others want to be. And those guys definitely looked like buyers."

"You mean the 'suits'?"

Steve grinned. "Yeah, the city suits. They're buying land. You can smell it. Either for themselves or for a developer. I'll bet on the developer."

"Well, one guy said Stackhouse was 'guiding' them through a deal, so maybe you're right." Kelly focused on the big black truck farther ahead.

Their plan had worked perfectly, much to Kelly's relief. She'd merged with the crowd behind Stackhouse and companions and followed him all the way from their goodbyes to his meandering stroll past the wool barns and a quick striding search for his parked truck. Once she'd glimpsed the mud-splattered vehicle and memorized the license plate, she phoned Steve and hastened to find him. They only had to wait a few minutes before Stackhouse's truck appeared, and they followed a safe distance behind. Now they were nearly out of the canyon leading from the national park and approaching the outskirts of the smaller towns surrounding Fort Connor.

"Should you speed up? We don't want to lose him when he gets to the edge of town," she urged.

"We're fine, relax. Besides, I've got some questions. You spent a lot of time explaining about this cousin Martha and how she got here from Wyoming and how close she was with Helen and how she was worried that someone from Helen's past came back to 'haunt' her. Then you searched the cottage and found the yearbook and Stackhouse's photo."

Kelly watched the mouth of the canyon open wide as the road straightened onto a rock-rimmed meadow. She sensed Steve zeroing in on the pertinent details she'd left unsaid. He didn't miss much, she'd noticed. "That's right."

"There's something you're not saying, I can tell. It makes no sense that a sweet lady like Helen would have done anything to cause a successful rancher like this Stackhouse to threaten her. Unless they were both involved in something illegal, like running drugs. But I kind of doubt Helen was a drug dealer." Steve glanced at Kelly. "So finish the story. Tell me what you're holding back. If you're worrying about Helen's privacy, don't. I promise I won't repeat what you say to a soul. Helen was pretty special to me, too."

Kelly believed him. "Yeah, you're right," she admitted with a sigh. "Sorry, it's hard to explain. That's why I'm being so closed-mouthed. I've only told my friends at the shop, because I don't want anyone to think less of Helen."

"That would be impossible. Unless she really was a drug dealer," he joked.

Steve's laughter helped Kelly let go. She proceeded to tell him the story.

"Wow," Steve said softly. "Any chance your Uncle Jim could be the father?"

"Nope," Kelly said with a shake of her head. "He told me he met Helen on a blind date when he arrived in town and bought the farm."

"Hmmm."

"Yeah, that's what I said, too."

"And Helen was worried about this person?"

"She was worried about something, according to Martha."

"And no trace of the child's records?"

"None. I went through every drawer and cabinet and crevice, believe me. The only clue I found was that yearbook photo and the inscription from Stackhouse."

Steve shook his head. "I gotta tell you, Kelly, that's pretty slim."

"Don't I know it, but it's all I've got," Kelly admitted.

"How does the money play into it?"

Kelly shrugged. "I don't know. Maybe this person was blackmailing her or threatened her somehow. Maybe she tried to pay him off to leave her alone."

"Have you thought about what kinds of questions you're going to ask this guy? I mean, how're you going to approach him?"

"I'm still working on that," Kelly confessed.

"Well, work on it faster, because Stackhouse just put on his turn signal," Steve warned. "Bet he's taking that county road on the left."

Kelly felt her throat tighten. What *would* she say? She had to be careful not to arouse his suspicions. "Oh boy, well, I know I have to ease into it. I mean, I can't make him suspicious." She watched the huge black truck ahead and, sure enough, it turned left on the next road.

Steve slowed down, too. "I'm going to drop back a little so we won't be right on his tail."

It was all Kelly could do to hold her impatience in check while Steve deliberately waited for a long line of cars to pass in the opposite lane before he turned onto the county road. As they created the hilly road, she relaxed. There, farther ahead, was the truck. "Thank goodness," she breathed.

"Okay, we've gotta have a cover story to explain why we're driving up on this guy's property."

"*We?*" Kelly shot him a quizzical look. "I don't need help asking questions."

"What were you expecting to do?" Steve countered. "Drive up his mile-long driveway, step out of the truck, and go ring his doorbell? Don't you think that would look a little strange? Who am I supposed to be, the taxi?"

Hmmm. He was right. That would definitely look strange. Rats. She hated it when he was right.

"Listen, I've got an idea," he said. "We've got a loom in the back, so why don't we say we're new to the area, just settling in, and you're a weaver."

"I can barely knit, now you want me to weave?"

Steve grinned. "Work with me, okay? We're newcomers, and we're buying land north of town. And we've been thinking about adding some sheep or alpaca—"

"I just saw an alpaca for the first time today. What if he asks me a question?"

"Just hand off to me, I'll answer. You're the weaver, and I want to start breeding alpaca—whoa, there he goes." Steve pointed ahead as the black truck turned onto a private road.

Kelly watched a dust cloud kick up in the truck's wake as they passed. There was a large, two-story white house in the distance and a sprawling red barn. She also noticed the fencing around Stackhouse's ranch was in good condition. Black and reddish brown cows dotted one pasture, and she thought she spied sheep in a far meadow backing up to the foothills.

"We'll go down to the crossing then turn around," Steve suggested.

"Okay, I'm a weaver, and we want alpaca, and we're ignorant. But how do we explain why we're there?"

"We can say someone at the shop told us that he'd be a good person to give advice about this business."

Kelly nodded. It might not be great but it was better than what she had, which was nothing. "Okay, let's go with it. Let's just get him talking. I'll take it from there."

Steve slowed at the intersection of the two county roads and turned the truck around. "Good luck. Any idea how you're going to ease into it?"

"Not a clue," she replied as they approached the private road to Stackhouse's ranch. "I'll play it by ear. See what happens."

They turned onto the road and slowed, a cloud of dust billowing around the truck. "This'll be interesting," he said.

It certainly will be, Kelly thought, her mind sorting through and discarding one question after another as they followed the driveway all the way to the barnyard. To her surprise, Stackhouse emerged from the barn and, seeing them, walked to the side of the split rail fence bordering his pasture as they drove up.

"Okay," Steve advised, parking the truck. "Just keep that great smile, and we're halfway there."

If only a smile would do it. Kelly jumped from the truck to the ground, straightened her T-shirt, and forced her brightest "meet the client" smile. Corporate life had its benefits. She could talk to anyone now without showing the emotion within. But this was not the corporate world, and she'd need a folksy, just-starting-out innocence to appear natural. She took a deep breath. That would be harder to pull off. Kelly hadn't felt innocent in so long, she'd forgotten how.

Steve met her beside the truck. "Okay, here goes," he said, smile already in place.

Kelly fixed the brightest smile she could find as they started across the barnyard. Stackhouse stood waiting, hands on hips, Stetson pulled low. "Hi there!" Kelly chirped loudly, waving her hand as they drew nearer.

"Good afternoon, sir," Steve called out. "I hope we found the right ranch. Are you Curt Stackhouse?"

"Yes, I am. What can I do for you folks?" Stackhouse replied as Kelly and Steve paused a few feet from him.

"Well, then, we found the right place, honey," Steve said, glancing to her before he reached out to shake Stackhouse's hand. Kelly bit her cheek to keep from frowning at the familiarity. "I'm Steve Townsend, Mr. Stackhouse, and this—"

"Kelly Flynn, sir," she said, offering her hand to the tall rancher, who was observing them closely. Stackhouse shook her hand firmly. His hand was big and warm and calloused, a working rancher's hand.

"We're gonna be married this summer, and we'll be buying some land north of town pretty soon, maybe thirty acres or so," Steve said, then put his arm around Kelly's shoulders, drawing her closer. Kelly nearly bit her lip in two this time. Steve knew she wouldn't blow their cover by pushing him away.

"Really?" Stackhouse said, brow quirking. "Whereabouts?"

"We've been looking at some acreage near Wellesly. I'm renting in Fort Connor now because it's close to my job at Advanced Tech. I'm an engineer there. I came to the university years ago, well, and I haven't been able to leave since." Steve glanced around with a guileless look. "It's so beautiful, I had to stay."

A smile tugged at the corners of Stackhouse's mouth. "I've heard that story a lot over the years," he said.

"And I've *always* wanted to come back," Kelly did her best to gush. "I grew up here when I was a little girl, until my dad had to take a job out of town. But I've always wanted to return. I've been working back East since college." She gestured, keeping her eyes Barbie-doll wide. "And then I met Stevie on a cruise, and it's just *so* wonderful! Now, I can come back home!" Her voice ran up a whole octave at the end of that sentence.

Stackhouse observed them both for a few seconds. Kelly held her Barbie pose, even though she felt her cheek start to twitch. "Well, that's a real nice story, folks, but I have to wonder why you're telling it to me."

Steve gave a chuckle. "Well, you see, Mr. Stackhouse, Kelly here is a weaver. In fact, that's a new loom in the back of the truck. We bought it from Sam Gepardson today. And—"

"You know Sam Gepardson?" Stackhouse asked. "He's a fine craftsman. A real artist."

"Yes sir, that he is, sir. We met him when we picked up the loom, but he was highly recommended by the folks at Kelly's favorite shop in town, House of Lambspun."

"Ohhh, yes!" Kelly jumped in, gesturing again. "They're *so* helpful. You see I'm new at all of this, and they tell me everything to do."

Stackhouse nodded, the skeptical expression Kelly first noticed no longer present. "They're good people. My wife's a spinner, so she knows the woman who runs the place, uhh . . ."

"Mimi?" Kelly supplied with another exuberant gesture. "Oh, yes, she's been *so* much help. And all the other people there, too. That's why we're here! It was one of them who suggested we come see you." She turned to her accomplice, Barbie still in place. "Stevie has alpaca questions." She could tell Steve was trying his best not to laugh.

"That's right," he went along with an agreeable nod. "You see, we were thinking we might add some alpaca once we move in, and this woman in the shop, right, honey? She said you'd give us good advice on the business. Even told us how to get to your ranch."

Stackhouse peered at them. "What was her name?"

At this, Kelly called up a Lizzie mannerism. Hand to her breast, she exclaimed, "Oh, my goodness, I simply *cannot* remember. But she was tall and blonde and very, very pretty," she volunteered Lisa's description.

Stackhouse shook his head and folded his arms across his chest. "Well, I wish I knew who it was, because that's kind of strange advice. You see, I don't have any alpacas. I've got a few hundred sheep, though. My wife has a small milling business in addition to her spinning."

"You don't?" Kelly squeaked, eyes wide. If they got any wider they'd pop out.

"Whoa . . ." Steve exclaimed, guileless still. "Well, I'm sorry we disturbed you, Mr. Stackhouse. I guess the lady was mistaken, honey."

"I'm sorry you folks wasted your time," Stackhouse removed his hat, running his hand through his pewter gray hair. "Listen, let me give you a couple of phone numbers to call—" At that, a familiar cell phone jangle sounded. "Uhhh, excuse me, folks," he said, then slipped the phone from his jeans and stepped away a few paces.

Kelly grabbed the moment. She turned to Steve with her most formidable frown. "You are *so* out of line, mister."

"Who, me?" Steve declared, all innocence. "What're you talking about?"

"You know what I mean. Move the arm. Now."

"Hey, I was just getting into the role," he teased.

"Sure, you were. Move it."

"But we're engaged, remember?"

"Move it or lose a rib. Your choice."

Steve backed away, laughing, arms in the air "hands up" style. "Hey, who was that a minute ago? I've never seen her."

"That was Barbie, and she's just your type," Kelly said, unable to suppress her own laughter.

"Sorry for the interruption, folks," Stackhouse said as he approached. "Let me give you a couple of names of breeders here in town. They can answer all your alpaca questions."

"That would be great, sir. Thank you," Steve said.

Stackhouse started to dig in his pocket, and Kelly realized she'd better act fast if she wanted more from Stackhouse than friendly conversation. Grabbing the most plausible line she could think of, Kelly plunged in. "Did you grow up here your whole life, Mr. Stackhouse?"

"Sure did." Stackhouse found his pen then withdrew a card from his back pocket. "So'd my father. We've ranched here since 1910."

"Oh, goodness," Kelly said. "My aunt grew up here, too. What year did you graduate from high school?"

Stackhouse smiled. "In 1955. A long time ago."

"Oh, my!" Kelly chirped, hand to breast again. "That's when my aunt graduated, too. What high school?"

"Fort Connor High."

"Goodness, what a coincidence. She went there, too. Maybe you knew her. She was Helen Flynn, then. Her parents had a small sugar beet farm east of town."

The change in Stackhouse's expression was barely noticeable, but immediate. Kelly would have missed it if she hadn't been staring at him intently with her wide-eyed pose. Barbie was useful after all. A light appeared in his eyes for a split second, then was gone.

He glanced down and wrote on the card. "You know, that name does sound familiar. But I can't bring back a face."

"Ohhhh, she was really pretty back then, I've seen her pictures," Kelly gushed. "She was petite with dark brown hair and bright blue eyes. And I'll bet she had a lot of friends!"

Stackhouse looked up and gave Kelly a guarded smile.

"I'm sure she did, Miss Flynn. But I just can't place her. Sorry." He turned to Steve and handed him the card. "Here, you go. These folks will tell you all you want to know about the alpaca business."

"Hey, thank you, sir," Steve said, shaking Stackhouse's hand again before he turned to Kelly. "You ready to go, honey?"

"Thank you so much," she said, letting Steve take her arm as they started to leave. "You've been very helpful, Mr. Stackhouse."

"I'm sorry I didn't remember your aunt." Stackhouse caught her gaze for a second.

Yes, you did, Kelly said to herself. But to Stackhouse, she simply waved and called out, "That's okay, thanks so much for helping."

Steve waved as well as they headed toward the truck. "He's lying," he said softly.

"You betcha," Kelly concurred with a vigorous nod.

Steve opened her door, and Kelly scrambled in." Hey, can Barbie come back for the trip home?" he asked.

"Not on a bet," she said and slammed the truck door shut.

Twelve

"**You** split the yarn into fourths, like this," Mimi directed, slowly pulling the strand of yarn apart. "Then, you'll use a darning needle and thread each little tail under and around and into the stitches to hide it."

"I don't have a darning needle," Kelly said, feeling deficient somehow.

"It's okay. We keep a supply right there in that little cedar box." She pointed to the center of the library table. "Megan, would you please hand me a needle? I'll get you started, Kelly, then you can finish."

Megan retrieved a needle. "Here you go. That's a great scarf, Kelly. I love those colors."

Kelly beamed with the pride of accomplishment. Considering how rocky her introduction to knitting had been, she was still amazed she'd created something so beautiful. She ran her hands over the colorful chunky-knit scarf. Now all she had to do was wait until autumn so she could use it. Or maybe not. April brought springtime temperatures and flowers, but springtime in Colorado was a fickle suitor. As likely to drop several inches of snow and freezing cold as seductively warm days that hinted of summer.

"There, now weave it in and around until there's only a little bit of yarn left, then tie a knot," Mimi said, demonstrating each step. "And snip, you're done."

"Wow. That's the first easy thing I've learned. Even I can do that," Kelly declared, taking the scarf and needle.

Slowly she replicated Mimi's movements. This step certainly was easier than the binding off process when her scarf was finished. Kelly wasn't sure how pulling one stitch over another would result in a finished edge, but darned if it didn't. Only a few maneuvers and she had a finished scarf in her lap. Except for the two dangling tails of yarn on each end and in the middle.

Mimi sank back into her chair and sipped her Earl Grey. "Thank you again, Megan, and you, too, Kelly, for what you did yesterday," she said, shaking her head. "Goodness, I had no idea it would become so . . . uh, challenging, shall we say?"

Jennifer snickered at the end of the table as she worked the emerald yard. "You gotta love Lizzie. She knows no shame. A woman after my own heart."

Megan scowled across from her. "Stop that, Jen. Don't you dare encourage her. Lizzie doesn't need any more ideas."

"Who, me?" Jennifer said, all innocence. "Never."

Laughter sounded over the hum of the wheel in the corner, as Burt interrupted his spinning long enough to tease. "You're incorrigible, Jennifer."

"I know, it's one of my finer traits."

"I still cannot believe Lizzie did that," Mimi said, smile winning out.

"Believe it," Kelly intoned, tucking in the fourth strand, only one dangling tail to go. Changing the subject, she added, "But the best thing that happened was our trip to the rancher's place after the festival."

"*Our?*" Lisa teased across the table.

This time it was Kelly's turn to scowl. "Well, I had no car, so I persuaded Steve to follow this rancher, Stackhouse."

"The hunky cowboy in the yearbook?" Jennifer pried.

Kelly nodded. "One and the same."

"Steve didn't know the family?" Mimi asked.

"No, he said the name was familiar, that's all." Kelly jabbed a tuft of red wool through the needle's aperture. "And to tell the truth, it worked better because there were two of us. We pretended we were ignorant alpaca breeders-to-be and were sent to him for information. He bought it, thank goodness, otherwise I wouldn't have been able to ask him questions."

"What kind of questions?" Megan ventured, binding off the edge of her turquoise sweater.

"Well, I wanted to see his response when I mentioned Helen's name, so I worked up to it. Asking him if he grew up here, where he'd gone to school, stuff like that. Then, I slipped Helen in."

"What'd he say?" Lisa prodded, examining the stitches on her coral sweater.

"He said he couldn't remember her even though the name was familiar, but the expression on his face said different. Even Steve saw it. It was subtle, but you could tell he knew Helen." Kelly gave a mission-accomplished nod.

"Kelly, I hope you're not suspecting this rancher on the basis of a facial expression," Mimi cautioned.

Kelly exhaled a sigh, listening to the rhythmic hum of the wheel behind her. She and Steve had discussed the same thing when they drove back to Fort Connor yesterday. It was obvious Stackhouse knew more than he was saying. He'd recognized Helen's name. He remembered her, but he wasn't admitting it. Kelly thought she saw a flicker of something else in his eyes. But nothing else was visible on that suntanned and weather-beaten face. "I know," she admitted. "A guilty expression proves nothing."

"Yeah, it might not be guilt at all. It could be heart-burn," Jennifer joked, causing a ripple of laughter.

Lizzie popped into the room then and bustled over to the bookshelves. "Mimi, we have those spring sweater patterns you showed me last week, don't we? Hilda is finishing her class and wants to show them the next project. Now, where are they?" she worried out loud as she removed a large three-ring binder and started paging through it.

"They should be there, Lizzie, I checked yesterday," Mimi advised, rising from her chair.

"Ohhh, here they are, dear," Lizzie declared, familiar smile returning. "Don't get up, I'll copy them."

"Hey, Lizzie, I hear you had a little field trip of your own yesterday," Jennifer tweaked.

"What do you mean, dear?" Lizzie replied as she slipped the plastic-encased patterns from the binder.

"Jennifer . . ." Megan warned ominously.

Jennifer continued, unfazed. "To visit the bonny lads of Scotland. A piper, too, I heard."

Lizzie beamed, hand to breast. "Ohhhhh, yes. He was an exceptionally handsome gentleman, tall and broad, with full gray beard."

"Tell me, Lizzie—"

"Jennifer!" Megan tried again.

Kelly knew exactly where this was going. So did Lisa and Mimi, she could tell from their smiles. Megan was wasting her time trying to divert Jennifer.

"Tell me, Lizzie, was he regimental or not?"

"Regimental, dear? Whatever do you mean?" Lizzie glanced over her shoulder as she headed toward the class-room.

"I've heard that when a Scotsmen is in regimental dress, he wears nothing beneath his kilt," Jennifer explained with a devilish smile.

Lizzie paused halfway to the doorway. "Oh, really? I shall have to remember that."

"Why do I even try?" Megan muttered.

"Beats me," Lisa said with a grin.

"Well? Was he, Lizzie?"

A light rose blush colored the little knitter's round cheek. Kelly spied a distinct twinkle in her eye as well. "It was green, dear," she said simply and headed for the doorway.

Kelly dropped her scarf. Mimi choked on her tea. Unflappable Lisa's mouth fell open, while Megan sank her head into her hand. Even Jennifer appeared at a loss for words, for a split second.

"*Green?*" she called out. "Lizzie, get back here!"

"Make her stop," Megan pleaded.

"Can't be done."

Kelly turned at the strangled sound of laughter behind her and saw Burt, red-faced, bent over his wheel, wiping his eyes. "You okay back there, Burt?"

"Oh . . . yeah . . ." he rasped and coughed. "But I spun a knot in my yarn."

"You asked something, dear?" Lizzie leaned around the corner.

"Did you say green?" Jennifer said, eyes alight.

"Yes, dear. His underwear was shamrock green." And she disappeared around the corner again.

Soft laughter bubbled around the table, as Kelly tucked away the last tiny strand of yarn. She held up her new creation and admired it all over again.

"I can't follow a great line like that," Jennifer said, stuffing her nearly finished sweater into the tote bag. "Time for me to get back to work. See you guys later."

Megan checked her watch. "Me, too. I've got to finish a tech article for this new client. I'm really trying to impress them so I can snag that account." She grabbed her knitting and shoved it into her bag as she rose to leave. "See you later."

Mimi rose as well, balancing her empty tea cup. "I'll check in with Hilda and see if her students need any help." Glancing to Kelly, she added, "Kelly, now that you know how to knit, you can sign up for Hilda's next sweater class. She's a wonderful teacher."

"Whoa, I don't know if I'm ready for that," Kelly hedged. "Sweaters look a lot harder than my easy scarf."

"You can do it," Lisa declared. "Pull out that first piece you were working on and start knitting. Get used to the smaller needles again. Then, we'll teach you how to do the stockinette. That's what you'll need for Hilda's beginning class."

"Stockinette? Is it hard?" Kelly asked, dubious already.

"No, not after you learn to purl," Mimi said as she headed toward the classroom. "I'll teach you how in just a minute. Let me check on Hilda first."

"Purl? I have to purl? Why can't I just knit?"

"Because that's how you do stockinette," Lisa explained. "You knit one row, then purl the next. And that makes this nice pattern, see?" She placed the scrumptious coral sweater on the table and pointed to the pattern. "That's called *stockinette*, and it's great for sweaters."

Kelly ran her fingers over the silk and cotton yarn, admiring the smooth interlocking stitches. "That is pretty. At least yours is pretty. I'm not sure mine will be."

"Hey, you'll do fine. You're a fast learner," Lisa encouraged and sat down again. "Now, take out your first piece and start knitting."

Digging into her own tote bag, Kelly found her homely first effort. She nearly flinched when she saw it. Compared to her pretty scarf, it was downright ugly. "Boy, these needles feel small now," she said.

"Start knitting. It'll come back. You were doing fine before."

Kelly did as she was told and proceeded to knit, slowly at first until the smaller needles and yarn started to feel familiar once more. Soon, she'd finished a row, then another. That peaceful feeling she remembered returned as well, heightened by the warmth of the morning sunlight streaming through the windows and the hum of Burt's spinning wheel.

"They're all doing a great job in there," Mimi announced when she returned. "Oh, good, you've gone back to your knitting."

"Oh Lisa's orders," Kelly joked.

Mimi sat beside her and scooted her chair closer. "Oh, good, you're at the end of a row. Now, if you'll give it to me for a moment, I'll show you the purl stitch."

Kelly handed it over and leaned forward to watch. "Go slowly, please."

"I will. Now, with the knit stitch you slid the right needle to the left of the stitch. Well, purling is the opposite."

"Opposite?" Kelly complained. "That'll mix me up, won't it?"

Mimi smiled. "You'll get the hang of it. First, the yarn goes in front of the needle, not behind as it did with the knit stitch. Then, the needle goes to the right of the stitch. Then, you wrap the yarn and slip the stitch like before." She moved slowly through each of the maneuvers over and over.

Kelly peered suspiciously as the new stitches moved from the left needle to the right. The whole maneuver was backward. Great. She had enough trouble going forward. And just when she thought she was getting the hang of knitting.

"And you'll have to tighten the stitches a little, too," Mimi continued. "Now, you try." She held out the yarn.

"Oh, brother, backward knitting," Kelly muttered as she reluctantly took the needles.

"You want that sweater?" Lisa challenged.

"You'll be able to do it," Mimi reassured. "It's easier than you think."

"Easy for you," Kelly joked as she started to replicate Mimi's movements—very slowly. Once again, the needles felt clumsy and awkward as she completed the new movements. But gradually the motions got smoother. Somehow she completed one row. Amazing.

"Great," Mimi enthused, rising from her chair again. "See? I knew you could do it. You were the only one doubting yourself. I'll check on you in a little bit." And she scurried from the room, heading toward the front of the shop.

Noticing the increase in customers browsing through the adjacent room, Kelly figured the sweater class had ended and now everyone was shopping. She glanced toward two young women, conferring beside the crates of wool, silk, and mohair. They squeezed the bundles as much as she did, Kelly noticed.

"Lisa, that's a particularly fetching color for you," a woman's deep voice boomed.

Kelly saw Lizzie's older sister, Hilda, stride into the room. As tall and broad as Lizzie was diminutive and plump, Hilda's raw-boned features were in sharp contrast to Lizzie's delicate ones. It always startled Kelly to see them side by side; they were so different, yet they were sisters.

"Thank you, Hilda. I'm finishing up now," Lisa said, then glanced toward Kelly. "Kelly wants to join your next sweater class. She's dying to make the same sweater." Lisa held up the gorgeous coral creation. It was beautiful. Short-sleeved, pretty pattern. *Perfect for spring and summer, too,* Kelly thought enviously.

"Excellent," Hilda decreed, approaching Kelly. "I see you've finished your scarf, Kelly. It's lovely. You've obviously mastered the knit stitch."

"Well, I don't know if *mastered* is an accurate term, but I am better than I was," Kelly admitted, purling away.

"Hmmm, what exactly are you knitting now?" Hilda asked, peering suspiciously at Kelly's practice piece.

Kelly glanced up, unable to stop the feeling she'd been called to the front of the class by the teacher for doing something wrong. "It's my practice piece," she admitted, a little embarrassed. "Mimi just taught me to purl."

"Ahhhhh," Hilda replied. "That explains it. Keep

going, my girl. Practice stockinette next, and you'll be ready for my class."

She gathered up the binder she'd placed on the table and turned as if to leave. Kelly was actually relieved. Hilda's presence was a bit overwhelming.

Suddenly Hilda spun about and boomed in her loud almost basso voice, "I almost forgot, Kelly. How is Helen's cousin, Martha, doing? She ran away like a little mouse after the services. I never had the chance to inquire after her."

"She's doing well," Kelly ventured, carefully choosing her words to protect Martha's privacy. "She doesn't really feel comfortable with strangers, that's why she avoids people. But, she's actually quite nice. I got to spend some time with her last week."

"That was thoughtful of you, Kelly. You're a good girl. Helen would be grateful, I'm sure," Hilda declared. "If you see Martha again, please tell her to call us if she needs help of any kind."

Kelly looked into Hilda's rugged stern face with its strong craggy features. A masculine face, really. She imagined Hilda must have found it hard to be the ungainly, almost ugly, sister of delicate, demure, and pretty little Lizzie.

"Why, thank you, Hilda. I'll tell Martha. In fact, I thought I'd drop over there tonight and check on her. See if she needs anything. Her left arm is somewhat paralyzed, and she has trouble doing things. I plan to help her when I can."

Hilda walked over and gave Kelly a strong pat on her shoulder. More like a good thump than a pat. "Good girl," she repeated. "Well, I must be off. Good day, everyone." And she swept from the room.

"Are you going over after dinner?" Lisa inquired.

"Probably. I have to finish this one account first. Hopefully, I'll finish by dinnertime." The clock insider her head prodded Kelly to check her watch. "Which reminds me,

I'd better get back to work. I'll see you tomorrow," she added as she stuffed her practice piece into her bag and rose.

"Not tomorrow. I'm swamped with appointments all day. But, we've got practice tomorrow night at the ball field. I'll see you then."

Practice. Kelly hadn't heard that word in a long time. It felt good. Outside. Sun setting over the foothills. Oh, yeah. She'd be there. "At the same field?" she asked, wrapping her new scarf around her neck despite the warm temperatures.

"No, actually, we're practicing on the junior high fields at the corner of Stover and Perkins. On the east side of town. Seven o'clock. And we usually go into Old Town afterward." Lisa said. "It's gonna be summer before you know it."

Summer. Kelly felt the word run all the way through her, leaving a warmth like a ray of sunshine. "Sounds good. I'll see you there."

Suppressing all desire to touch and squeeze fibers and fabrics, Kelly hurried from the shop. Nearly eleven. She needed to get on task. This telecommuting was fine as long as she kept track of her time. Tick tock inside her head.

As she scampered down the steps toward the driveway, she noticed a man step out of his car and wave. "Well, hello, Ms. Flynn. I just stopped by to see you," Alan Gretsky called out and headed toward her, bright smile in place.

Great, Kelly thought, suppressing a frown. She wanted to get back to work, but she owed it to herself to hear what the realtor had to say. After all, she would be selling the cottage someday, wouldn't she? That question niggled in the back of her mind then darted away. "Hello, Mr. Gretsky," she managed.

"Ms. Flynn, I've got great news for you," Gretsky declared, clapping his hands together. "I've been discussing

your property with my out-of-town client, and they are extremely interested in purchasing. And when I told them
the particulars of the present loan arrangement, they were
undeterred, Ms. Flynn. Undeterred," he repeated as if it
were a new word.

Gretsky fairly reeked with enthusiasm. His eyes
danced with excitement, his suntanned face glowed, and
he looked ready to dance in place. Kelly couldn't help but
smile. It was hard not to like such a friendly fellow, especially when he wanted to give you money. "What exactly
does that mean, Mr. Gretsky?" she asked.

"My clients want to make you an above-market offer
on your property, Ms. Flynn. *Above* market," emphasizing
the repeated word this time.

Kelly held her smile in check. "How much above market?"

Gretsky folded his arms across his chest and grinned
wider, if that was possible. "Thirty thousand above market, Ms. Flynn. That should more than cover your ex-
panded loan plus penalties and fees. More than enough."

Her mouth dropped open. Kelly couldn't help it. The
amount shocked her. "What? Why would anyone pay that
much money for this little piece of land and the cottage?"

Clearly enjoying her reaction, Gretsky rocked back on
his heels. "The buyers have their reasons, Ms. Flynn. This
land would be perfect for some high-end townhomes beside the golf course. Those are very popular nowadays."

Kelly stared across to the quaint little cottage. Thirty
thousand over market. That meant she could pay off the
entire loan, including the extra twenty thousand Helen had
borrowed. And pay off the penalties, too. She wouldn't
even have to dip into her meager savings. The idea was
tempting, she had to admit.

"And, I believe they can be persuaded to pay your closing costs, too, Ms. Flynn," Gretsky added. "I took the lib-
erty of mentioning the unfortunate situation with your

aunt's demise and, well, they said they'd help you any way they could."

"Boy, that's a lot to think about, Mr. Gretsky," she said, shaking her head. "I hope they're not in a hurry for a decision."

"I think they're willing to wait for a while. Shall I tell them you would seriously consider their purchase offer?"

Even though part of her fought the idea, the accountant in Kelly responded, "An offer like that is definitely worth consideration, Mr. Gretsky."

She'd be a fool not to. All of the financial concerns that had bedeviled her for the last few weeks would be gone in a twinkling. She could return to her former life. Everything would be back to normal. Why didn't that feel better?

Gretsky nodded knowingly. "I was hoping you'd say that, Ms. Flynn. I'll tell my buyers. You have a good day now." He tipped his fingers to his forehead in a minisalute and returned to his shiny black Lexus.

Kelly watched him drive away and wondered why such good news didn't feel better. Why didn't *she* feel better?

Thirteen

"**Are** you sure I can't do anything for you while I'm here?" Kelly asked, succumbing to the familiarity of Uncle Jim's overstuffed armchair. She let herself sink in.

"No, dear, but thank you for asking," Martha replied, rocking in her straight-backed rocker. "I may take you up on the offer later, though. Mr. Chambers notified me the other day that my late husband's estate was nearly finished probate. And when it is, I'll be able to retrieve some of my treasured family possessions." She sipped her tea as a worried frown pinched her face. "I can't imagine Ralph would've sold my family keepsakes. Lord, I hope not. They're of no value, except to me."

Glancing about Martha's tidy but sparsely furnished living room, Kelly tried not to slosh the tea in her cup. "Did you have a large house in Wyoming? If so, we can bring back some of the furniture." Giving in to a smile, she added, "It's a little Spartan here, Martha. I'm sure you'd feel more comfortable with your family keepsakes on the shelves."

Martha nodded. "You're right, it is, and I *would* like to see my family pictures on the mantle once again. And my china." Her eyes lit up. "Oh my, Kelly, I had some beautiful pieces I'd collected over the years. Goodness knows if they're still there. And my quilts. Oh my, yes. Mustn't forget those. Wedding ring, Dresden plate, little Dutch girl," she murmured as she rocked.

"Don't worry, Martha," Kelly reassured. "We'll retrieve them all as soon as Mr. Chambers says we can. How far away is it? Were you in Cheyenne?"

"No, we were farther west, almost to Laramie."

"Is it a large house? We may need to rent a moving van."

"Oh my, I can't imagine needing that much, really. I've learned to do with a lot less these past few years." Her gaze shifted toward the lace-curtained windows. "It's a good-sized house, Kelly, indeed it is. We can probably give most of the furniture to the church. Or, the Sisters of Charity. Yes, they could sell what they don't need and keep the proceeds. Now, as for the equipment outside, well, I guess we'll just have to have an auction?"

"Equipment? What kind of equipment?"

"Why, all the ranch equipment, naturally. We had more than three hundred acres when I left. And about five hundred head of cattle. Mr. Chambers said he'd hired on some folks to manage the place until all this is settled. I don't know what I'd do without that man." She shook her head. "Mr. Chambers has handled every little detail so I don't have to. Even drew up a will for me. Goodness, I've never had a will."

"He certainly is thorough," Kelly agreed. "You said he'd hired ranch hands?"

"Oh my, yes. Livestock can't be left unattended. They have to be fed and watered and looked after, especially in the winter. We'd get snowdrifts six feet deep out there sometimes. I imagine our neighbors, the Simpsons, did it after Ralph died. I'll have to thank them." Martha closed her eyes, as if picturing. "Cattle will have to be sold at auction this summer, I imagine."

"No desire to continue ranching?" Kelly probed, wondering if Martha's desire to sell off everything from her former life stemmed from unpleasant memories or a genuine desire to continue her new, simpler life.

Kelly felt protective of Martha already, and she'd only known her for a week. But it was enough for Kelly to feel drawn to help the wiry little woman. She recognized the same feelings she'd had for her aunt's well-being surface within. Their connection might be slight and only recently formed, but it was there. Kelly could feel it resonate inside herself.

"No, Kelly, I truly don't. In fact, I want to do something different with the land. I'd like it to stay open and wild. No houses. We're losing too much of our open space to development, nowadays."

Kelly was surprised at her response. "Wow, that's a great idea, Martha."

A tiny smile tugged at the corners of her mouth. "I've been thinking about this ever since Mr. Chambers said I'd inherit everything. And I've decided I want to donate the land to the Nature Conservancy, so it'll remain a natural area forever."

"That sounds wonderful. Is Mr. Chambers working on that, too?" Kelly asked, admiring Lawrence Chambers' thoroughness and attention to detail. He'd not only taken great care with Helen's legal affairs, but he was now aiding Martha.

Martha reached to the table beside her and poured herself another cup of tea. "Not yet. He has to have some tests done on the land first. More tea, Kelly?" she offered.

"No, thanks, I'm good," Kelly chirped, holding the half-finished cup of tea. Oh, what she wouldn't give for a cup of coffee right now. "What kind of tests?"

"Mineral tests, to see what may be out there. Ralph never had it done. Wanted to run cattle and that was that.

But Mr. Chambers says there may be oil or gas out there, and we need to find out before it's donated. That would change the arrangement."

It would, indeed, Kelly thought, impressed again with Chambers' thoroughness. "Absolutely, Martha. You could section off any income-producing acres from the rest of the natural space. And that income could be placed in a trust for your lifetime, then pass on to the conservancy."

Martha's face brightened with the broadest smile Kelly had seen so far. She didn't know Martha could look that happy.

"Ever the accountant, aren't you, Kelly? You're going to be such a help when I have to handle all those details."

"Don't you worry about a thing, I'll be right there," Kelly promised.

"I appreciate that more than you know."

Noticing the darkness outside the windows, Kelly decided now was as good a time as any to ask the other questions she'd brought with her. "Uh, Martha, if you don't mind, there're some questions I'd like to ask you. About Helen."

Martha leaned back into her rocker, teacup nestled against her injured arm. "I could tell there was something else on your mind, Kelly. Go ahead. Ask me anything."

"Could you think back to those months Helen lived with your family in Wyoming and you two grew so close? Do you remember anything, any detail at all, that Helen may have mentioned about who the father might be? Did she ever let something slip in a wistful reminiscence?"

Martha closed her eyes and was silent for several minutes, her rocking slowed as well. Kelly held her tongue so as not to disturb Martha's reflections.

"I recall she said they always had to slip away to see each other. Once, she mentioned their favorite hideaway was a cabin up in Poudre Canyon. They'd pretend to be hiking with a church group, then go off by themselves instead. Helen said that cabin was her favorite place on earth."

Kelly pondered that for a moment. "Whose cabin was it? I know Helen's family was poor, so it definitely wasn't theirs."

"She wouldn't say, but I sensed it belonged to him or his family." She glanced toward the darkened windows. "I always felt that he was from a wealthy family that wouldn't have approved their relationship. Even though Helen never said so, I just sensed it."

"Hmmmmmm." Kelly tapped her teacup, causing the cold tea to slosh. "You could be right. Or, there's another possibility, even though it's one I don't like to entertain. Helen could have been seeing a married man. Perhaps that's the reason for her secrecy."

Martha frowned. "I never allowed myself to consider that possibility. It wouldn't be Helen. But I suppose anything can happen. And in those days, reputations could still be ruined by a messy affair, especially in a small town. Marriages certainly were."

Pausing for a second, Kelly tried to find the right words to ask the next question. It was definitely ugly, but she had to ask. "Is there any possibility that Helen had more than one boyfriend? I remember her telling me once that she 'used to keep the boys guessing' when she was in high school. I know this sounds awful, but do you think Helen might have had, uhhh, relationships with several boys?"

Shock claimed Martha's face. "You knew your aunt better than that, Kelly!"

Embarrassed and a little ashamed for having asked, Kelly apologized. "I know, Martha, she wasn't like that. Please forgive me for saying such things, but I'm simply trying to look at her murder from every angle I can."

"I know you are, Kelly. It's just . . . it would be unlike her to do that."

"Did she ever mention knowing some handsome young cowboy?" Kelly probed in her last effort.

Martha's bright smile returned. "They were all handsome young cowboys back then, Kelly. Every boy in my high school class was determined he'd go on to be a rodeo star and win that big silver belt buckle." She laughed softly.

Kelly gave up with a sigh, remembering the top prize at Cheyenne Frontier Days, awarded to the best rodeo cowboy each year. "You're probably right. I'd just found an inscription in her high school yearbook that looked promising. Some young wrangler-type wrote over his picture, 'Yours, always. Curt.' I was hoping maybe Helen had let something slip about him."

"Curt, Curt," Martha murmured, eyes closed. "No, Kelly. I would have remembered that name. Sorry."

"That's okay, Martha," Kelly said with a loud sigh. Setting the teacup aside, she pulled herself from the comfy chair. If she left now, she could still run over some account totals before bedtime.

"Don't try to take this on your shoulders, Kelly. It's not your burden, you know." Martha said, rising from her rocker as well. "You've done more than enough as it is."

"I wish I believed that, Martha, I truly do. But thanks for saying it anyway," she said, then kissed Martha's thin cheek and waved good-bye.

Balancing her oversized metal mug of Eduardo's coffee, Kelly dropped her tote bag and several plastic binders on the library table. They landed with a solid thump. "The new girl, Suzie, asked me to bring these to you," Kelly said as she sank into the chair beside Mimi. She'd been surprised, actually, to see Mimi alone, rocking quietly in the shop's main room instead of bustling about, managing. A peacock-blue skein of yarn lay in her lap and was slowly coming to life on Mimi's expert needles.

"Thank you, Kelly. I'll get to them in a few moments. After I knit a while longer." She sent Kelly a quick smile then returned her attention to the yarn.

"What are you making?" Kelly asked, reaching out to touch the brilliant blue. Was it wool? Silk? Cotton?—A combination? She rubbed the strands. "Hmmm, feels like . . . silk?"

"Very good. Silk and cotton. Exactly what you'll use for that sweater you're dying to make. And I'm making one of our popular sweater designs to put out in the store. We've sold every one of these. Incidentally, how's the purling?"

"Better." Kelly sipped her coffee. "And I've started the stockinette. Knitting one row, purling the next. I have to admit, it looks halfway decent."

Mimi laughed softly as she rocked, fingers working the yarn. "Are you always so hard on yourself, Kelly? Give yourself credit. You're doing quite well."

"Thanks. Coming from you, that's a compliment." Kelly pulled out her practice piece, which was growing to the size of a lopsided placemat. That idea was ludicrous, though. Kelly was certain the sight of it would put off her appetite.

Checking her stitches, Kelly started the new row. After she and Mimi had spent several tranquil moments in silence, knitting, Kelly spoke up. She sensed Mimi was worrying about something.

"Mimi, are you all right? You're awfully quiet this morning."

"I'm fine, Kelly. Something's on my mind, and I wanted to think about it for a while, I guess."

"Knit on it for a while?" Kelly offered Mimi's word for unraveling problems. "What sort of problem are you unraveling? Is it something you can talk about or would you rather not? I'll understand, either way."

Mimi chuckled. "You've got a good memory, Kelly. No, I haven't unraveled anything, and yes, I can talk about it." She took a deep breath and kept knitting for another minute before she continued. "I heard from my landlord yesterday, and the news isn't good."

"Raising your rent?"

"I wish that were it. No, it's more serious. He sold the property this week. His health deteriorated so last year, he simply had to cut back and is closing his property management business. Selling all his properties."

It was impossible to miss the worry on Mimi's face, as if an invisible cloud darkened. "Whoa, what does that mean for you and the shop?"

"That's what has me worried, Kelly," she admitted. "There's no guarantee the new owner/landlord would renew the shop's lease this fall. Mr. Jeffers, the former owner, tried to reassure me on the phone, but I could tell he wasn't sure what the new owner will do."

"Have you heard from the new landlord yet?"

Mimi shook her head. "And that's what concerns me. This all happened so quickly. Usually, when there's to be a transfer, the tenant receives a letter advising them of change of ownership. Not that they can stop the sale or anything, but as a courtesy. I received no notification until yesterday with Mr. Jeffers' phone call."

"Hmmm," Kelly thought. "Is that breaking any terms in your contract? Have you checked?"

"Yes, and all it says is 'notice will be given' but no time frame." She chewed her lip. "I guess I'll be smarter with the next contract I sign. But Mr. Jeffers was an old family company and they had an excellent reputation in town."

"Mimi, now it's your turn to stop being hard on yourself. Most people wouldn't have caught that, either. Tell me, who's the new owner?"

"Some company called A&G Management. That's another thing that bothers me. It's not listed in the phone directory, so I'm wondering if it's an out-of-state company that's trying to buy up land. Rumor has it the Big Box discounter is looking for more land parcels."

Kelly wondered if Big Box was also the buyer who was interested in her property. Gretsky said his clients wanted to build townhomes. "What does Big Box want to build?"

"Companion stores, an upscale restaurant, some office space, boutique shops."

"Hey, Mimi, you're 'boutique'," she teased. "The shop is definitely trendy. Maybe they'd give you prime space."

"I don't think so, Kelly. The word is that Big Box has lots of plans for Fort Connor. Somehow I don't think my little shop is part of it."

Mimi's poignant tone stole Kelly's smile. "Worst case scenario, if you had to move, where would you go?"

Mimi's busy fingers stilled and sank into the peacock blue yarn in her lap. She stared toward the wood-trimmed paneled windows, morning sunshine pouring through. "That's what I've been trying to sort through, Kelly. I made a few calls and was startled at the rental prices I've been quoted. I knew Mr. Jeffers was reasonable in his pricing, but, goodness, I had no idea he was beneath market."

"Would you be able to afford the new rent? Is your profit margin able to handle that increase?" Kelly pried, unable to stop being an accountant.

"Yes, but it'll take all the extra I'd planned to use for investing in more new looms. And, of course, my retirement plan will have to wait. Again." She exhaled a long sigh.

"Mimi, I will help you with your new accounts. No problem. I'm really good at that. Don't worry, I won't let you fall through the cracks," Kelly promised and patted Mimi's arm. After weeks of receiving reassurances on all things large and small, it felt good to be able to give it as well. Completing the circle.

The new part-time helper, Suzie, hurried into the room. "Mimi, that pattern company is on the phone," she announced. "Can you talk with them now, or should I take a message?"

Mimi nearly sprang from her chair, tossing the yarn to the table. "Now! I'll talk now. I've been trying to reach them for over a week and the phone is always busy," she complained. Hurrying from the room, she nearly ran into Burt. "Oooops, sorry, Burt," she apologized before she headed for the front.

"Looks like she's busier than usual today," Burt observed to Kelly, placing a can of diet soda on the table.

"You might say that," was all Kelly said. Mimi could announce the news in her own time. "How're you doing, Burt?"

"Fine, fine," Burt answered and surprised Kelly by taking the chair beside her instead of setting up the spinning wheel in his favorite sunny window. He clasped his hands together and leaned toward her. "Actually, I'm glad I found you alone, Kelly. My contacts in the department shared what they could with me, and I thought you'd be interested."

Kelly stopped mid-purl, dropping the knitting needles to her lap. "What'd they say?" she whispered, leaning closer.

Burt glanced over both shoulders before he spoke. "I talked with the coroner and judging from the marks on Helen's neck, she was probably seated when she was strangled."

"Seated?" Kelly asked, incredulous. "That doesn't make sense. Why would she be sitting when this drunken vagrant invades her house?" Burt looked her in the eye, and suddenly Kelly understood. "She must have known the killer. Otherwise, she wouldn't be sitting down, would she?" Kelly's heart beat faster at this new information.

"It's unlikely," Burt replied.

"Did the coroner tell Morrison? I mean, are they paying attention to this new information?" she demanded, voice rising.

Burt placed his finger to his lips and glanced over his shoulder again. "I'm sure they are, Kelly. Morrison is sharp."

Kelly held her tongue, even though she disagreed with his assessment of the lead investigator.

"And you'll be relieved to know they're doing extensive tests on the yarn that was found beside the river. Apparently, there were tiny specks of blood on the yarn. That caught their interest because they also found blood droplets on some of the carpet fibers they took from the cottage."

Kelly caught her breath. Now here was news. Bless the crime scene investigators. "Whose blood was it? Helen's?"

Burt shook his head. "Nope. My crime lab informant told me she was type A. The blood was Type O. Same as the suspect."

The elation Kelly felt evaporated. "Darn it! I was hoping we'd find something that proved he wasn't the killer."

"Don't give up yet," Burt advised. "Only blood typing was done so far. DNA tests are still pending."

Kelly sank back in her chair, the new information swirling inside her head, sending up one new theory after another. "When will they be done, Burt?"

"In a few days, so be patient," Burt said and gave her a fatherly pat as he rose. "Now, I'd better check on the new fleece Mimi mentioned yesterday." He headed toward Mimi's office until Kelly's voice stopped him.

"Thanks, Burt," she called after him. "You're a prince."

Fourteen

Lisa poured the tawny ale into her glass and took a sip. "How's your shoulder doing?" she asked Kelly.

Kelly leaned back into a wicker chair and stretched her legs, enjoying the warm spring night. Midnight, and the outdoor cafés sprawling through the heart of Old Town were still filled with customers. They spilled out into the historic plaza.

"It's sore, but it's a good sore, you know?"

"Oh yeah," Lisa grinned. "I know what you mean. With me, it's my elbow. When I don't pitch regularly, it stiffens up. Sounds like your shoulder was ready for some action."

"I'd forgotten how much throwing helps." Kelly sipped the most famous of the local microbrewed boutique beers. "And I'd also forgotten how good this tastes. Yum." She ran her tongue over her upper lip, licking off the creamy foam.

Lisa motioned her boyfriend, Greg, to the table. "Did you talk to Sully? Can he make it this weekend?"

Greg, tall, blond, and marathon-runner lean, sauntered to their table and leaned over Lisa's chair. "Nope. He's gotta work in Denver." Glancing to Kelly, he gave her a bright smile. "You wouldn't be up for a three-day trek to Diamond Peak, would you? We need an eighth person to even it out."

Kelly stared wide-eyed for a second, letting her expression answer for her.

Lisa laughed out loud. "Okay, I guess not. Wait a month, and you'll change your mind. It's great up in the canyon on a summer night, lying under the stars, staring up, counting—"

"Mosquitoes," Greg teased and kissed the top of Lisa's head.

"Hey, there weren't that many last year. Not at that altitude."

"They were all in our tent, then." He laughed. "You ready to leave?"

Lisa nodded, drained her glass, grabbed her bag and rose. "Good practice tonight, Kelly," she said, sliding her arm around Greg's waist. He did the same. "See you at the shop."

"Night," Kelly said, raising her glass. They both waved as they walked off.

She felt an old familiar twinge inside, watching Lisa and Greg together. Both tall, blond, slender, and handsome. Two nice people. They made a nice couple. She wondered if that might be in store for her someday. The last time she thought it was right, it proved wrong, and she had her heart broken.

Draining her beer, Kelly grabbed her wallet, shoved it in her jacket pocket, and rose to leave. The sound of salsa music spilling from a nearby club captured her attention, and she turned to see several couples moving to the beat near the outdoor fountain. One of the girls looked a lot like Jennifer. Kelly wove a path through the outdoor tables, eyeing the girl.

Sure enough, it was Jennifer—margarita in one hand and dancing her heart out. Kelly scrutinized the guy pulsating to the music beside Jennifer. Tall, spiked black hair, and hotter-than-hot looks. If ever a guy had Bad Boy written all over him, he was it. Kelly smiled to herself as she walked out into the soft spring night, the seductive Latin rhythms floating after her.

Kelly placed Carl's food dish on the cement patio as the doorbell rang. *Darn,* she thought, heading inside the house. She was about to start her early morning run. Sunshine streamed through the cottage's lacy white curtains. A perfect day.

Yanking open the front door, she was surprised to see Mimi standing there, newspaper in hand. "Hey, good morning. What brings you over so early? Is the shop opening at six A.M. now?" Kelly joked.

Mimi didn't return Kelly's smile. In fact, the worry lines crossing her attractive face deepened. "Kelly, there's something in the paper you need to read. I've been hoping and praying I'm mistaken, but . . ." Her voice trailed off.

"What is it?"

Mimi didn't reply, but handed over the newspaper instead. Kelly took it and could not miss the front page lead article: "Second elderly woman slain in home."

She caught her breath and read on. Was this a copycat murder? the reporter speculated. Victim was found strangled in her modest Landport home. Kelly's heart skipped a beat. Oh, no. Please, no. She poured over the article, searching for some identifying detail that would confirm what Kelly already feared inside.

And then it jumped out at her. At the end of the article, the reporter mentioned the "bright red, yellow, and purple tulips" lining the walk to the victim's white frame house on Maple Street. Kelly's heart sank. It had to be Martha. Kelly'd noticed the glorious display of tulips lining

Martha's walk the last time she'd visited. And the absence of such a colorful arrangement at the neighboring homes along the street.

"Oh my God," she breathed. "It's Martha."

"Ohhhh, no," Mimi whispered, wrapping both arms around herself. "I was hoping it wasn't true, hoping—" She shut her eyes and turned away.

Kelly felt sick to her stomach. She sank down on the front step, the newspaper dropping to her feet. She had done this. She was responsible for Martha's death. It was her questions and search for answers that got Martha killed. No one in town even knew about Martha, not even her church. Helen had protected her cousin well—until Kelly came along. All those years of carefully protecting Martha's whereabouts from an abusive husband, all for nothing. Kelly managed to blow Martha's cover in a few days. She led the killer right to Martha's door.

Kelly's gut wrenched, and the tears started to flow. Damn. There were still tears left. She'd never run out of tears, would she? She sank her face in her hands and let them fall.

"I'm so sorry, Kelly," Mimi soothed, voice beside her which indicated that Mimi had joined her on the concrete step. "I could tell you'd grown fond of Martha in the short time you knew her." She rubbed Kelly's shoulder comfortingly.

"I killed her, Mimi. I'm responsible," Kelly said through the tears.

"What? Don't be ridiculous, Kelly—"

"The killer must have been watching and followed me to her house. I got her killed. It was me . . ." Kelly choked on the last words as another flood of tears washed over her.

Mimi kept rubbing Kelly's shoulder without speaking, all the while Kelly wept softly. Grief for Martha mingled with the still-raw grief for Helen. And her dad, even though that was three years ago. Everyone was gone.

She'd just found a new family connection in Martha, only
to have it yanked away before she'd even gotten to enjoy
it. Why was it loved ones didn't stay in her life? Was it
her? Was she poisonous, or something? Even her old
boyfriend left.

Now that she was waist-deep in the swamp of recrimi-
nation and guilt, more hurt bubbled to the surface. Old,
old wounds. *Don't forget your mother,* an ugly voice whispered. *She left you, too. And you were only a baby.* The
well that ran deep opened then, and tears continued to
pour forth hot on Kelly's cheeks.

"Kelly, Kelly . . ." Mimi said. "You are not responsible
for someone else's actions. Least of all, this vicious killer
who committed these crimes. Maybe he learned of Martha
from Helen. Maybe there's some connection between
them all. Who knows? And we certainly don't know
what's going on inside that sick mind."

Cried out at last, Kelly lifted her T-shirt and wiped her
face, drying her eyes, wiping her nose. She had to move.
Run. She couldn't sit still anymore. She needed to chase
away the dull ache inside. Push it back way down deep
where she didn't have to look at it or feel it. She pulled
herself to her feet.

"I've got to run, Mimi. I . . . I need time to think," she
said, brushing grit from the back of her latex shorts.

"I understand," Mimi said as she rose. "I'll tell the others when they come into the shop, if you want me to."

"Yes, please. I don't want to have to say it." She
reached over and gave Mimi a quick hug. Mimi squeezed
back. "Thanks for everything, Mimi," she said, breaking
off before the tears returned.

"I'll tell Burt, too, when he comes in this morning,"
Mimi called as Kelly started off.

Kelly waved, heading for the edge of the golf course,
which she followed until she picked up the river trail.
Once on the paved pathway, Kelly decided to forego the
scenic route she usually took. She wasn't in the mood for

too much beauty this morning. Instead, she went the opposite direction, knowing it would lead through an open, almost barren wilderness area, then skirt past an abandoned industrial site before winding through a deeply wooded and shaded passage beside the river once more. Traffic on this section of trail was sparser, which suited Kelly just fine. She wanted to think. Needed to think.

She settled into her running rhythm and picked up her pace, early sun at her face. The sun felt good, and so did the rhythm. Dense trees started to thin and traffic sounds grew fainter as she ran. Each stride, each breath helping to ease the ache. Like rubbing a cramped muscle slowly, slowly, walking it out. Running it out.

Who did this? Who killed these sweet women? Who was that vicious? And why? What threat could they be to the killer? What did Helen and Martha know that caused their death? Kelly sorted through one idea after another, discarding them right and left. None made sense. Trees thinned to disappearance, open grassland now. Three ravens, obsidian black, cried their complaint at being disturbed and took to the sky. What leftover feast had they found in the brush?

Helen withdrew money to ward off the threat. It hadn't worked. Was Martha lying when she said she didn't know who the money was for? Kelly rounded a curve, startling more birds, flushing them into the air. No, no, that wasn't right. Martha's concern about the money withdrawal was too real.

Maybe . . . maybe it wasn't about the money. Maybe it was something else that made Helen and Martha a threat. Perhaps they knew something about someone. Information that could harm that person. Kelly let the thought simmer for a while as she headed out of the grassy area and toward the old factory site. Broken windows gaped in the concrete block walls like gouged out eyes, staring without seeing.

It had to be about the baby and Helen's hidden love af-

fair, Kelly mused. Who would be threatened by that?
Someone who had a position of respect in the community,
perhaps? Someone who had secrets to hide. A face sur-
faced. A furtive glance that hinted at secrets. Stackhouse.
Kelly's breath quickened, even in the midst of her stride.
She remembered Curt Stackhouse's guilty denials about
Helen. He was lying. Why would he lie unless he was try-
ing to hide something?

Kelly picked up her pace, rounding another curve that
bordered the abandoned site. Far from the highway, no
sounds of people or cars carried on the breeze. No one
around for miles. Was Stackhouse the one? He was certainly a successful rancher. Land buyers and sellers court-
ing him long distance even. Real estate deals right and
left, Kelly surmised, caught up in this scenario. He mentioned his wife owning a business. Maybe he was afraid
she'd divorce him if the truth came out. Maybe that would
destroy his investment business, maybe—

A raven's shrill cry overhead startled Kelly from her
creative imaginings. Suddenly, she felt a warning chill
ripple through her. *Turn. Turn now,* her instinct said. Still
running, Kelly whipped her head around to look over her
shoulder and was shocked to see a hooded cyclist bearing
down on her—only a few yards away.

Kelly leaped to the side of the trail with a surprised
yelp as the cyclist whizzed by, a blur of gray sweatshirt
and sweatpants. She couldn't even see his face, it happened so fast. Or was it partially covered? Sunglasses.
Yes, he wore sunglasses. And the gray hood covered everything else.

Breath coming fast now, the workout's disciplined
breathing was gone, replaced by an adrenaline rush.
Thanks to all those years of softball and sports, Kelly's reflexes were razor sharp. She stood, hands on hips, wondering how any responsible cyclist would ignore the basic
courtesies of the trail. The normal calling out of "coming

up on the left" that one heard so regularly it was as familiar as early morning birdsong.

Kelly already knew the answer. That was no ordinary cyclist. And he deliberately did not call out a warning because his intent was to run right into her. At the speed he was going, she'd have been knocked unconscious on the side of the road. Who knows how long she might have lain there in this desolate section before she was found?

Something caused Kelly to look up then, and she swore she saw the raven perched on the roof of the gutted building. "Thank you," Kelly said out loud to the bird. Its warning cry had brought her back from deep reverie in the nick of time.

Kelly peered down both directions of the trail, comprehending for the first time how isolated she was right now. A cold chill ran up her spine. *Get off the trail now,* her instinct warned. Kelly glanced at her watch. She'd been running for more than thirty minutes. It was a long, desolate run back on the trail. What if the cyclist returned?

The realization that the cyclist and the murderer may be one and the same resonated inside. It had to be Martha's killer come back for Kelly. After all, the vagrant suspect was still locked up. Who else but Martha's killer would come looking for her?

Kelly didn't need any more convincing. She took off into the scrubby, rutted terrain beside the trail, heading north. The trail ran diagonally through Fort Connor from the foothills northwest of the city to the southeast edge of the county, following the river most of the time. Kelly knew the highway lay to the north of the river at this point, and highway meant cars and people. She might have to hike a few more miles to the shop and home, but she'd be surrounded by traffic. Who would have thought she'd ever welcome traffic?

The ruts became crevices and filled with prickly bushes. Kelly plunged through them all, keeping the morning sun on her right shoulder as a compass. She felt the thorny branches tear at her legs but didn't even look down. Blood would wash off. At least the cyclist couldn't ride out here. Heck, she could barely walk out here.

At that moment, her left foot sank into some oozing ground, more muck than mud. *Yuck,* Kelly thought, as she yanked her foot free and tested for drier ground across the barren area. *Up ahead,* she thought she spied barbed wire. Instead of trepidation, it brought elation. Barbed wire meant boundaries. Fences. And probably the highway.

Sure enough, Kelly heard the glorious sound of trucks, the *whoosh* and the rumble of heavy rigs on asphalt. Amen, she breathed, right before she tripped over a rock and tumbled forward. Splat. Face first into the dirt and grit. Muttering some of her dad's favorite curses from his "navy days," Kelly scrambled to her feet again. Brushing grit off her filthy T-shirt, she bent over to brush her knees and stopped. Why bother? Long bloody scratches marked her legs from knees to ankle. Might as well add skinned knees to the mess.

Climbing the incline to the highway's edge, Kelly released a huge sigh of relief. Yes. She was only a couple of miles from home. All that was left was the barbed wire. Kelly scanned the expanse of rusty wire, then took a deep breath, and gritted her teeth as she grabbed hold. Yanking two of the wires in opposite directions, she struggled through, feeling her expensive running shorts catch, then rip, as she yanked herself free—on the other side at last. Thank God her tetanus shot was up to date.

Not wasting a moment, Kelly set off running alongside the highway. The thought of Eduardo's strong coffee was enough to bring back her strength and her stride as she headed home.

"Oh my gosh! What happened to you?" Megan exclaimed when Kelly finally stumbled into the shop.

"Coffee . . . please," was all Kelly said as she leaned over, hands on bloody knees, to catch her breath.

Megan snapped into action. "Suzie, would you get Kelly a mug of Eduardo's strongest? Put it on my tab," she directed, gesturing toward the front of the shop. "And tell Mimi to come quick, if you see her." Approaching Kelly, she offered, "We need to get you cleaned up."

"No, it's okay," Kelly said when she caught her breath. She'd sprinted the last half mile to the shop, dodging cars at intersections. "I'm going home to . . . to shower in a minute."

Mimi raced into the foyer and her mouth fell open at the sight of Kelly. "Oh, no! Kelly, did you fall down? What happened?"

"I've been climbing through scrub brush and barbed wire to reach the highway," Kelly said, straightening at the sight of Eduardo's coffee headed her way. She reached out both hands as Suzie delivered the treasure into her grasp. "Ohhhh, Suzie, you're a lifesaver." With that, Kelly took a big drink, causing teenaged Suzie to flinch.

"Oooooo, watch out, it's hot," she warned.

Kelly didn't care. What was a burned tongue compared to all the other scrapes and bruises she'd received this morning? Another big swallow and she'd begin to recover, she was sure.

"Why were you climbing through brush?" Mimi demanded, concern still evident. "I thought you were running on the trail."

"I was, but I got chased away." She had to have another long drink before she could tell this story. But before she could begin, another voice interrupted from the adjoining room.

"Mimi, do you want to take a look at this first cabinet and tell me if you like the angle?" Steve said as he rounded the corner. "I can move it another inch—whoa! What happened to you?" He stared at Kelly.

"Someone chased her on the trail," Megan announced.

"What?" Steve cried. "Did he hurt you, Kelly?"

"Look at her," Suzie interjected, eyes round. "She's all torn up."

Kelly held up her hand, quieting the speculation. "I wasn't actually chased. Some guy on a bicycle nearly ran into me on the trail. And I decided it wasn't an accident, so I got out of there the best way I could. Unfortunately, I was in the section down by the abandoned beet processing plant, and the trail veers pretty far from the highway at that point. So, I had to hike through some nasty brush to get out. Plus, barbed wire."

"Oh, Kelly," Mimi's voice trembled. "Was he actually following you?"

"Probably," she nodded. "I don't think it was by chance he caught up with me in that deserted stretch." She took another sustaining drink of the rich dark brew and felt strength returning to her strained legs.

"Did you get a look at him?" Steve asked in a low voice.

"I did, but he was all covered up in a hooded gray sweatshirt and sunglasses, so I couldn't tell features. Plus, he was going so fast, he was just a blur." Her mouth hardened. "Bastard. He was headed right for me. No warning, nothing. If I hadn't turned when I did and saw him coming, I'd be lying unconscious beside the trail right now."

Mimi shuddered, Megan's pale face got even paler, while Steve's features darkened into a scowl.

"Kelly, you have to tell the police," Megan insisted.

Kelly made a dismissive noise. "And listen to Lieutenant Morrison tell me it was my overactive imagination. No thanks. I'll tell Burt. He'll believe me, then maybe he can get the message to Morrison." She drained the cup.

"Burt should be in shortly, Kelly," Mimi said. "I was planning on telling him about Martha, too."

"Yes, please do, and ask him to make sure the information gets to Morrison, would you?" Kelly placed the empty mug on a table spilling over with tidy bundles of yarn. Her bloodied hand looked garish among the bright spring colors. "I'm going home to shower and clean up all these scrapes. I'm a mess." She brushed her hands down her filthy shirt and shorts.

"You're coming back over here afterward, right? I mean, Burt will want to talk with you, I know he will," Mimi declared.

Kelly nodded. "I'll come back later. I've got to log on to my office site and get some work done. Ask Burt if he'll hang around till lunch."

Without another word, she was out the door and down the steps. She'd come back all right. Check with Burt, get his opinion, and grab some more of Eduardo's coffee before she took the long drive out to Stackhouse's ranch.

Fifteen

Kelly shifted her coffee mug and tote bag to one hand and yanked open the shop's front door. Smoothing her light-weight sweater over her jeans, she stood for a moment and let the familiar surroundings sink in. It always felt so good here. Everytime she stepped inside, she could feel the difference immediately. Soothing, relaxing, she couldn't quite put it into words. But it felt good.

Recognizing Jennifer's voice, Kelly headed toward the main room. Jennifer and Lisa both sat at the library table, knitting as usual. Lisa was offering assistance to a woman twice her age beside her. And Jennifer had something other than emerald-green yarn in her lap.

"Hey, are you finished with the sweater?" Kelly asked as she settled into a nearby chair.

Jennifer looked up at Kelly with a concerned expression. "Yeah, I finished yesterday. Listen, how are you? Mimi told us all about your . . . your . . ." Jennifer paused, watching Kelly's finger to lips then pointing to the new knitter across the table.

"I'm fine," Kelly said brightly. "My legs are a mess and they sting like crazy from the alcohol, but they'll heal. I'm gonna have new scars to join the ones from softball."

Jennifer clearly wanted to hear more, but Kelly shook her head no and mouthed "later." Steve rounded the corner from the classroom area, hammer in one hand and a cabinet door in the other. Spying Kelly, he immediately came over.

"How're you doing?" he asked quietly when Kelly gestured to the newcomer with Lisa.

"I'm okay," Kelly said, noticing the worried look. Everyone was worried. She almost felt guilty for causing such concern. "I used every bandage in Helen's cabinet. But I'm okay. Now I'm getting mad."

"At the guy?"

"Ohhhh yeah."

"That's good. But maybe you'd better run on the creek-side trail from now on. There're lots more people all the time on that trail." He motioned around the table and toward Mimi's office. "We all think you'd be safer there. You don't want to give Mimi heart failure." He smiled wryly.

Kelly could tell he was forcing a smile for her sake. "I think that's a good idea," she agreed, reaching for her tote bag. "I don't feel like scrambling through brush again any time soon."

Steve turned back to the half-finished cabinets hanging against the wall. "Promise me you won't do anything crazy, okay?" he said over his shoulder.

Kelly hesitated. *Define crazy,* she thought, but answered, "No plans to. But I will find out who he is. Depend on it."

Just then Burt strode into the main room and headed for Kelly. "Ahhh, there you are. Are you okay?" he asked as he drew up a chair.

Another concerned face, Kelly observed. Now, she was really starting to feel guilty. Everyone in the shop was worried about her. She wasn't used to that. "Yeah, a little scratched up, but that's okay."

Burt glanced to the newcomer who was gathering her things together and thanking Lisa for her help. "I called my old partner and asked him to get the message to Morrison about Martha. And about your encounter on the trail this morning," he said softly.

Kelly noticed Jennifer leaning closer to hear. "Thanks, Burt. Let's hope Morrison doesn't dismiss Martha's death as a copycat or try to explain it as another robbery gone bad," she said with a sarcastic tone.

Burt smiled at that. "Cut him some slack, Kelly. He's a good man. He'll figure it out."

Kelly didn't need to register her doubts at that comment. Jennifer gave a disdainful snort. "I don't know who this guy is, but he sounds like he couldn't find his you-know-what with a flashlight."

Burt ducked his head, clearly trying to hide his grin. "Ohhh brother, you girls are brutal. Time for me to leave, before you pick on me."

Noticing Lisa's student waving good-bye, Kelly brought her voice back to normal. "We'd never pick on you, Burt."

"Yeah," Jennifer said with a grin. "You're one of us."

"Thanks, Jennifer. Coming from you, that's a compliment," Burt said as he rose to leave. "Kelly, take care of yourself, okay? Take it easy the rest of today, why don't you?"

"Will do, Burt," Kelly lied, picking up her knitting where she left off. "I'm going to sit here and knit."

"Good girl." Burt nodded in satisfaction and waved as he left.

True to her word, Kelly sat and knitted one row, then purled the next, getting her rhythm back, watching the neat rows of stockinette stitch appear.

She'd sit here and knit—for a while. Long enough to lull everyone in the shop into relaxing. Then, she'd slip away and head to Stackhouse's ranch while it was still afternoon. That's when she and Steve found him there last week.

Glancing to the side, she noticed Steve immersed in cabinetry. Jennifer concentrated on the scarlet bulky knit yarn she was knitting. Her needles were almost as large as the ones Kelly used for her scarf.

"What're you making?" she asked, purling easily now.

"I thought I'd try that open-weave vest Megan showed me."

"We were all worried about you, Kelly," Lisa's voice interrupted across the table. "Megan told us all about it." She shivered. "You really think it was, you know, the . . ."

"Killer?" Jennifer finished the sentence. "Had to be. Who else would follow her out there?"

A cell phone's melodious jangle sounded. Lisa finished winding her long blonde ponytail and secured it with a rubberband before she grabbed her phone.

Kelly waited until Lisa was absorbed in conversation before she leaned toward Jennifer. Instinct told her she should tell someone where she was going, just in case. Kelly deliberately didn't think about the "in case" part.

"Jen," she whispered, glad Steve had left the room. "I'm going to run an errand, but I don't want you to freak out when I tell you what it is, all right?"

Jennifer's large brown eyes widened even more. "Oh brother. This doesn't sound good."

"It'll be okay," she said as much to convince herself as Jennifer. "I'm driving out to Stackhouse's ranch in a few minutes. I'll be back by dinner."

"Why? I thought you guys talked to him already."

"We did, but both Steve and I could tell he was lying when he said he really didn't remember Helen. I think he remembered her a lot, judging from the look in his eyes."

"So?"

"So, I want to ask him some more questions. Maybe he remembers something from the past that might help."

"There's something you're not saying. I can tell."

"Yeah," Kelly admitted. "I want to see the expression on his face when I ask him about Martha."

"Are you crazy?" Jennifer retorted, clearly horrified by Kelly's plan. "What if he's the killer?"

"Well, I'll play stupid and jump in my car and drive home fast," Kelly joked, hoping to deflect Jennifer's objections and ease her own fears.

Jennifer glanced over her shoulder and lowered her voice. "Yeah? And what if he doesn't let you? What if he attacks *you* this time? Face it, Kelly, somebody was out to hurt you this morning."

The overwhelming sense of Jennifer's objections began to override Kelly's bravado. Frustration and anger and determination had all boiled together this morning while she'd showered and dressed. Adrenalin kicked in as well as she formulated her scheme. Perhaps it was crazy, but at least it had helped bury the grief and guilt over Martha's death. Now, they were shoved down deep where Kelly couldn't feel them.

She let out a long sigh. "Yeah, I've thought of that, too," she admitted.

"Good. Now I know you didn't get stupid overnight. You'd be crazy to go over there alone. If you want me to, I'll go with you."

"No, he'd probably clam up—" Suddenly Kelly got a new idea. "Wait a minute, I know! I'll take Carl with me. I'll have him on his leash. Nobody in his right mind would try to attack me in front of my dog."

Jennifer opened her mouth as if to object, then closed it again. "Okay. But he's gotta be on his leash right beside you. Promise?"

"Promise," Kelly agreed with a grin and put her knitting back into its tote bag.

• • •

Carl shoved his smooth black head right beside Kelly's as she headed down the road to Stackhouse's ranch. She reached up and stroked a smooth ear. "Hold on, boy, we're almost there," she promised her excited dog. Carl had been pacing the back seat since they left. Pacing and falling flat, of course. Every time she turned a corner, he's slip on the upholstery and lose his footing. Doggie wipe-out.

Approaching the open barnyard area, Kelly scanned the outbuildings for Stackhouse. His huge black truck was parked on the graveled spot, so she figured he was home. But what if he wasn't? Would she turn around and head back into town? Kelly admitted she didn't have an alternate plan.

Fortunately, that wasn't necessary. Stackhouse appeared in the barn door, watching Kelly bring the car to a stop nearby. Parking swiftly, she grabbed the dangling end of Carl's chain lease. With a dog as strong as Carl, she used an industrial-strength metal leash. "You have to behave, Carl," she admonished him as she stepped out and opened the door for her dog. Carl bounded from the car, yanking Kelly at least two feet. She reined him in, glad she was strong, otherwise she'd be lying face first in the dirt right now.

Kelly saw Stackhouse slowly approaching, so she went into the routine she'd practiced on the drive over. She hoped it sounded convincing.

"Hello, Mr. Stackhouse," she called cheerfully, waving her hand as she went to meet him.

"Afternoon, Miss, uh, Ms. Flynn, isn't it?" he replied, stopping a few feet away. "Nice dog. What's his name?"

Kelly noticed a wary expression on the rancher's weather-beaten face, so she ramped up the wattage of her smile. "This is Carl, and I wanted to bring him out so he could see this gorgeous place you've got here. I can't wait till Stevie and I can have some acreage of our own like this." She glanced around appreciatively. Carl took one look at Stackhouse and pulled forward, clearly anxious to do a meet-and-sniff.

Stackhouse smiled, just a little. "Hey, fella, how're you doin'?" He held out his hand close enough for Carl to sniff.

Carl sniffed thoroughly, then slurped with his long pink tongue. Stackhouse chuckled. Kelly took note that he'd passed her dog's test. Carl was a good judge of character.

"Don't slobber on Mr. Stackhouse, Carl."

"That's okay, Ms. Flynn." Stackhouse caught her gaze. "Surely you didn't drive all the way out here to show your dog the scenery. Is there something else, Ms. Flynn?"

Kelly took a breath and plunged in, hoping she'd find her way. "Well, yes, Mr. Stackhouse, I, uh, well . . . I wanted to ask you again about my aunt, Helen Flynn Rosburg. You see, I kind of got the impression when we spoke last week that you really did remember her. But something was holding you back. Or maybe you were embarrassed or something."

She was desperately hoping Stackhouse would volunteer a comment at that point, which she could use to bounce off of, but he didn't. He stood there, observing her with his Stetson pulled low over his eyes, shading his face. He said nothing. So Kelly stumbled on.

"You see . . . I'm trying to find anyone that might have known my aunt all those years ago. I've got this . . . this strong feeling that her death was caused by something in her past. Perhaps something that happened."

Still no reply from Stackhouse. He stood like a cowboy statue, staring at her. Kelly felt the sweat start to bead on her forehead. She distracted herself by patting Carl's side. He was busily checking out ground smells. A lot more than squirrels lived in these pastures.

To her immense relief, Stackhouse finally spoke. "That was a long time ago, Ms. Flynn. What makes you think I know anything?"

Kelly met his steady gaze and gambled. "Instinct, Mr. Stackhouse. My gut tells me you did know Helen. I saw it in your eyes," she said, hoping blatant honesty might earn her a few points.

Stackhouse held her gaze for an excruciating minute, then glanced toward the forest edging his pastures. "You've got good instincts, Ms. Flynn. I'll give you that."

Kelly blinked, surprised that her honesty had been matched. "You knew Helen, didn't you?"

"Yes, Ms. Flynn, I knew her. In fact, I'll never forget her. She was the first girl I ever fell in love with. And the only one to break my heart."

This time, Kelly couldn't contain her surprise. Stackhouse clearly noticed, and a wry smile tugged at the rancher's mouth. "Why don't we take a walk," he suggested, pointing toward the pasture. "That way Carl can chase what he's smelling."

He led the way into his open pasture, Kelly and Carl following. Now that she was knee-high in the spring grass, she noticed the varied shadings of early green, from chartreuse to lime. Approaching a small clearing, Stackhouse stopped and grabbed a stick at his feet. He held it up to Carl. Carl was already two steps ahead of him and began to yelp, eager to play.

"You want this, Carl?" Stackhouse tempted. "Go get it." And he tossed the stick in an arching throw.

Not a bad throw, Kelly had to admit, and released the leash just as Carl lunged forward. Watching her "protection" race off into the high grass, Kelly hoped this new feeling she had about Stackhouse was correct. There was an honesty coming off the man, and she didn't think he was faking it. Her antennae were sharp, and she had yet to pick up any uneasiness or deception on his part.

That surprised her. She'd convinced herself all morning that Stackhouse's wary expression last week signaled something dark. Now that she was here, she felt no threat whatsoever. She'd better be right, because Carl had disappeared into the grass now. If Stackhouse really was a clever killer, he could dispose of her out here in the pasture. No one would find her in the grass, save Carl and the ravens. The memory of the huge bird's warning caused a secondary pause.

She decided to break the ice, hoping Stackhouse would explain his tantalizing comment. "That sounds like you and my aunt had some, uhh, shared history together."

"Yeah," he said with a nod. "We shared a few moments of history, you might say. I wanted a lot more than that, but Helen didn't."

This time it was Kelly's turn to stare silently, waiting for Stackhouse to continue.

"We went through high school together." He stared off into the grass, where Carl's head bobbed occasionally. "And I had a crush on her the whole four years. I must have asked her out a thousand times. Helen would laugh and tease me, but never say yes to a date. In fact, I don't think she dated anyone. I never saw her with any other boys, either."

Kelly kept her silence, not wanting to interrupt the reminiscence. Obviously, Aunt Helen had cleverly concealed her real affections from everyone.

"But, I sensed there was someone else. I'd swear to it."

"What made you think so?"

He turned to Kelly with a wide smile. "Instinct, Ms. Flynn. Same as you."

"Did she drop any clues about this person?"

He shook his head. "Nope, not a one. But I got the feeling that she was protecting him for some reason. Can't explain it. Just a hunch."

"And you never saw her dating any of the other boys?"

"Nope. She'd flirt with some of them, but nothing more. Hell, she wouldn't even talk to most of the boys. I felt kind of special. Helen liked to talk to me. She'd let me walk her to and from class. I don't know why she picked me and none of the others."

"I do," Kelly declared with a grin. "I saw your photo in the high school yearbook. You were a handsome devil, Mr. Stackhouse." She figured Lizzie's vocabulary would come in handy about now. "Matter of fact, you're still handsome."

Stackhouse slanted a look her way. "You've got your aunt's charm, that's for sure. And you can call me Curt. I don't stand on much formality."

"Kelly," she offered in kind.

"You even resemble her, you know? There's a look that comes in your eye that's pure Helen." He grinned. "Maybe that's why I'm talking like a damn fool right now."

"It's never foolish to admit falling in love, Mister, uhh, Curt. And I find your honesty refreshing. Some boys would have dropped a girl like Helen once she turned them down. Yet, you two stayed friends."

Stackhouse gazed past Kelly's shoulder toward the sprawling ranch house in the distance. "We were close until summer of our senior year, then she stopped talking to me."

Kelly did some mental arithmetic. Early spring would have been when Helen conceived the child she later gave up. "What happened to change your friendship?" she probed.

Stackhouse stared into the pasture for a long moment. The only thing that broke the silence were the cries of annoyed birds that Carl had unwittingly flushed. "I guess it won't be disloyal to talk about it," he said in a subdued voice. He drew in a breath. "We . . . well, we became intimate one night. The night after graduation, in fact." He shook his head. "I still remember as if it were yesterday. It was a warm spring night in late May." He gazed off toward the mountains this time, clearly reminiscing.

Kelly, meanwhile, was making an effort not to let her jaw drop. She hadn't expected to hear this, especially after he'd emphasized that Helen refused to even date him. Waiting as politely as she could while Stackhouse enjoyed his memories, Kelly couldn't hold her curiosity a moment longer. "Wow. That's quite a bombshell, Curt. I trust you're planning to explain Helen's sudden change in behavior. You can't just leave me hanging like this."

He looked up and grinned sheepishly. "Well, I reckon I owe you an explanation."

"Damn right."

He laughed. "You get more and more like Helen the longer I talk to you. She didn't mince words, either."

Remembering her aunt's occasional "salty" language, Kelly smiled. "Thanks, but get back to explaining. What made Helen change her mind? She wouldn't even date you before. Did something happen at graduation?"

"Not that I remember. It was just all us kids surrounded by our families, posing in those caps and gowns, feeling awkward and proud at the same time."

"Did you see her there with her family?"

"Yep, she looked happy like everyone else, posing for pictures."

"How'd you get together that night, then? Did you call her or meet her?" Kelly prodded.

"Nope," he said with a bemused expression. "That was the strangest part. She came over to see me. Drove over in her father's old Ford truck. My family had just returned from the high school as I recall. Then, there's Helen ringing our doorbell. You could have knocked me over with a feather."

"What'd she say?"

"She didn't say much. It was her face that did the talking. I could tell she was angry. And she'd been crying, because her eyes were red. She never admitted what was bothering her, but I could tell it was something really important. To her, at least." He paused. "She wanted to go out for a drive and talk, so we did."

"What'd you talk about?" Kelly probed, hoping to keep Stackhouse remembering the pictures inside his head.

"You know, she didn't say much. Just kept asking me questions the whole time she drove. What was I going to do after school? What kind of summer job? Had I decided which college? I wound up doing most of the talking, as I recall."

It was clear to Kelly that Stackhouse had enshrined these memories of Helen, otherwise he wouldn't have such clear recollections. "Where'd you drive?" she continued to probe.

"Up into Poudre Canyon late at night." He shook his head, as if still amazed by the youthful bravado. "We drove past Rustic, then she pulled off the road. Wanted to take a walk, she said. It occurred to me then that she was headed somewhere."

"Was she?"

"Yep." He nodded. "Up through the trees there was a clearing and a cabin that just happened to be unlocked. It was a beautiful place, it truly was." He smiled ruefully. "We stayed the rest of the night. Came back at dawn. I lied to my parents and told them Helen had dropped me off with some of my buddies after midnight. Didn't want to add to the trouble I was sure she'd be getting when she got home."

"Were her parents upset? Did you ask her?"

He shook his head. "Didn't need to. Nice girls didn't stay out all night in those days. It was a different time. I'm sure she caught hell from her dad. He was pretty strict." Stackhouse stared past Kelly's shoulder. "I thought that evening was a whole new beginning for Helen and me. Turned out to be the end."

"Why? What'd she say?"

"Not much. In fact, she barely spoke to me after that. Acted like there was nothing between us, like nothing had happened. Even when I proposed to her, she'd just look away and say no, she couldn't. Or wouldn't." He sighed heavily. "I must have asked her to marry me at least a hundred times."

Kelly puzzled over the scene he'd painted. What was going through Helen's mind for such erratic behavior?

"She was working at a soda fountain that summer, and I came over every afternoon after I finished working the fields. Must have consumed several gallons of cherry limeade talking to her." The memory brought back his smile. "I'd go over, talk to Helen if she'd let me, drink cherry limeades, and propose. Just like clockwork every day. Until July."

"What happened in July?"

"Suddenly one day, she was gone. The owner of the drug store said she had to go to Wyoming to help take care of her sick aunt and cousin. Her dad's brother owned a cattle spread up there. I figured she'd be back pretty soon, so I waited all summer and fall. When she didn't return, I went to ask her family. They weren't too friendly, and they said Helen was staying in Wyoming 'indefinitely.' That's when I finally gave up. I realized she couldn't really care for me, or she'd have tried to contact me. Write or something. But I never heard from her, so . . . I let her go. Had to."

Kelly watched his face and the remembered emotions register there. His sincerity appeared genuine. Kelly swore she could feel it. But her skeptical side roused itself from the remembrances and shook awake with a question.

Was it possible Stackhouse was faking? Was he inventing this whole story to lead her astray and away from suspecting him from complicity in Helen's death? That thought didn't resonate inside, but Kelly felt compelled to follow it up, anyway. There was only one thing she had left to test Stackhouse, but she had to work up to it.

"When did you learn she was back in town?" she asked.

"When a friend told me she saw an engagement announcement in the paper that next year. I didn't even contact her. By then, I'd finished my freshman year at the university. I was glad she'd found someone who made her happy. That made it easier for me, too." He smiled. "I met my Ruth that fall."

"You know, Helen's cousin, Martha, came to live in Fort Conner a few years ago. Helen helped her start over after she left her abusive husband back in Wyoming."

"Sounds like something Helen would do. How's she taking Helen's death?"

"Pretty hard," Kelly answered. "That is, while she was still alive. She was the elderly woman who was just murdered in Landport the other day."

Stackhouse stared at Kelly, shock written on his face. The last doubts Kelly had about his guilt disappeared. He couldn't fake that reaction.

"My God," he breathed. "What do the police say?"

"They're looking into a connection between the deaths," Kelly said, fervently hoping Morrison was doing exactly that.

Stackhouse scowled. "I thought police caught the man who killed Helen."

"They have a suspect in jail. He's a drunken vagrant who's been causing trouble in Old Town for years. The police saw him on the golf course near Helen's house that night, and they're convinced he did it."

He peered at Kelly. "But you're not."

"Nope. It's too easy and doesn't explain everything. There were some personal items and money stolen from the house that night, yet the drunk didn't have a thing with him except a hangover."

"Hmmmmm."

"Yeah, exactly."

"What do you think happened?"

Kelly paused, choosing her words carefully. "I don't know, but I'm going to find out. That's why I'm poking around in Helen's past. Sorry about all the questions, but I was hoping you'd know something."

She broke off her sentence when she spied a familiar

red truck barreling down the road to the ranch. Her cover was about to be blown.

"Here comes your fiancé. How're his alpaca plans coming?"

Kelly made a quick decision. "He's . . . he's not my fiancé. He's just a guy I know from the wool shop. We thought it might be easier to come out here and ask you questions if we looked like a nice young couple moving into town." She gave him a wry smile, as the truck drove into the barnyard.

Stackhouse eyed her carefully, sizing her up all over again, Kelly sensed. "Soooo, you came out here to ask me questions because you thought I might have something to do with Helen's murder, right?"

Kelly took a deep breath. "Initially, yes," she confessed. "But our conversation has convinced me you had nothing to do with Helen's death."

"How can you be sure, Ms. Flynn?" he challenged.

She met his steady gaze. "Instinct, Mr. Stackhouse." Then, she gambled and gave him a wink.

Stackhouse's smile returned and he chuckled then nodded toward Steve, who'd leaped from the truck and was crossing the barnyard. "So, you and Stevie aren't engaged?"

"Lord, no, I barely know him."

"Could've fooled me. You two look like a couple."

Kelly did her best to look appalled, which seemed to amuse Stackhouse. "No way. My friend at the shop must have told Steve where I was going. He was there building cabinets for Mimi."

"So he doesn't work for a computer company?"

"Nope," she said, watching Steve head through the pasture.

"Building cabinets? Is he a carpenter?"

"Actually an architect, but he's a developer now. Likes building houses."

"Thought you said you hardly knew him."

"People at the shop talk."

"Uh huh."

Kelly eyed Stackhouse and saw the amusement. Surprisingly, she didn't mind his teasing.

Steve was coming closer. However, Carl also noticed and was headed straight for him, galumphing through the grass in huge leaps. Steve spotted Carl coming at him, and they both disappeared down into the grass. Doing the slobber and roll, no doubt, Kelly decided. Had to be a guy thing.

"Well, your dog sure likes him."

"He bribes him with golf balls. Carl can be bought."

"Well, he's a good judge of character. He liked me," Stackhouse said with a laugh.

Kelly had to join him as they watched Steve distract Carl by throwing a stick, then head their way.

"Good afternoon, Mr. Stackhouse," Steve called as he drew nearer. "How're you doing, sir?"

"Real fine, now that Kelly explained why she's here," he replied.

Kelly watched Steve's reaction. Relief was still mixed with concern. "It's okay, Steve. I've grilled him already, and he's off the hook," she deliberately joked.

Steve visibly relaxed. He advanced toward Stackhouse and extended his hand. "Well, in that case, Mr. Stackhouse, let me re-introduce myself. Steve Townsend."

Stackhouse clasped his hand. "Call me Curt. And I gather it's not Stevie. I'll bet Kelly does that just to annoy you."

"Sounds like her." Steve agreed with a grin.

"Hey, payback for the arm," Kelly retorted, unwilling to let the jibe stand.

"I hear you're a builder. Now I know where I heard your name," Stackhouse said. "One of the Wellesley town council told me about your new site out near county road sixty-four. Smart move. We need more affordable houses. Keep it up, son." Checking his watch, he glanced back at the ranch house. "Well, folks, once again I've really enjoyed chatting with you, but I've gotta get back. I promised Ruth I'd take her to dinner in town tonight, and I'd better get cleaned up." He started walking toward the sprawling frame house, Kelly and Steve falling in step behind. "Ruth and I'd love to have you two over for dinner some time. Why don't you stay in touch, okay?"

Surprised by his kind offer, Kelly agreed quickly as did Steve. "I'd like that, Curt," she said. "You've been really polite with my, uh, investigation."

"Wish I could have helped more, Kelly. Keep on asking questions," he said over his shoulder. "And keep in touch." He picked up the pace, heading for the ranch house.

Instead of returning to his truck, Steve leaned on the hood of Kelly's sporty sedan. "Don't give Jen a hard time when you get back to the shop, okay? She didn't want to tell me, but I sensed you were going to do something like this. So, I made her talk."

Kelly laughed. "What'd you do? Bribe her with a cinnamon roll?"

"That works? I'll use it next time." His smile disappeared. "You had us all worried. I had to swear Lisa and Megan to secrecy so they wouldn't tell Mimi. She would've called the cops. And I guarantee Curt wouldn't be so friendly if the cops came racing up his road."

Feeling prickly and defensive, Kelly retorted, "I'm perfectly capable of taking care of myself."

Steve glanced away. "Listen, I wanted to talk to you about something else. Something serious."

Caught off guard, Kelly stared at him. And in a moment of complete honesty confessed, "Steve, I'm about to choke on serious. It's been nothing but serious since I returned to Colorado. Helen's death, now Martha's. I can't take any more. Honest to God."

Steve looked out over the pasture. Carl's head bobbed up at a crow's angry caw then disappeared into the grass again. "Don't worry. It isn't about you or Helen or anyone you know. It's a story about my best friend and me when we were growing up here years ago."

"Is it short?" she asked.

He didn't smile, simply folded his arms and leaned back against her car, still staring out into the grass and trees in the distance. "Yeah, it's short. Bill and I were best buddies all through junior and senior high. We were gonna be roommates at the university our freshman year. We'd party together, hike, take our girlfriends camping up in the canyon, all that."

Kelly leaned against the car as well, listening, deliberately not interrupting. Sounded good to her.

"Our plans were all set. Until that June, right after high school graduation," Steve continued. "Some guy was having a party at his folks' place up in Estes Park. Bill really wanted to go. I had an early call at my summer job that next morning, so I didn't want to. No way would I get back home till three A.M. from their place. My job at the golf course required me to be there at six A.M. every Sunday."

"Wow, that must have put a crimp in your social life," Kelly interjected, hoping to dispel this cloud that seemed to settle over Steve as he talked.

"Yeah, kinda. My girlfriend was pretty understanding, though. Anyway, Bill begged me to drive him up there, even if I had to leave early. His car was in the shop. He'd broken up with his girlfriend, Lauren, and really had it for this girl he'd just met. She'd asked him to show up, since it was her cousin who was throwing the party. So, I agreed. Told Bill I'd drive him up, stay for a while, then he'd have to find another way home. Or, stay with the new girl, whatever." He paused.

"Did he stay?"

"Yeah," Steve said, then drew a deep breath. "He was having a great time dancing with this girl when I left about eleven. So, I waved good-bye, and that was the last time I saw him alive."

Kelly held her breath. She'd sensed this story was not going to have a happy ending.

"Seems after midnight, the host brings out his own little stash of designer drugs, and Bill joined in. Most of them don't even remember much after that, they were all so wasted. But the parents returned the next day and found Bill lying dead on the rocks below the cliff. Who knows what happened. He either walked out onto the cliff and fell off or was pushed or whatever. Hell, maybe at that point he thought he could fly."

Steve's face darkened with the memories, Kelly noticed. She held a respectful silence for several long minutes, then gently offered, "I'm so sorry, Steve. That was an awful way to lose your best friend."

"Yeah. It was."

"I'm curious, though. Why did you want to share it with me? And why now?"

"Because I don't want you to make the same mistake I did after Bill's death. I blamed myself for years, convinced that if I'd been there, he never would have died. He'd have gone home with me like he always did when we partied late. And he'd be alive today."

He turned to face her. "And I can tell you're blaming yourself for Martha's death. Thinking you're responsible. None of us is responsible for someone else's actions, Kelly. I know now that Bill would've stayed at the party no matter what I did. He was crazy about that girl. It was his choice to stay. I couldn't have stopped him. And you couldn't know there was a killer lurking around Martha, watching and waiting. It's not your fault."

Kelly met his direct gaze and stared back, saying nothing. She could feel the truth in what he said, but part of her still didn't want to accept it. Not yet, anyway. She looked away, twisting the leash into a coil. "Yeah," she admitted. "Part of me knows that. And part of me doesn't accept it."

"I know. It takes time. Enough said." Steve shoved away from the car and put his fingers to his lips and let out an ear-piercing whistle.

Carl's head popped up from the grass, and he started galumphing toward them. Kelly wished she could whistle like that. She'd tried but it never worked.

"C'mon, big fella," Steve said as Carl broke through the grass and headed their way. "I'm heading back to the shop to finish up some adjustment on the cabinets. I'll tell Mimi and the others you're okay. Hey, how're ya doing, boy?" he said, bending over an exuberant Carl.

"Thanks, I appreciate it," Kelly said, attaching Carl's leash. "I've got to get some work done on my accounts before nightfall. C'mon, Carl. We've gotta go home." She yanked Carl's leash and opened the door.

Steve was already walking to his truck. "See you, Kelly," he called over his shoulder.

Kelly jumped in her car, revved the engine, and headed down the ranch road, noticing the sun was about to kiss the tops of the foothills. Dusk would settle soon. Steve had already turned his truck in the same direction but waited for her to pull ahead of him.

Kelly stopped as she came parallel with his truck. Something was niggling in the back of her mind. She signaled him to lower the passenger window and when he did, she spoke up. "Listen, I really appreciate your confiding in me. I could tell it was a hard story to tell. It was a hard story to listen to. But I'm curious about something. Have you ever told that story to anyone else?"

Steve waited a moment before answering. "Only one other person. That was Mimi. Bill was her son." With that, the window closed and Steve's big red truck moved down the road.

Kelly opened the sliding glass patio door and Carl raced outside into the darkened backyard. Night creatures surely must be afoot. Kelly leaned against the doorframe and gazed up into the silky blue-black sky. Now that it was nearly midnight, much of the surrounding commercial lighting had gone dark. The stars were brighter, she noticed as she sipped a hot chocolate. As die-hard a caffeine addict as she was, coffee and midnight did not go together.

Arching her back, she indulged in a long satisfying stretch, grateful to be off the computer at last. These investigative excursions were taking quite a toll on her work schedule. So far, she'd juggled both.

Drawing the blinds, she stepped out into the patio, enjoying the blanket of total darkness that enveloped her. Looking past the golf course, she could see the shadowed mountains in the distance, looming. Silent and protective. She stared at them for a long while, in hopes their silence would calm her restless mind.

She'd overlooked something. She must have. Stackhouse wasn't involved in these murders. And Kelly was still convinced the vagrant wasn't guilty, either, even though he'd been charged with Helen's. Was Morrison going to try and explain away Martha's death as well? She had to find something, some information somewhere that would convince him the real killer was still lurking about. Kelly wasn't about to spend the rest of her time in Fort Connor looking over her shoulder whenever she found herself alone on a trail or roadway.

Swirling the last of the hot chocolate, Kelly sorted through the ideas churning inside her head. She needed to ask more questions. Maybe . . . maybe she could find someone from Helen's high school who knew Helen all those years ago. Someone who still lived in Fort Connor. There had to be some clue as to who Helen's mystery lover was. Was he really some wealthy son of an important family like Martha suspected? And what happened on graduation night that upset Helen so she'd run to Curt for consolation? Did the rich boy reject his poor girlfriend now that he was headed to college? Did Helen tell him about the baby? Did he reject her?

Kelly visually traced the Big Dipper, letting the stars' vastness calm her. Then the image of Helen's high school yearbook came to mind. That was a good place to search. Perhaps she could tell from some of the messages who Helen's close friends were. It might not be much, but it was all she had.

Draining the hot chocolate, she went back inside and grabbed the yearbook off its bottom shelf. She plopped down on the Oriental carpet like before and began paging through the book. Scanning the written messages, deciphering swirls and cramped scrawls, Kelly slowly perused the pages until she came to what she and her friends had always called the "mug shots," those stiff, lookalike photos that revealed every flaw.

Starting with the A's, Kelly scrutinized page after page until she reached the end. There she paused, and studied one photo. She leaned closer, examining it, then she smiled. Closing the yearbook with a satisfied snap, she shoved it back onto the lower shelf and headed to bed.

Sixteen

"**Kelly,** how are you?" Mimi asked, peering over a box of crinkly, lacy yarns.

Must be a new shipment, Kelly guessed, since the brilliant colors and textures didn't look familiar. "I'm fine. A little tired from having to work so late last night, but okay. What kind of yarns are they?" she asked, pointing to the blaze orange, fire-engine red, and bubble-gum pink brimming from the box. "I don't recognize them."

"Probably because they don't last long enough for you to even see them," Mimi said. "It's called 'eyelash' because it's got all these little fibers that knit up into these great trendy scarves and tops, whatever." She started arranging the profusion in a crate along the wall. "Girls just love these yarns. They'll be gone in two weeks."

"Wow," Kelly said, sinking her hand into the pile. "They're soft and yet they look spiky."

"I know. They're such fun," Mimi said with a youthful giggle. "I whipped up a scarf for my thirteen-year-old niece last week for her birthday. 'Electric limeade' was the color. Then I knit little strands of crimson silk through it as well. I called it cherry limeade." She grinned, pleased with herself.

Remembering Curt's comment about his summer of cherry limeades, Kelly had to smile. "Great idea, Mimi. Why don't you make another and wear it so we can see."

"Maybe I will," she said as she headed back toward the checkout area.

Kelly stroked the eyelash once more, then headed to the main room. Megan was already there, knitting with a neon pink cotton that nearly glowed it was so bright. "Wow, that's a great shade for you, Megan," she said, dropping her tote bag and settling in. "What are you making?"

"I thought I'd make the shell that's hanging over there." She pointed to a red sleeveless top dangling from the ceiling of the other room.

It was almost as pretty as the top Kelly would make someday. She wasn't sure when "someday" would arrive. Maybe she could actually start now. After all, she finally felt comfortable doing the stockinette stitch, she thought, as she pulled out her practice piece and started knitting. Maybe.

"You know, we were all worried about you yesterday," Megan said softly without looking up.

Kelly let out an audible sigh. This would take some getting used to. "I know, and I'm sorry. I didn't mean to concern anyone. After all, I had Carl, and he'd be more than enough protection."

"Steve told us about Carl."

Busted. "Okay," Kelly admitted with a laugh. "He was a little distracted by, well, by everything. But it turns out I didn't need protection. Trust me, if I felt anything questionable about Stackhouse, Carl would never have gotten off his leash. I swear."

Megan glanced up, and Kelly was surprised to see so much concern still. "I believe you. Just promise you'll take one of us along next time you're sleuthing. We can lurk in the background while you're asking questions, so we won't cramp your style."

Kelly laughed out loud, picturing Megan lurking, as well as herself 'sleuthing about' à la Sherlock Holmes. "I'll think about it, I promise."

"You don't have to do everything alone, Kelly," Megan said as she returned to the neon pink rows of stitches.

Letting that thought play through her mind, Kelly kept up her knitting and purling, row after row of stockinette forming in the variegated wool. After a few minutes, she checked her watch. Lizzie should be arriving with Hilda any minute. Hilda's advanced knitting class began at eleven.

Just then, she heard the front door's jangle and Lizzie's birdlike soprano voice and Hilda's rich contralto in the foyer. *Right on time,* she thought. Sure enough, Hilda sailed into the room like a cruise liner—tall, substantial, impressive bulk. Lizzie followed in her wake, skimming the water like a sailboat, darting and quick to respond to the wind's whim. "Good morning, ladies," Kelly greeted them both.

"Ah, good morning, Megan, Kelly. Still laboring on that practice piece, I see," Hilda observed as she steamed past.

"Good morning, dears," Lizzie chirped as she floated by.

"Morning, Hilda, Lizzie," Megan replied.

"Lizzie, when you have a minute, could you help me with some of my stitches?" Kelly asked.

"Surely, dear," Lizzie agreed. "Let me get Hilda settled, and—"

"I'm fine, Lizzie," Hilda decreed. "Go help Kelly."

"Well, if you're sure, dear." Lizzie set her knitting bag, fabric bag, and purse on top of the library table and started to draw up a chair.

"Why don't we go into the café and have some tea, all right? That way we won't be distracted by Hilda's class.

Megan, you'll excuse us, won't you?" She deliberately caught Megan's gaze and winked.

Megan glanced to Lizzie then said, "Absolutely. I have to go back and work as well. See you later."

"What particular problem were you having, dear?" Lizzie asked as Kelly led her to the café.

Choosing a quiet table in an empty corner, Kelly offered Lizzie a chair and settled in herself. "Well, to be honest, Lizzie, I think I'm doing pretty well with my stockinette. Take a look and tell me what you think." She handed over her misshapen practice piece.

Lizzie observed the stitches with a professional eye, checking both sides of the piece—knitting and purling sides. "Very good, dear. I can see where you got the hang of it, so to speak, and your stitches improved."

"Thank you," Kelly said, feeling the flush of accomplishment. "Coming from you that's high praise."

"Flattery, flattery," Lizzie dimpled.

Kelly signaled a waitress over. Jennifer was scouting property this morning for her real estate office, apparently. *Just as well,* Kelly thought. She wanted privacy for this chat. "Tea, Lizzie?"

"Oh, yes, thank you, with cream and sugar," she told the waitress, showing another dimple.

When the waitress scurried off, Kelly set her knitting aside and leaned forward slightly. "Actually, Lizzie, I have other questions I'd like to ask you. Not about knitting at all, if you don't mind?"

"Why, certainly, dear. What is it?"

"I was paging through Aunt Helen's yearbook last night, and I couldn't help noticing your picture there, too. You were in the same class, right?"

Lizzie beamed. "Yes, we were. We both were graduated the same year. In fact, Helen and I shared several classes together. She was clever with math like I was. Sometimes we were the only girls in the class." Her eyes lit up in amusement.

Better and better, Kelly thought. "That's wonderful, Lizzie, because I'm trying to find out everything I can about Helen's last year in high school. The people she knew, what groups she joined, who were her friends, and all that."

Lizzie cocked her head. "Why are you asking, dear? Do you think it has something to do with her death?"

Kelly smiled at Lizzie's perceptiveness. "Perhaps," she hedged. "I'm simply trying to look everywhere I can for information."

"Well, of course, I'll be glad to help. What would you like to know?"

"Did she have a lot of girlfriends? Anyone close to her?"

Lizzie closed her eyes. "Not really. Helen always kept to herself. Almost aloof. I admired that quality in her. She always looked so ... so self-contained." She gave a wry smile. "And of course, that quality never sits well with the popular girls. They like to think every other girl is jealous of them. So when they see someone who isn't, well ... they tend to get mean-spirited."

"So, Helen wasn't one of those popular girls you're talking about?" Kelly moved her arm so the waitress could serve their tea and coffee.

"No, indeed. Helen seemed in her own little world most of the time."

"You two were friends, weren't you?" she asked when the waitress left.

"I'd say we were acquaintances. We went to the same church, so our families knew each other, but Helen and I didn't really even talk much until high school. That's when we shared classes together."

"Were you one of those popular girls, Lizzie?" Kelly ventured with a smile.

Lizzie dimpled and blushed at the same time, clearly delighted to be considered. "Oh, my gracious, no! I was never one of them. Why, Hilda and I weren't even allowed to date. Oh, no. Papa was much too strict for that. And having boyfriends was absolutely required for those other girls. They were always whispering and giggling and telling tales about all the boys and each other, of course."

"Did they talk about Helen?"

A devilish smile teased Lizzie's mouth. "Oh, yes. It used to infuriate them that the boys paid so much attention to Helen when she didn't pay attention to them. Helen had this way about her. Ohhhh, it was hard to define . . . she was saucy without actually flirting. But it was fascinating to watch her. She didn't lead them on, like the other girls. Helen was smarter than that." Lizzie gazed at the white porcelain teapot, obviously reminiscing.

Kelly was just as fascinated by Lizzie's vibrant recollections of her high school years. Clearly, those were golden years in Lizzie's mind, enshrined forever. Kelly was struck once again that Helen held such an important place in the memories of both Stackhouse and Lizzie. Her aunt clearly carved out a niche for herself on her own terms.

"Was there any boy she paid particular attention to?"

"Well, she would walk to and from class with that handsome Curtis Stackhouse practically every day. You know, I believe I spied Curtis at the Wool Fair when we visited. And he's still a handsome man." Lizzie gave an appreciative nod, as if judging a fine wine.

Kelly grinned. "I saw him yesterday, and you're right. He's still a handsome man and a successful rancher now. He also remembered Helen." She left it at that.

Lizzie perked up. Her pink hair ribbon bouncing on her neat silver hairdo. "Well, I'm sure he did. That poor boy worshipped the ground Helen walked on. Wore his heart on his sleeve, too. That used to drive those other girls wild. One of them, Julie Fisher, had her cap set for Curtis, but he wouldn't give her the time of day." Lizzie giggled.

Surprised again at Lizzie's observations, Kelly decided to probe a little deeper. "So, Curtis Stackhouse was

Helen's boyfriend, then. You said they walked to class
every day, and he worshipped her."

"Oh no, dear," Lizzie corrected, wagging her head.
"I'm sure Helen liked Curtis, but she didn't love him. He
was simply a decoy, so no one would notice the boy she
really loved."

Boy, Lizzie didn't miss a trick, Kelly thought in admiration. "Who was that? Do you know?"

Lizzie lifted her dimpled chin proudly. "I most certainly do. I saw them kissing behind the library. Lawrence
Chambers stole Helen's heart. Poor girl. She knew he belonged to another."

Kelly stared in surprise. She wasn't expecting that answer. "*What?* Lawrence Chambers? Her lawyer?"

"One and the same."

Kelly wagged her head in amazement. "Brother,
Lizzie, you missed a career in journalism. You should
have been a reporter. I'm impressed."

Lizzie blushed in pleasure at Kelly's praise. "Thank
you, dear, but Hilda and I were destined to be school-
teachers. Papa said so. And he was right. We were excellent teachers."

"Let's get back to Lawrence Chambers, okay?" Kelly
picked up the thread. "What made you think he 'belonged' to another?"

"Well, it was common knowledge. Lawrence was from
an old established and very wealthy Fort Connor family.
He was already pledged to Charlene Thurmond. She was
the daughter of his father's oldest friend and business associate, Henry Thurmond. I heard they'd been promised
to each other as children." Lizzie shook her head sadly.
"Poor Helen. She was just the daughter of sugar beet
farmers, and not very successful ones at that. She never
had a chance. But Lawrence loved her. There was no
doubt about it. I could tell by the way he gazed at her in
class. I'd catch him watching her in algebra."

Kelly sat quietly, sipping her coffee while her mind

churned. Chambers. Lawrence Chambers. She'd never have guessed. Recalling the stark high school photo of an owlish, homely Chambers peering out from behind huge glasses, Kelly had to marvel. Judging from Lizzie's account, Helen could have had any boy she wanted. In fact, she had a heartbreakingly handsome young cowboy following her around like a puppy. Yet she spurned them all for the bookish and unattainable Chambers.

Helen had always referred to him as her oldest and closest friend, Kelly remembered. Close was right. That explains the tremendous care and concern Chambers had always demonstrated toward Helen. *And it explained his intense grief at her death,* Kelly thought, recalling his emotional reaction in his office.

Or, did it? Kelly stared into her empty cup, as a niggling little thought wormed its way from the back of her mind. What if upstanding and trustworthy Lawrence Chambers was deliberately misleading her? Perhaps that emotional distress was cleverly designed to deflect further scrutiny? Clearly, Chambers had secrets to hide. Was he afraid his position in the community would be jeopardized if Helen's story got out? Helen would never reveal it, Kelly was certain.

Perhaps it's not about the story, the niggling thought whispered. Perhaps it's about money. Lots of money. Helen's property is worth a lot of money now. And Martha's, too. In fact, Martha's property could be worth a great deal if there's oil and gas beneath. And who was it that suggested the land be tested for minerals and other riches? Chambers.

Kelly recalled Martha's comments the day before she died. How Chambers was 'taking care of everything.' What if he had been surveying all of Martha's subterranean wealth and Helen found out? What if she felt betrayed and threatened to reveal his scheme? Had Chambers murdered Helen and Martha for their land? Did he try to run Kelly down on the trail to get her out of the picture or, at least, out of town?

Kelly set her cup back into its saucer, letting her thoughts settle as well. The image of frail-looking Chambers riding a bike at top speed would not come into focus. She was beginning to go in circles now, and all the theories were running into one another. She needed to sort through them all, to see which ones deserved further scrutiny and which ones made no sense.

"Do you have any more questions, dear?" Lizzie inquired. "If not, I need to check on Hilda's class. I'm in charge of copying patterns for everyone, and I think it's that time." She checked her watch.

"Oh, definitely. Thanks, Lizzie, you've been a great help," Kelly said, pulling some bills from her wallet and dropping them on the table. "I really appreciate your openness. And your memory is simply fantastic. I still think you'd have made a great reporter."

"Oh, hush, dear," Lizzie said with a giggle and a little wave as she walked toward the shop doorway.

Kelly gathered her things and headed back to the shop's main room. The library table was deserted, which suited her just fine. She needed time to think about Lawrence Chambers and all those theories that swirled inside her head. What better way than to use Mimi's method? She'd knit on it.

Pulling out her ever-expanding practice piece, Kelly picked up the stockinette where she left off. Knitting the remainder of that row, she purled the next, getting her rhythm back. In the adjoining room she heard the sounds of Hilda's class dismissing themselves and noticed several students wander into the room, checking pattern books and yarns. She was comfortably settled in and feeling positively meditative, until a loud voice shattered her peaceful state.

"Good heavens, girl! Are you planning to make a blanket of that thing?" Hilda boomed from across the room. Kelly jumped in her chair and dropped a stitch.

"Darn it, Hilda, don't scare me like that," she exclaimed, annoyed that her peaceful interlude had been interrupted. "You made me drop a stitch."

"Let it join the others. Surely you don't plan to use that piece," Hilda said as she came to stand beside Kelly's chair.

Kelly could feel Hilda's penetrating gaze and wondered how she could be considered such a good teacher. Did she intimidate her students into succeeding?

"Of course not," Kelly protested, not a little defensive. "I told you this is my practice piece. I'm practicing stockinette so I can—"

"Good Lord, girl, you've practiced enough," Hilda decreed, and reached over to yank the piece from Kelly's hands.

So shocked at Hilda's quickness, Kelly just stared at her for a few seconds. "Hilda!" she cried. "I was in the middle of a row!"

"Your stockinette looks fine," Hilda decreed, examining the stitches much as Lizzie had done. Then, to Kelly's amazement, Hilda whipped out a pair of small scissors and snipped the length of yarn that attached the piece to the remainder of its skein.

"*Hilda!*" Kelly protested, ignoring the students who were hiding their laughter behind pattern books. "Do you treat all your students this way?"

"My students don't need prodding. You do. It's time you started your sweater." She dropped the forlorn practice piece on the table.

"What?!" Kelly protested. "I can't do that sweater yet. It's too . . . too complicated. It has a pattern . . . and . . . and I've never followed a pattern before."

"You can read, can't you?" Hilda peered overtop her spectacles, her pale blue eyes hawklike.

Kelly couldn't believe it. She'd fallen into the clutches

of the Nazi Knitter. Where had helpful Hilda gone? She managed to scowl back. "Patterns are different. They look strange. All those little lines and squiggles."

"That's only because you've never done one before. Everything new is strange at first. You simply need to choose a simple pattern. Come with me."

Hilda turned smartly on the heel of her industrial-strength nurses' shoes and headed toward the other room where all the new sweaters and tops were dangling from ceiling and cabinet doors and draped across shelves. Kelly gave in and followed after.

"Now, look at all you have to choose from," Hilda said, gesturing to the multitude of yarns spilling from crates and piled on shelves. "You need something to build your confidence, Kelly. I suggest you choose one of those bulky knit yarns you used so successfully with your scarf. We'll find a simple pattern, and you'll have a sweater before you know it. Then, you'll be ready to tackle that sweater you're pining for."

Kelly stared at Hilda, shocked at the clever suggestion as well as her uncanny read of what was causing the hesitation. The suggestion resonated within, but pride reasserted itself. Kelly wasn't going to capitulate that fast, so she forced a frown, even though her fingers were itching to dive into the crates and start touching.

"Wellllll . . ." she demurred.

"Stop stalling, girl, you know you want to do it."

Rats. Hilda was outsmarting her at every turn. Kelly wasn't used to that, but she gave respect where it was due—albeit grudging. "How long would it take to do a sweater with these yarns?"

"Not much longer than it took to knit your scarf. You remember how fast that went, don't you?"

Kelly nodded.

"And how proud you felt when you finished? And how—"

Kelly held up her hand. Only total capitulation would

satisfy Hilda. "Okay, okay, you've convinced me, Hilda. I'll make the sweater. Brother, you're relentless, you know that?"

"I pride myself on it." Hilda said, and Kelly could swear she detected a twinkle in that stern gaze. "Now, look up there. See the sweaters with the larger pattern? They were knit with those yarns. Tell me which one strikes your fancy, and I'll find the pattern."

Kelly scanned all the sweaters that were displayed, searching for a simple design. She found it hanging in the corner. A sleeveless shell with wide neck. No scalloped edges to maneuver, no fancy edging. No frills, just row upon row of neat stockinette top to bottom. Plain and simple. "How about that one," she chose, pointing to the light pink creation.

"An excellent choice. Now, you choose a yarn you like while I find the pattern," Hilda ordered before she headed for the pattern books.

This time, Kelly eagerly complied with Hilda's instructions. She dove into the bins, squeezing and stroking yarns fat and thin. Obediently concentrating on the chunkier wools, Kelly found some of the variegated yarns she used for her scarf. But these were spring colors—pale azures, cool lavenders, and minty greens.

Eyeing the sweater once more, she noticed how even the stockinette looked and realized the chunky yarn that was so perfect in her scarf would not yield the same effect in the sweater. She needed an even thickness all over this time. She began to plunder other bins of solid colors—creamy oatmeal, lime sherbert, cherry parfait.

Caressing the pudgy bundles she noticed the different feel and checked the label. She was surprised to see that it was a blend of cotton and merino wool. Checking the tag that dangled from the sweater, Kelly saw that it was also a cotton blend. That settled it in her mind.

She grabbed four skeins when Burt approached. "Hey,

Burt," she said, noticing his worried expression. *Not him, too,* she thought, bracing herself for another lecture.

"Do you have a minute, Kelly?" he asked, glancing over his shoulder. "I've got something to tell you."

Kelly sensed it had to do with Helen. "Certainly, Burt. Why don't we talk while you spin," she suggested, heading back to the main room. She dropped the roly-poly bundles of cherry parfait onto the library table while Burt settled at the spinning wheel in the corner. Kelly grabbed a pattern book and spread it out at the end of the table.

"You talk, and I'll listen," she suggested as she leaned over the book, pretending to read. "Hilda's about to descend on me with a pattern. So you better make it quick." She nodded toward Hilda, who was across the room busily flipping through pages.

Burt picked up his spinning where he'd left off, hands deftly working the roving as the wheel hummed. "I heard from my contact at the crime lab again. The DNA tests are final now, and the blood on the carpet and the remnant of burned purple wool are a match."

"Does it match the vagrant's DNA?" she ventured, already sure of the answer.

"Nope."

Kelly exulted inside, even though she couldn't reveal her reaction. "Told you," she whispered.

"Yeah, you did."

"What's Morrison going to do now? He has to let that guy go, doesn't he? He can't still cling to that worn-out intruder theory now, can he?"

No answer at first. Just the hum of the wheel. "Actually my former partner says Morrison is checking everything out, but the guy's staying in jail for the time being. A hearing's been set for next week, and he'd already been assigned a public defender. If there's not enough evidence, he'll be released."

"Sheeesh," Kelly complained scornfully. "Morrison cannot admit he's wrong, can he?"

"The intruder theory could still be the right one, Kelly," Burt pointed out. "Just a different intruder. It's clear someone else was in the house and left blood specks on the carpet. Who knows? Maybe that's why they took the purple wool. They were bleeding and they grabbed whatever was handy." The wheel picked up speed.

Kelly paged through the book, ostensibly reading. "I've thought the very same thing, Burt. And I think I know why there's blood on the carpet. Helen fought back. She stabbed her attacker. I'll bet that's why there was a broken needle on the floor. That's what she used to defend herself."

"Could be—"

"Finally!" Hilda boomed across the room, smothering Burt's voice. "I knew that pattern was here." She snatched the plastic page and strode toward the office.

"Isn't there any way we can light a fire under Morrison?" Kelly complained. "Every day he wastes makes it harder to find the real killer."

"Morrison's doing his job, Kelly. He's just thorough. Meanwhile, don't go poking around all by yourself anymore, okay?" Burt warned. "Otherwise Mimi will have heart failure. You really gave her a fright the other day. She won't admit it to you, but she was a basket case until Steve returned and reported you were safe and sound."

"I promise," Kelly said with a nod, spying Hilda headed her way. "We'll talk later."

"Here, you go," Hilda announced, presenting the pattern with a flourish. "And I see you've chosen a beautiful yarn. Well done, my girl."

Kelly didn't even hear Hilda's compliment. Her attention was focused on the well-tailored gentleman who now stood in the entrance to the main room. Kelly's gaze settled on the legal-sized leather portfolio in his hand, and her stomach tightened.

"Ms. Flynn, I have some wonderful news for you,"

Alan Gretsky announced, flashing his brilliant toothy grin.

"Why, hello, Mr. Gretsky," she replied. "How are you?"

Gretsky's grin got even wider if that were possible. "Fabulous, Ms. Flynn, especially now. My clients have made you a most generous offer. A most generous offer, indeed." He approached, leather portfolio in his outstretched hand.

Kelly stared at it, reluctant to accept the portfolio. She knew what was in there. A generous offer to buy Helen's cottage. Her cottage, now, but still—the cottage of memories.

Forcing herself to accept the portfolio, Kelly forced a lukewarm smile. "I bet I know what this is."

Gretsky chuckled. "Yes, I bet you do, Ms. Flynn. But I bet you'll still be surprised by the generosity of their offer. They were most sympathetic to your situation, what with the recent death of your aunt and all. So they were exceptionally generous with the purchase price. They wanted to make sure you did not share any unnecessary financial burden."

"I confess I haven't made up my mind yet," she said. "I've committed to staying here for three months. So, I'm not sure that will work with your clients' plans."

Gretsky dismissed her concerns with an expressive wave of his hand. "They're totally flexible, Ms. Flynn. Remember, they wouldn't be moving into the cottage. So, don't worry about it. You take the time you need to think it over. You'll notice the acceptance date is a month away. And if you haven't decided by then, why, I'm certain they'd be amenable to extending the date."

Brother, Kelly thought. *They want this land badly.* She turned the portfolio over in her hands. Gretsky had skillfully boxed her in. Now, she had no reason not to consider the offer. To refuse to even examine it would be financially irresponsible, her accounting voice piped up. She owed it to herself to see what kind of money Gretsky was so excited about.

"All right, Mr. Gretsky, I'll take a look," Kelly agreed. "But I can't promise you when I'll have an answer."

"That's to be expected, Ms. Flynn," he replied. "The clients are totally comfortable with that, as I said before." Glancing about, he added, "Please excuse the interruption, folks. I'll let you all get back to your business. You take care now, Ms. Flynn. Have a good day." He gave a friendly wave and left.

Kelly stared at the portfolio, then stared at the cherry parfait bundles on the table. She really wanted to sit down and start that new sweater, but she couldn't. She had to examine the contract offer. And that would take time.

She checked her watch. Brother, noon already. Even without the offer, she'd have to leave and get back to her corporate accounts this afternoon. Cherry parfait sweaters and following up Lizzie's tantalizing information about Chambers would have to wait. She glanced at Hilda, who was standing stoically, pattern in hand, and saw the sympathetic gaze meet hers.

"Well, Hilda, I guess that sweater will have to wait a while, okay?"

"Don't you worry, Kelly," Hilda reassured. "I'll have everything in a bag in Mimi's office waiting for you. Whenever all of this business is finished."

"Thanks, Hilda," she said, scooping up her belongings. Glancing over her shoulder to Burt, she smiled. "Thanks, Burt. We'll talk again later. And don't worry, I'll be too busy for a while to get into trouble."

"I'll hold you to that, Kelly," Burt called as she left.

Seventeen

"**So,** the offer's legit?" Jennifer asked as she poured Eduardo's fragrant dark coffee into Kelly's stainless steel mug.

"Yep," Kelly replied, leaning against the side of the café's outside door. Pale, early-morning sunshine filtered through the wide windows in the corner where they stood. Daylight savings time said eight o'clock, but the late-April sun was still bashful. Another month would bring the brilliance and summerlike warmth. "I searched the company name listed as the buyer, and it's authentic. It's Big Box's property acquisition division," she said, savoring the delectable aroma right beneath her nostrils. She couldn't wait another moment and took a long drink.

Jennifer scanned the nearly empty café and asked, "How generous was the offer? Burt told us Gretsky raved about his client's generosity."

"He wasn't exaggerating," Kelly admitted. "They really did offer above market price. Way above, which would allow me to pay off that horrible mortgage plus penalties and fees for early sale and still walk away with money."

"Any contingencies?"

"None. They really want this property, Jen."

"Well, if you want me to take a look at the offer, let me know. Those clauses can hide tricky things."

"Thanks, Jennifer. I'd appreciate your help." She exhaled a deep sigh. "You know, I wasn't expecting to have to deal with something like this on top of everything else that's happened. I mean, I can't really think about the offer because these murders have totally claimed my attention. Even my work is taking a back seat. The only way I'm keeping up is to work way late at night." She took another deep satisfying drink.

"No wonder you need Eduardo's coffee," Jennifer commented with a wry smile. "I'd better get you one of our spare mugs to fill up as well. Where're you off to this morning?"

Kelly glanced around to make sure no one was close enough to hear their conversation. No worries. Eduardo was noisily preparing omelets at the grill, while Pete rang up receipts across the room. The other morning waitress was serving the only customer in the café.

"I'm going to see Lawrence Chambers, Helen's lawyer," she confided. "Lizzie was a gold mine of information. She wasn't allowed to date, so she kept meticulous notes on everyone else's social life, including Helen's. And she knew who the mystery boyfriend was."

"The hunky cowboy, I hope."

"Nope. He was just the decoy so no one would notice the boy she really loved."

"Well? I'm waiting. I may get a customer in my section any minute. Hurry up," Jennifer ordered.

"It was Lawrence Chambers."

"Really? Was he hunky back then?"

"Hardly. His school photo makes him look like an earnest owl," Kelly said, unable to hide her smile.

Jennifer sighed. "Well, if Helen chose him, he must have been special. Helen was a great gal. So, why're you going to see him?"

"I'm just fishing. See what I can pry out of him. If not, then I'll see if I can get him to take a stroll down memory lane. See what happens."

Jennifer wagged her head. "There you go, again. Stirring up trouble, poking around. Burt told us you promised to behave."

Kelly fixed Jennifer with a wicked grin. "*You're* telling *me* I should behave?"

Jennifer started laughing. "Okay, okay, you got me. I won't say another word. But I'm not gonna cover for you. You can go in there and tell everyone yourself what you're up to."

Suddenly Kelly remembered something. "Whoa, thanks for mentioning that. I've got to touch base with them. I may be a little late for practice tonight. Won't know until I log on to my office site." She headed toward the shop.

Lisa and Megan were still sitting at the library table, as were some other knitters. "Hi, folks," Kelly greeted them all as she settled into a chair. "Lisa, I may be a little late for practice tonight. I won't know how heavy my workload will be till I check with my office later, okay?"

Lisa glanced up. "Yeah, but if you make it a habit, we'll beat you."

"Severely," Megan added.

"I'll remember that." Kelly let herself relax as the soft laughter rippled around the table. But as Mimi entered and sank into a chair, one look at her expression swept all humor away. Her face was ashen.

"Mimi, what's wrong?" Lisa asked.

"I've just been notified by the new landlord that the shop's lease won't be renewed this September. The property's being sold," Mimi said solemnly.

Stitches and yarns were forgotten, dropped unnoticed

to laps, as everyone stared at Mimi, clearly horrified at the announcement.

"But I thought your old landlord said that wouldn't happen," Megan protested, her pale face registering her shock at the news.

Mimi chewed her lip. "He said they 'probably' would extend the lease, but I could tell he didn't know for sure, even when he said it. That's why I've been so . . . so worried lately, wondering if this would happen."

Kelly leaned forward, wishing she had an answer. "Mimi, I'm so sorry. I know how much work you've put in here." She glanced around, feeling a little sick that strangers would soon own Helen and Jim's farmhouse. "I can't believe this is happening."

"Neither can I," one of the knitters spoke up.

"Is there any way around the lease?" the other asked.

Mimi shook her head. "No. All leases are renewed at the discretion of the landlord."

"Mimi, we'll help you look for another place, honest," Lisa offered. "And Jennifer will scour the multiple listings for you. She'll find something—"

"What will I find?" Jennifer inquired as she marched up to the table and deposited another full mug of coffee in front of Kelly.

"Thanks, Jen," Kelly said, glancing up. "Mimi's losing her lease in September. The farmhouse will be sold. You're gonna have to help her find another place."

"What!" Jennifer protested. "Who's the new landlord? How dare he throw you out. What's his name?"

"Some company called A&G Management. I've already checked the directory, and it's not listed. Who knows if they're local or out of town. Maybe they're from Denver." Mimi gave a dispirited shrug.

Jennifer frowned and stared out the wood-trimmed paneled windows. "A&G Management, A&G Management. I think I've heard that name somewhere. Let me look into it, Mimi. I'm curious." She slipped off her apron. "Listen, I"m leaving early. It's dead in there. I'm going to the office to start checking. I want to know who this A&G Management is." She turned to leave.

"Jennifer, I appreciate that, dear, but there's nothing that can change the lease. I don't want you wasting your time," Mimi said sadly.

"Don't worry, Mimi, I do this research all the time," Jennifer declared. "I'll get back to you later." With that, she was gone.

Kelly stared after her, then let her gaze drift slowly around the farmhouse that Mimi had transformed into a wonderland of color and texture. The thought of it being sold and possibly torn down made her sick to her stomach. She checked her watch and rose from the chair. If Chambers passed her scrutiny, maybe she'd ask him about Mimi's predicament. Maybe there was some legal loophole only lawyers knew.

She leaned over and patted Mimi's arm. "Mimi, I have to go ask Lawrence Chambers some questions. I'll see you later."

Kelly sped from the shop, eager to leave the pall that had settled over everyone inside.

Lawrence Chambers laced his fingers together and rested them against the polished walnut desk as he fixed Kelly with a sympathetic look. "I'm afraid Mrs. Shafer has no option but to leave at the end of August," he said. "I wish there was some legal loophole, Kelly, really, I do. I know how much that shop meant to Helen and to Mrs. Shafer."

Kelly let out a loud sigh, partly for effect. The lease discussion had established a friendly tone. Now, it was time for her to start probing. "Thank you, Mr. Chambers. I was afraid as much, but it never hurts to ask. Particularly since I have an offer to sell my property as well. I'm not sure yet what I'll do." She deliberately left it hanging.

Chambers' eyes popped wide. "Someone is offering on your house? Who is it? Do you know them, Kelly?"

"I researched the buyer name and it's the property acquisition division for Big Box." Another deep sigh. "I really don't know what to do. They've offered above-market value, which would allow me to pay off that awful loan plus penalties and fees. I confess, I'm tempted."

"Good heavens, Kelly!" Chambers leaned over his desk. "What are you hesitating for? Grab that offer and run all the way to the bank. It would provide a reasonable solution to that horrible loan problem."

Kelly surveyed Chambers. His expression radiated sincerity. Clearly, if he'd been trying to keep Helen's and Martha's land under his control, he would have registered some trace of dismay, even subtle, that the land was slipping from his control. But there was no hint of that anywhere in his expression.

"Well, I told the realtor that I was pretty busy now, and he'd have to wait on a decision. It could be over a month, I don't know."

"Well, speaking as Helen's former adviser, I'd cast my vote to accept the offer. You've had your life disrupted far too long with this whole ordeal, Kelly. It's time you returned to pick up the pieces."

Kelly pondered his answer as well as his expression and concluded his sincerity was genuine. "I'm thinking about it," she admitted, then sipped her coffee as she tried to decide how she could possibly turn her questions toward the past and his shared history with Helen. How to broach such a delicate subject? "It's hard to concentrate on anything else, Mr. Chambers. I'm still so caught up with Aunt Helen's death."

Chambers settled back into his black leather armchair, his lined face gaining even more wrinkles now. "I understand, Kelly. It's the same for me," he admitted. "I still cannot believe Helen's gone."

Surprised by his sudden honesty, Kelly observed

Chambers' somber mood. Her glance drifted to the vibrant quilted mountain scene that hung on the paneled wall beside them. An idea came suddenly, and Kelly gambled. "Was that the cabin you and Helen visited back in high school?" she asked in a quiet voice.

Chambers' face paled in an instant. His eyes grew huge. "Wha-what do you mean?"

Now he really did resemble a startled, blue-eyed owl, Kelly observed. "Martha told me that Helen and her boyfriend would escape to a mountain cabin up in the canyon all those years ago," she said, truthfully repeating Martha's piece of the puzzle. "Helen never revealed your identity, Mr. Chambers. Someone else did."

Gripping the arms of the black leather chair, Chambers stared at Kelly, rigid, clearly horrified by what he heard. "Wh-wh-who?"

"A high school classmate of Helen's who had a keen eye for people-watching. That person once saw you two together and remarked that you were obviously in love." She glanced to the quilt. "I'm guessing that's Helen's gift of shared memories and a remembrance of lost love."

Chamber's face regained some of its color, much to Kelly's relief. She didn't want to send the frail lawyer into cardiac arrest with her visit.

He gazed at the quilt, and his lower lip trembled. "She was the love of my life, my true love," he whispered. "But I was too scared of my father to stand up for her. God help me, I was such a coward. My family had my life all arranged, and my wishes meant nothing. I told Helen I'd confront my father and tell him I'd choose my own wife. Yet, every time I tried, I . . . I lost my nerve. That steely gaze of his would lock onto me and . . . and I would freeze."

His head sank to his chest. "I still remember Helen standing alone in the shadows behind the bleachers, watching my father and Charlene announce our engagement to all their friends. I'll never forget the stricken look on her face." A huge shudder shook his shoulders.

Riveted by his account of the story, Kelly now understood what had driven Helen into Curt Stackhouse's arms that night. "Was that graduation night by any chance?"

The question seemed to rouse him. "Yes, yes, it was. I remember now, we were wearing our caps and gowns."

Chambers' obvious remorse and regret tugged at Kelly. "Now I know why you took such good care of my aunt over the years," she ventured in a gentle voice. "And if it's any consolation, Mr. Chambers, Helen and Jim had a good marriage. I know because I was there growing up and visited regularly throughout my life."

He glanced down at his clasped hands. "Yes, thank God for that," he said with a sigh. "And I've tried to be a good husband to Charlene all these years. She's a good woman, and a wonderful mother. We have three grown daughters and eight grandchildren now."

That last image seemed to cheer him a bit, Kelly noticed. "Well, Mr. Chambers, you've been truly fortunate. You have a growing, healthy family. You should be thankful." Then added, pensively, "Helen and Jim weren't quite as lucky. They lost their only child when he was only five years old, and they couldn't have any more, Helen told me. They sort of adopted me as their daughter, especially after my own father died."

Chambers nodded. "I know how much Helen loved you, Kelly. Truly like her daughter."

Kelly felt another tug within. "Well, I felt the same way. She was the closest thing to a mother I ever knew. I don't know if Helen ever told you, but my mother walked out on my dad and me when I was a baby, so Helen was really important in my life."

"Yes, she told me."

Feeling old memories encroach, Kelly swiftly changed the subject. Now that Chambers was composed again, Kelly wanted to explore a theory that had recently surfaced in her mind. Deciding it might be easier if she wasn't looking directly at him, she glanced to the quilted mountain cabin and wondered how to probe yet another delicate subject. Once again, she jumped in.

"I'm sure Helen regretted giving up the baby years ago, especially since she and Uncle Jim couldn't have any more children. Helen had never hinted at the child's existence. As close as we were, she never let on. It was Martha who told me. Forgive me for stirring up these old memories, Mr. Chambers, but I thought you might have some information about the man. He's in his late forties now. And I've wondered if he was the reason Helen withdrew all that money."

She took a deep breath and continued, still focusing on the quilt. "Perhaps, he found out his real mother's identity. Adopted children do that, I've heard. And maybe he appeared suddenly and said something to frighten Helen. I don't know. Maybe she didn't want to have any contact with him. I do know she was worried those last few days, because she wasn't herself when I spoke—"

The rest of Kelly's explanation died on her lips at the sight of Chambers. This time he really looked like he might have a heart attack. His face was pasty white, nearly gray, and his hand clutched at his chest.

"Mr. Chambers, are you all right?" Kelly cried as she sprang from her chair. "Should I call a doctor? Is it your heart?"

Chambers stared ahead, eyes glazed, for an excruciating moment, before he whispered, "A child . . . she never told me . . . my God . . ."

Kelly sank back into her chair, amazed that Chambers didn't know and feeling guilty that she'd dropped the dramatic bombshell so abruptly. "I thought you knew," she ventured when she saw Chambers revive once again. "I mean, I assumed . . ." Her voice trailed off, realizing again how foolish assumptions could be. And how misleading.

"When . . . where . . ." he struggled.

"Helen's father sent her to Wyoming and Martha's family the summer after graduation. Martha said the baby was born in December. December eleventh, I believe."

Chambers stared, stricken, so Kelly continued. "Apparently Helen stayed throughout the holidays with Martha's family and the baby, then gave him up for adoption to the Sisters of Charity in Cheyenne. She came home to Fort Connor in early winter, I think." Seeing the guilt shimmer in Chambers' eyes, she drew another breath and reached for whatever reassurance she could find. "Helen met Jim that spring, and they were married the following fall. So, she started a new life, too, just like you, Mr. Chambers," she offered gently.

Tears welled in Chambers' eyes and splashed down his cheeks, as if a hidden dam deep inside had broken at last. "Oh, dear God, what did I do . . . ?" he cried, a sob catching in his throat. "Oh, Helen, Helen . . . forgive me . . ." He sank his head in his hands and wept. "I abandoned you and the child . . . forgive me . . . forgive me . . ."

Kelly sat, unable to move, wishing she had not been the one to cause such distress. Maybe her friends were right. She shouldn't be poking around in other people's lives.

Nothing, no amount of questions, could bring Helen back alive. Or Martha. She had mucked about for more than two weeks, intruding herself in other people's business and their personal lives, and she still wasn't any closer to discovering the killer's identity than she was when she started. Burt was right. Morrison would look into everything and find the truth. Surely, he would. She should stay out of it.

Chambers' sobs rose and fell now, the voice of lamentation. Kelly's heart squeezed. She had to leave. Chambers' grief was too raw and real to be witnessed. She quietly rose from her chair and slipped from the office. Once outside, Kelly took a small notepad from the secretary's desk and wrote her apology for causing him such pain. She folded the sheet and gave it to his puzzled secretary with instructions that Mr. Chambers was not to be disturbed.

Eighteen

Kelly dropped her tote bag on the floor of the middle room, then carefully set her empty coffee mug beside it on the polished wooden floor. She'd indulge in her morning ritual of Eduardo's coffee in a few moments. Right now, Kelly wanted to feel. Needed to feel. Touch. Sink her hands into the softness that spilled from every corner of the room.

She started with the round maple table in the center, its rich burnished wood peeking through the colorful bundles that covered the surface. Kelly sank both hands into a bin of silk and cotton yarns, luxuriating in the softness. Next, she fingered the gorgeous long-sleeved crimson sweater that appeared on display yesterday.

Silk and cotton or was it that special cotton she was hearing about? Whatever it was, it was beautiful, she thought, wondering if she'd ever get good enough to attempt sleeves like those. They were bordered at the wrist with a knitted ruffled effect. *How on earth did they do that?* she wondered.

One step at a time as Lisa would say, Kelly reminded herself, then let her hands disappear into a crate of boa yarns—frothy, softer-than-soft, and bold primary colors. They knitted up into flirty, sassy accent scarves she had seen flung over shoulders of old and young alike.

The coffee craving gene began to protest the delay of its morning caffeine rush. Kelly reluctantly left the tactile paradise and grabbed her things. She'd drop her stuff at the table, get a fill-up with Eduardo's blessing, then she'd be ready to apologize to her friends for all the worry her recent activities had caused them. *Mea culpa*s all around.

Last night's softball practice had helped release some of Kelly's frustration. With each throw, each swing of the bat, she let go. Afterward, she'd used work as an excuse to skip the get-together and gone home to a soak in the tub. Her corporate accounts had consumed the afternoon. Late night was hers.

She turned the corner into the main room and was surprised to see Jennifer talking excitedly to Mimi. Megan sat wide-eyed across the table, her knitting in her lap, which was a sure sign Megan was engrossed in the subject.

"Hey, guys, what's up?" Kelly asked, plopping her things on the library table.

Jennifer whipped around, amazing Kelly again how fast she could move if she wanted to. If only she could throw a ball. "Kelly, I discovered who A&G Management is," Jennifer announced. "You'll never guess."

"I'm sure I won't. Who is it?"

"None other than Alan Gretsky. He formed the company last year, and apparently that's when he began meeting with this Big Box associate. I heard from another agent in his office that Gretsky met this guy socially. Some connection with his wife's family in Denver or something. Anyway, he's been wining and dining this guy, hoping to work into a deal where he can score big. And this is it."

"Whoa . . ."

"Yeah, my thoughts exactly. Now you know why he wants the cottage. He needs both parcels to make this deal work. Big Box won't want one without the other."

"Mimi, when did A&G buy out your landlord?" Kelly probed. Mimi stood at the end of the table, her hands clasping a cone of novelty yarn. Her expression a mixture of uncertainty and confusion, with worry thrown in for good measure.

"I'm already ahead of you," Jennifer cut in, grabbing a legal-sized document from the table. "April fifteenth, just a week ago."

Kelly caught up with Jennifer. "So, no surprise that my offer appears this week. Once Gretsky had this parcel under control, Big Box could offer on the cottage."

"Exactly. He's probably already drawn up the contract to sell this parcel to Big Box, and he's just waiting for you."

Kelly frowned, picturing Gretsky and his big friendly grin. "Of course, he knew that I wouldn't want to stay once I learned the shop was leaving. He figures all he has to do is wait. Wait until I leave. Son of a . . . sailor."

Jennifer chortled. "What was that again?"

"One of my dad's sanitized navy curses." Kelly threw up both hands. "Coffee. I need coffee. Right now. Brain cells are shutting down, and I need to think about this."

Once again, Jennifer jumped into action. "Hold everything, I'll be right back." She snatched Kelly's mug and was gone in a flash.

Kelly stared after her, remarking, "Wow, look at that speed. If only we could teach her to throw. What do you think, Megan?"

Megan grinned, picking up her pink cotton blend again. "We could teach her to throw."

"And batting? You think?"

"Probably, but that's not the problem. It's the base running. Jen would never make it around because she'd stop to flirt at each base," Megan said with a wink.

At that moment, Jennifer slid into home, depositing Kelly's mug and her own on the table without spilling a drop.

"Impressive," Kelly observed. "We're thinking of offering you a spot on the team."

"Thanks, but no thanks. I don't like to stand in the sun and sweat."

Even Mimi smiled at that. Kelly picked up her mug, inhaled Eduardo's nectar, and drank deep. Once, twice, thrice, to the sound of soft laughter.

"Okaaaaay," Kelly said, sinking into a chair. "Alan Gretsky, A&G Management. Who doe this guy think he is? Buying up land under one name, hiding identities—"

"It happens, Kelly," Jennifer declared. "Especially when there's a lot of money involved. And my friend from his office told me Gretsky's really hungry. Seems he's been trying to run with the top dogs and always falling behind. He's missed out on some important deals the past few years, consequently he's been particularly anxious to score big so he can get in the 'club,' so to speak."

"There's a club?" Megan jibed.

"Yeah, and a secret handshake, probably," Jennifer said with a laugh. Checking her watch, she added, "Listen, I have to get back to the café. We're swamped this morning. Feast or famine, you know. I'll try to stop by after work. See ya." She raced off.

Mimi sat on the edge of a chair, still clutching the fat colorful cone of novelty yarn. "Mr. Gretsky didn't do anything wrong, Kelly," she said in a quiet voice. "I know you want to help, dear, but there's really nothing you can do. A&G is a legitimate company, and it bought this property. It's all totally legal. Don't worry about me. I'll find another place."

Kelly scowled into her mug. That may be true, she mused, but that wasn't the point. Gretsky thought he could outsmart them. Kelly, however, prided herself on not being outsmarted. And thanks to her good instincts, she seldom was. This time would not be the exception, she vowed, as an idea swam through the caffeine to the surface.

"I know that, Mimi," she said. "But I don't like Gretsky trying to force us both out. He has control of your place, yes. But he doesn't have mine."

"Uh oh, I see that look on your face," Megan warned.

"Don't worry," Kelly warned. "I'm not going to do anything crazy. Or anything I'd need a Rottweiler for, either." She grinned. "I'm just going to see if I can shake up Gretsky."

"Oh, no . . ." Mimi whispered, clearly horrified.

"It's okay, Mimi, honest," Kelly explained, waving her hand. "I'm simply going to tell him that I've changed my mind, and I'm staying in Fort Connor for good. So, I won't be selling the cottage, after all." Kelly felt the idea resonate inside her with a surprising intensity.

"Why?" Megan queried.

"I'm hoping my announced change of plans will throw a wrench into Big Box's plan and they'll pull out of the deal. Then, if Gretsky's dreams of development riches go down the drain, maybe he'll change his mind about leasing."

"Boy, that's a stretch," Megan observed.

"Yeah, I know, but it's all I've got. So, I'm gonna run with it." With that, Kelly jumped out of her chair and grabbed her tote bag. "See you folks later," she called over her shoulder as she headed for the door, leaving Megan and Mimi staring after her.

"Caffeine rush," Megan decreed.

"Lord, I hope so," Mimi breathed.

METROPOLITAN REALTY proclaimed the large stainless steel letters on the wall behind the receptionist's desk. Kelly had already switched her demeanor when she pushed through the glass doors. She deliberately hesitated in front of the enclosed area, waiting for the receptionist to speak first.

"May I help you?" the attractive young blonde asked.

"Yes, please," Kelly answered in a breathy voice. "Is Mr. Gretsky here? I spoke with him last week about selling my house."

The young woman's face brightened. Sold houses meant paychecks. "Let me check with his assistant, Laura." She quickly dialed a number and waited. "Laura? One of Alan's clients is out front. Is Alan here? Ohhhh, all right." She hung up the phone. "Laura will be right with you if you care to wait." She indicated some plush leather armchairs and sofas in warm caramel and chocolate tones in the corner of the lobby.

"Thank you," Kelly replied politely, then spied a tall, thin woman hurrying down a corridor, headed her way.

"I'm Laura, Mr. Gretsky's assistant, may I help you?" she asked. Wisps of graying hair had escaped from the neat bun and feathered around her face, softening the lines and wrinkles.

"Well, I was hoping to speak with Mr. Gretsky," Kelly said, feigning a worried look. "I'm Kelly Flynn, and we spoke earlier this week about selling my home, and I—"

"Why don't we go to Alan's office, Kelly. It's more comfortable there," Laura suggested, gesturing to the corridor.

She ushered Kelly into a spacious office with huge windows overlooking tall cottonwoods bordering one of Fort Connor's waterways that crisscrossed the city. Called ditches by old-timers and canals by the newbies, they were a reminder of the city's early agricultural history.

"Please sit, Ms. Flynn, and I'll get your file." Laura settled across the room at an antique secretary's desk, which had obviously been restored with great care because the mahogany shone rich and golden.

Kelly settled into a rust-colored leather chair, relaxing into its comfortable embrace. Gretsky might not be running with the big dogs yet, but he knew which signals to send. Both his wardrobe and his office décor spoke volumes. Admiring his huge antique polished wood desk, she couldn't resist asking, "Mahogany? Walnut?" and glanced to Laura.

Laura smiled as she sorted through the files on her desk. "Walnut. Eighteen eighty, I believe."

"My compliments. It's beautiful."

"Here it is," Laura declared, opening a file folder. She scanned the contents for a moment. "Your property hasn't been listed for sale, has it, Ms. Flynn?"

"Uhhhh, no, not yet," Kelly demurred. "In fact, this is all so sudden, I . . . I really need to speak with Mr. Gretsky. You see, I told him I would need time to think, but then things have been happening, and . . . oh, gracious!" Kelly made an exasperated gesture. "Everything's changed suddenly. When's he coming back? I have to leave in a few—"

"He's out with clients right now, showing property. But he should return—" The ringing phone stopped her midsentence. She reached over, punched speakerphone, then went back to paging through the file. "Alan Gretsky's office. May I help you?"

"Yes, this is Main Street Frame Shop," a woman's high voice announced. "Is Mr. Gretsky there?"

"Not at the moment. I'm his assistant. May I take a message?"

"Yes, of course. Please tell him that the family quilt he brought in last month is all framed and ready for him to pick up. It'll be three hundred and forty-seven dollars. Tell him to ask for Sandy. I'm the one in charge of framing."

Laura started scribbling on a nearby notepad. Kelly, meanwhile, had perked up at the mention of the words "family quilt." Her buzzer went off inside.

"Sandy, I'll make sure to tell him. How late are you open?" Laura asked, continuing to scribble.

"Until five, oh and be sure to tell him it looks absolutely beautiful," Sandy's voice oozed pride. "We were very careful with the little fabric pieces that were sewn into the middle of all the squares, and the embroidery, too. Oh yes, and that tiny lock of baby hair. Simply precious. We were extremely careful. That's why it took so long to frame."

"I'll be sure to tell him," Laura promised. "Bye." She clicked off.

Kelly watched Laura examine the file's paperwork but didn't see her. All she could picture was Helen's quilt hanging on the cottage wall, each square filled with treasured pieces of Helen's early needlework, embroidery, crocheting, even tatting. And—in one square, a tiny lock of blond hair from their young son who died.

Her heart pounded so hard, Kelly was afraid Laura might hear it. That was Helen's quilt Gretsky took to the frame shop last month. And there was only one way he could have gotten it off her wall. He killed her. Gretsky was the murderer. He had to be.

Kelly fairly leaped from her chair. "Ohhh, my goodness, will you look at the time," she announced as she checked her watch. "I have got to get back to work. Consulting hours, you know. Have to be online when my boss is. Listen, you tell Mr. Gretsky I'll give him a call later and we can set a time to talk."

"I'm certain Alan will call any minute now, and I'll have him give you—"

Kelly waved no. "No, no, when I go online I don't even pick up my phone. I'll call him." Spying the open card holder, she snatched one of Gretsky's business cards. "I'll take his card to make sure I've got the number. Thanks so much. You have a good day, now," she said as she escaped through the doorway before Laura could say a word.

Speeding through the lobby and out the glass door,

Kelly headed for her car—then on to Fort Connor's Old Town and the Main Street Frame Shop. With Gretsky's card in hand, she could pass herself off as his assistant, sent to pick up the family quilt for her boss. Having overheard the phone message, she already knew to ask for Sandy. Kelly would gladly pay $347 to have Helen's treasured heirloom quilt back in the cottage where it belonged. She would deal with Gretsky later.

Nineteen

Spying her friends' cars parked outside, Kelly raced up the brick walkway to the knitting shop's entrance. She patted the key in her pocket. Now that Helen's quilt was back on the wall safe and sound, Kelly wasn't taking any chances. She'd locked both front and back doors. Heart still racing, she fairly burst through the shop's doorway and rushed into the main room to find Jennifer, Megan, and Lisa knitting around the table. Burt looked up from his spinning in the corner.

"Kelly!" Lisa greeted her. "Jennifer told me about—"

Kelly silenced her with a finger to her lips, then announced in a hushed voice, "I'm glad you're all here. We've got to talk." She pulled out a chair closer to Burt and gestured for the others to move to that end of the table.

"Well?" Jennifer prodded when they settled. "We're waiting. Megan told us where you went. What'd Gretsky say?"

"He wasn't there. I spoke with his assistant instead."

"And?" Jennifer gestured. "C'mon, Kelly, keep talking. Do you want me to run back to the café and see if Eduardo saved some coffee?"

"No, I don't need any coffee. I'm wired enough as it is."

"Uh, oh, this is gonna be bad, I can tell." Megan screwed up her face.

"While I was in his office talking to his assistant, this call comes in. She puts it on speakerphone, and the message is from a frame shop in Old Town. The family quilt Gretsky brought in last month is ready, the woman says. The quilt with all the little needlework and embroidery pieces in the middle of the squares and the lock of baby hair." Kelly paused deliberately to let the message sink in.

Lisa and Jennifer stared intently as did Burt, but Megan drew back with a gasp. "Helen's quilt!" she cried. "How did he get it?"

Kelly leaned over the table and the others followed suit. Even Burt's wheel stopped spinning. "The only way he could. Gretsky murdered Helen. He's the killer."

"What? That's crazy!" Megan cried. "You can't seriously believe he'd kill Helen for a quilt."

"No, of course not. I think he took the quilt after he killed her," Kelly explained. "I think—"

"Wait a minute, wait a minute," Lisa exclaimed. "Are you sure it's the same quilt?"

"Yes. I took one of Gretsky's cards and went to the shop. Passed myself off as his assistant picking up the quilt for my boss. It's Helen's all right, and it's hanging back on the cottage wall where it belongs."

"Clever girl," Burt observed. "But you're a long way from proving his guilt, you know that, don't you? Gretsky could always say Helen sold it to him before she died, and you couldn't prove differently."

"I know," she said, nodding. "But my gut tells me he's the killer. Now we have to prove it."

"Hold on," Jennifer interrupted this time. "Why do you think he killed Helen? What reason would he have?"

Kelly glanced toward the browsing customers. "I believe he's Helen's illegitimate son, the baby she gave up for adoption years ago. And I'll bet anything he discovered Helen was his birth mother and tried to force himself into her life. Especially after he discovered she owned a prized piece of real estate."

"Hmmmm," Jennifer mused aloud. "That makes sense. But it still doesn't explain why he'd kill her."

"I'll bet he tried to weasel the land out of Helen," Lisa jumped in. "And Helen didn't like it. In fact, I'll bet she didn't like him. Helen never did like pushy people."

"Yeah, you're right," Megan agreed. "But, still, that's not enough reason to kill."

"Look, I'm not sure what happened," Kelly continued. "Maybe Gretsky tried to intimidate Helen or threaten to expose her past or whatever. But something happened to worry Helen so much she deliberately took out a top-heavy mortgage in order to withdraw $20,000. And I'll bet next month's salary that money was meant for Gretsky."

"For what?" Megan queried.

"To leave her alone," Jennifer supplied.

"And Gretsky wouldn't do it," Kelly picked up the thread. "Plus, I'll bet she also refused to sell her property. Chambers said Helen called before she died and told him she wanted to change her will. She wanted the land to be turned into gardens if I didn't want it."

"When did she call him?" Lisa asked.

"The day she was killed."

"Whoa."

"You know, you're right," Jennifer said with a nod. "That could have pushed Gretsky to the limit, especially if he'd made promises to Big Box."

"Absolutely," Kelly agreed. "I'll bet he'd been making plans the moment he discovered his birth mother's identity. And when she didn't cooperate, he killed her. Maybe in anger, who knows?"

"All of that is possible, Kelly, but you still have to prove it," Burt reminded. "How do you propose doing that?"

"We'll have to trap him," she said simply.

"Trap him!" Megan croaked. "Are you kidding? How do we do that?"

"With information, that's how," Kelly whispered. "First, we'll dig up everything we can on Gretsky. Then, we'll figure out how best to confront him with it."

"That'll be harder than you think, Kelly," Burt observed sagely. "I should know. I spent a lifetime doing it."

"I think you've been watching too many of those movies," Lisa said with a little smile. "But count me in. What do you want me to do?"

Kelly hunched closer. "I thought we'd each search something different. Megan, how about you doing a Web search on everything you can find on Gretsky. Google him, whatever."

"Will do," she said. "I've got even better sources than that."

"Megan 'Deep Throat' Smith," Jennifer joked. "Okay, I'll not be outdone by our resident geek. I'll turn over every real estate rock I can find and see if there's any dirt on him. Also, I'll check on his financial status. I've got friends who can help me there."

Burt leaned over. "And I'll ask my partner to run a discreet check on Gretsky."

"Boy, I wish we had a blood sample from Gretsky, then we could match it with the blood from the carpet—" Kelly said.

"Is it an unusual blood type?" Lisa interrupted. "If so, I have a friend who works at the hospital blood bank."

"Type O was found on the carpet and the wool. Same type as the suspect in jail," Burt offered.

"And nearly half the population," Lisa added with a shrug.

"But," Burt continued, "the crime lab also did DNA tests, and they show absolutely no match with the suspect."

"That's okay, Lisa," Kelly said. "You can check if he's a member of the health club or if he had a personal trainer. People gossip with trainers." She looked around at her friends. "Boy, I don't know what I'd do without you guys."

"We just don't want you working alone," Jennifer teased. "What are *you* checking?"

"I'm going to look into that Wyoming adoption agency, the Sisters of Charity. I'll also check if there're any state agencies that keep records on adoptees looking for birth parents." She looked at her watch. "It's almost evening now. Why don't we touch base tomorrow afternoon after lunch and see what we've turned up. Is that possible? Can we all meet here?"

They all nodded. Then Megan spoke up. "Who's gonna tell Mimi? Anyone brave enough?"

"I will," Burt volunteered.

"Bless you, Burt," Kelly said and kissed his cheek. "See you folks tomorrow."

Mimi was rearranging the antique trunks and wooden crates in the foyer when Kelly pushed open the shop's front door. She fairly pounced on Kelly when she entered.

"Kelly, what's this I hear about your trying to trap this vicious murderer?" she croaked in a whisper, so the customers browsing in the adjacent room wouldn't hear. Her gray eyes were as round as demitasse saucers.

"Shhhhh," Kelly reminded, finger to lips. She didn't have to wonder if Mimi was worried. She radiated anxiety, reeked with it. Kelly took a deep breath and endeavored to calm her. "Don't worry, Mimi. We're all working on this together. I'm not going off alone to confront anyone. Even Burt's helping."

Mimi's attractive face puckered into a worried frown. "I know, he told me. But I still don't understand why you can't just let the police handle it. After all, you've found new evidence—"

"Which is entirely circumstantial, Mimi. Nothing I've uncovered proves anything. Gretsky's been too clever for that. We're hoping to confront him and maybe he'll slip and let out the truth."

Mimi stared horrified. "How?"

"We're still working on that," Kelly hedged as she headed for the main room. "But don't worry, Mimi. No one's doing anything crazy. I promise."

Everyone but Lisa was already seated around the library table as Kelly entered. Even Burt was in his corner, spinning, a large plastic bag at his feet overflowing with golden-blond wool. Kelly was reminded of the fairy tales from childhood. Damsels spilling golden hair from castle windows, witches casting spells on maidens, dwarves spinning straw into gold. She had to smile at the image of Burt beside a basket of straw.

"Hey, everyone," she greeted them, then let her things drop to the table and sat down. "When's Lisa coming? Anyone know?"

"Right now," Lisa's voice sounded as she sped into the room.

Jennifer looked up from her knitting and checked her watch. "Whoa, that's the fastest you've ever been able to get away from the health center. What'd you do? Put all your clients in the therapy pool and leave?"

Lisa grinned. "Naw, they'd turn into prunes before I got back. I merely switched some appointments with another therapist so I'd be freed up." She plopped into a chair.

Megan glanced up over her pink wool, which had grown considerably since yesterday. If Megan knitted when she was worried, she'd have that sweater finished tonight, Kelly figured. "Did you see Mimi pacing the foyer?"

"Ohhhh, yeah," Kelly said. "I tried to calm her down."

"Don't worry about it, Kelly. She's simply being a mom. You gals are family to her, you know," Burt said over the relaxing hum of the wheel as his fingers worked the roving.

"Okay, folks," Kelly said, retrieving a spiral notebook from her tote bag. "Now that we're all here, let's see what we've got." Glancing over her shoulders at the browsing customers wandering about, she added, "And remember to keep it down. We don't want to alarm the locals."

"I'll start," Burt said, letting the wheel slow to a stop. "The subject's record is clean. Only minor traffic offenses. Speeding. Parking fines. No scrapes with the law. No complaints from neighbors. Belongs to the country club, various professional organizations, community, philanthropic, etc., etc. The usual. Nothing suspicious whatsoever."

Kelly made notes as Burt spoke. "Okay, I might as well go next," she volunteered. "I turned up nothing useful. The Wyoming agency, Sisters of Charity, no longer handles adoptions, and the Church Diocese was absolutely no help. All they said was they 'think' the adoption records are still in sealed boxes in the Diocese basement, but they're not sure. And even if they were available, only the parties immediately involved would have access. Like the mother or the child. Also, my search for state agencies ran into a brick wall. Privacy rights and all that restrict access." She gave a sigh. "So, I turned up nothing."

"Well, I guess things really do come in three's, because I came up empty, too," Lisa remarked as she flipped open her water bottle and took a drink. "No record of Gre—" She caught herself. "Of the subject ever giving blood. At the hospital or at the Red Cross. So, nothing there. Also, he's not a member of the health club. I even asked some of the freelance trainers if they knew him, and no luck there, either."

"Well, I had *very* good luck," Megan crowed discreetly and leaned over the table. "I found biographical info from when he was a speaker at a real estate convention. He's married twenty-three years, has two teenagers, was born and raised in Cheyenne, Wyoming, and his birth date matches exactly. December 11, 1955. He went to the University of Wyoming and moved to Colorado twenty years ago. I even found an interview he gave to a business magazine where he mentions that he was *adopted*." Megan's eyes danced with obvious delight at her discoveries.

"Whoa, great job, Megan!" Kelly congratulated her and scribbled the information on her notebook.

"A-*hem*," Jennifer spoke up. "Megan's not the only one who hit pay dirt. I discovered that Gretsky's been trying to recover from some bad real estate deals that went sour during the last couple of years. He puts on a good show, but it's just that. Expensive tailoring, all flash and sizzle, but no steak. According to my source, who knows everything there is to know about every realtor in this town, Gretsky is hanging on by his fingernails, hoping for a break. And he's depending on the Big Box deal to rescue him from financial disaster."

Kelly sat quietly, absorbing what Jennifer said. Reason enough to kill in her book. "Great job, Jennifer," she said. "That sounds like the key to Gretsky. Threat of financial collapse. I'd say that's motive enough for murder." She stared through the window outside. "We can use that to push him into confessing."

"Whoa, Kelly, hold the phone," Burt said, spinning wheel picking up speed. "Don't get ahead of yourself. Do you actually think a smooth operator like Gretsky is simply going to confess if you start asking him questions?"

"No, of course not," Kelly admitted, then leaned over the table even more. "I've been thinking about this since last night. And asking questions isn't going to get us anywhere. So I don't plan to ask." She gave an enigmatic smile.

"What are you going to do, then?" Lisa probed.

"I'll let him do his realtor spiel, then I plan to go on the attack. Confront him. Shake him up. Accuse him. I want to wipe that phony smile off his face and make him mad."

"Are . . . are you sure that's a good idea?" Megan ventured.

Kelly nodded. "Remember, I'm not alone with him. You guys will be situated in adjoining rooms in case he threatens me."

"Except for me," Burt declared. "I'm staying in this corner."

Kelly shook her head. "Sorry, Burt. He'll clam up if he sees another man in the shop. I sense it. You can go into the spinning room right there," she pointed to the corner room, jutting off the main area. "You can even fix a mirror on the shelves so you can keep an eye on us if you want."

Burt scowled, clearly unhappy he wasn't closer, but acquiesced. "Okay, but only if I can rig up a mirror. I want to make sure this guy doesn't try something."

Megan's eyes grew huge. "Oh my gosh! Burt, do you think he'd try to hurt Kelly? I've got a bad feeling about this whole thing."

"I'd like to see him try," Kelly challenged.

"Don't worry, Megan, I'll come prepared," Burt reassured.

"Whoa, this is getting more serious than I thought," Lisa observed. "When are you planning on setting this up, Kelly?"

"I'm going to call Gretsky this afternoon and ask him to meet me here early tomorrow morning, say eight o'clock. That way, we'll avoid having customers in the shop."

"Hey, wait a minute," Jennifer spoke up. "We'll still have customers because the restaurant opens at six thirty

A.M., so people will be here. How do you want to handle them?"

"I figured we could use those wooden screens Mimi uses to close off sections of the shop for classes. We could block off access going to the classroom area and the weaving room. So, your job, Jennifer, would be to make sure none of the café customers slips through into the shop, okay?"

"Gotcha. I can do that." Jennifer nodded.

"Megan and Lisa, why don't you two sit at the end of the classroom by the windows, so you can see but are too far away to hear our conversation." Kelly pointed, indicating the adjacent room. "Sit and knit and talk normally. I want Gretsky to feel totally comfortable. I'm going to be sitting at this end of the table alone when he arrives. He can join me here."

"Where are you going to put Mimi?" Megan asked.

"We'll make her stay in her office. And you and Lisa will have to make sure she doesn't peek out, okay?"

"Sounds like a plan," Lisa agreed. "What time do you want us here tomorrow?"

"Why don't we all get here a little after seven, okay?" Kelly glanced around and watched her friends nod in agreement. "I'm going to call Gretsky right now and tell him he has to come at eight o'clock tomorrow morning if he wants to talk to me about selling my property. He's got one chance."

"He'll be here," Jennifer concurred.

"And so will we," Burt added, gray eyebrows knotting.

Kelly caught Jennifer's eye and smiled. "Better tell Eduardo to make an extra pot of coffee tomorrow morning. We're going to need it."

Twenty

Kelly stroked the gathered bunches of mohair that draped along the wall beside the bookshelves of the main room. She tried not to pace, but it was impossible. So, she'd stop every few steps and squeeze a tempting yarn, caress a silky sweater, or fondle a frothy shawl.

Glancing over her shoulder, she observed Lisa and Megan doing the same. They were all too keyed up to sit down. Only Burt seemed calm, as the sound of his spinning wheel hummed steadily from the corner room. Craning her neck, Kelly spied the mirror Burt had discreetly wedged between the wools. Sure enough, she saw Burt spinning away, hands methodically working the roving into strands to feed the hungry wheel.

Jennifer's voice sounded behind her. "I think we have a visitor," she said, glancing toward the windows. "Here comes a black Lexus, and it's one minute to eight. He's right on time. Good luck." She sped through the middle room and was gone.

"Okay, folks, black Lexus at eight o'clock. It must be

him," Kelly announced and headed for her spot at the end of the library table. The morning sun felt good as she picked up her practice piece and needles, pretending to knit.

The door jangled as it opened, and Gretsky's voice sounded, "Hello? Ms. Flynn, are you there?"

"In here, Mr. Gretsky," Kelly called out. "The main room with the fireplace, to your left." Her heart speeded up its already fast pace.

Gretsky appeared in the archway and gave Kelly a dazzling grin before he approached. It was all she could do not to gag. He was dressed as if he were about to be named realtor of the year, she noticed, mentally adding the wardrobe's likely cost.

"Ah, Ms. Flynn, how good to see you again." He glanced about. "I didn't think the shop opened this early."

"It doesn't. We're here to help Mimi start sorting and packing. She has to leave this location. Apparently the new landlord doesn't want to rent. They want to sell." Kelly kept her attention on moving her needles through already-completed stitches, hoping Gretsky wouldn't notice that she was knitting nothing—thanks to Hilda.

"Oh, that's a shame," he replied in a sympathetic tone as he sat in the closest chair. "She's had this shop for several years, hasn't she?"

Smarmy bastard. We're going to nail you to the wall. She took a deep breath. "Yes, it's really sad."

"I gather you had time to examine the purchase offer, Ms. Flynn. May I call you Kelly? I like to be on first names with people."

Kelly gritted her teeth. "Please do."

He leaned back into the chair and withdrew a small notepad and fountain pen from his breast pocket. A Mont Blanc, no doubt. "I'm sure you had time to consider the generous nature of my clients' offer, Kelly. You can rid yourself of that high-rate mortgage with the proceeds and leave here with money to spare. I know you'll be glad to get on with your life."

Kelly couldn't listen to another word. She set her pretend knitting aside and fixed Gretsky with a glare. Using her coldest corporate voice, she asked, "Why didn't you just take the twenty thousand dollars and leave Helen alone? Why'd you kill her? Did she refuse to sell her property? Was that it? What drove you to murder your own mother?"

Gretsky went white in an instant. He opened his mouth but no words came out. He stared at Kelly with huge blue eyes. Helen's eyes, Kelly realized in that same instant. So that's why she'd liked him at first. He has Helen's eyes. Son of a . . . even her dad's full-blown navy curses wouldn't do justice now.

She leaned forward defiantly. "Did she threaten to tell her lawyer, Lawrence Chambers, about you? He told me she called him the day she died and said she was coming in to change her will. She wanted the property to become gardens for the city if I didn't want it. Helen did that because of you, didn't she, Gretsky? Because you were threatening her, pushing her—"

Gretsky sprang from his chair, face flushed with rage now. "What madness are you spouting, woman? Are you insane? Accusing me of . . . of *murder!* How dare you?"

Flushed with her own sense of righteous indignation, Kelly sprang from her chair and faced off with him, toe to toe.

"How are you going to explain having Helen's heirloom quilt in your possession when her will states it belongs to me?" Kelly pointed toward the cottage. "It's back on my wall where it belongs, Gretsky. But the woman in the frame shop will be glad to testify that you brought it in the day after Helen's murder. Your name's on the invoice. How are you going to explain that?"

Gretsky's lips twitched. "I . . . I bought it from her. When I went to see her about her property . . . several weeks ago. I admired it and she sold it to me." His features composed themselves once again as he glared at Kelly.

Kelly crossed her arms in front of her. "Sure you did. How much did you pay for it? Did you pay in cash? Did you write a check? If what you're saying is true, then there'll be proof. A paper trail, Gretsky. Even if you paid with a wad of cash you carry around in your pocket, Helen would have deposited any money given to her. I should know. I kept her accounts. And there would be a record of it."

His eyes darkened as they narrowed. "I don't know what you're talking about."

"Just like there'll be a record of the twenty thousand dollars you took from the house that night," she kept on pressing. "There's proof Helen had all twenty thousand in cash that night, yet not one bill was found. The vagrant in jail didn't have a dime on him when arrested. Police found nothing. That's because you had it. And unless you stuffed all twenty thousand in your mattress, there'll be a paper trail of that, too, Gretsky. Even if you tried to send it offshore, we can find it."

"You are truly insane, Ms. Flynn, and I'm not continuing this conversation a moment longer." He turned on the heel of his expensive Italian loafers, but Kelly's reflexes were quicker. She kicked over his chair, startling Gretsky long enough so she could run in front of him, blocking his escape.

"Do you know what I do for a living, Gretsky? I'm a corporate CPA. That means I know how to tie your finances into so many knots you won't be able to access your assets for years. Do you have enough cash reserve to support yourself and your family for two or three years until this case comes to trial? Of course you don't. I know how precarious your financial situation is right now. That's why you were so desperate to do this deal with Big

Box. But Helen was in the way, wasn't she? That's why you killed her."

Gretsky's color began to fade again, and his mouth twitched. "I don't know what you're talking about. I'm going to talk to my lawyer right now and bring charges against you, Ms. Flynn. For defamation of character and slander. You should be committed."

Kelly didn't miss a beat. "While you're at it, ask him how much it costs to defend against a civil suit. Because that's what I'm going to ask Lawrence Chambers to bring. We may not have enough to force the police to bring a criminal case against you, Gretsky, but civil court is a whole different ballgame. All we need is a preponderance of evidence to prove wrongful death in Helen's case. That's easier for a jury to decide. A majority is all that's needed."

She watched fear flash across Gretsky's pale face, then was gone. He was on the brink. All she had to do was push him a little more. Kelly closed in on him, right up to his face, deliberately challenging. "What happened that night? You were already on the edge. What pushed you over?" she prodded.

An ugly sneer twisted Gretsky's mouth, and Kelly had no doubt she was the focus of his rage. "You conniving bitch," he hissed as he raised his hand to strike.

Kelly didn't flinch. "Careful, Gretsky, I don't go down as easily as Helen."

Different emotions played across his face now, Kelly noticed. The rage was gone, but fear had taken its place. Gretsky dropped his hand. "I'm getting out of here. I'm going to see my lawyer." He turned and headed for the foyer.

Kelly spotted Burt slipping through the weaving room, obviously heading for the foyer the back way. She had to stop Gretsky from leaving. Shake him up to slow him down. She'd used everything she had, and he still stonewalled. There was only one thing left, and it might not work. Kelly gambled and threw the dice anyway.

"Is that bandage on your hand from where Helen stabbed you? There was a broken knitting needle lying beside her body. She defended herself the only way she could. It must have been a deep wound, because it bled a lot."

Gretsky's step slowed, and he paused near the doorway.

"You tried to wipe up the blood with the purple wool, didn't you?" Kelly continued, slowly walking up behind him. "Blood specks were found on the carpet. Police did DNA tests and have the results now. They don't match Helen or the jailed suspect. That's because it's your blood, isn't it, Gretsky?"

This time Gretsky paused at the doorway, and his hand reached out to a nearby crate filled with canary-yellow yarn. He appeared to brace himself as his head bent forward. Kelly sensed he was balancing on the edge, but the ground was crumbling beneath his feet.

She gave the last nudge. "If you're innocent, you'll want to prove it, won't you? That's easy. Just give police a blood sample, and this will all be over."

Something inside collapsed, and Gretsky seemed to fold in on himself. He leaned against the doorway to the foyer. Burt appeared behind him and stepped forward, slipping his arm beneath Gretsky's, holding him up.

"Why don't you sit down and get this off your chest, Mr. Gretsky," Burt suggested gently, as he guided him back to the main room. "Tell us what happened. I'm sure you didn't mean to do it. What went wrong that night?"

Kelly picked up the fallen chair, and Burt guided Gretsky straight to it. He sank into the chair and leaned his head back, eyes closed. Kelly spied Megan and Lisa edge around the library table, and Jennifer peeked from the classroom.

Burt caught Lisa's attention and made a telephone sign

with his hand. Lisa stealthily retreated to the classroom
once more, calling the police, Kelly figured.

Gretsky heaved a huge sigh, more a shudder than a
sigh. "It wasn't supposed to be like this . . ." he whispered
at last. "She should have sold me the land. It was so
easy . . . why didn't she? None of this would have happened. Oh, God . . ." He bent forward and sank his face
into his hand.

Kelly waited for the sound of weeping, but it didn't
come. Instead a bitter, rancorous voice emanated, full of
rage and pain. "Why? Damn it, why? I've tried so hard.
Done everything that they did. Wined and dined the same
people, boozed and kissed ass, and still the deals didn't
come. Why? I did everything they did. Looked the same,
talked the same. Never good enough. Always falling
short. Never quite measuring up. Smug bastards. Keeping
me out."

Not sure who the "smug bastards" were, but Kelly
guessed he meant the top dogs, the real estate elite. Burt
sat in the chair beside him and leaned forward. "But you
had a deal with Big Box, didn't you?" he ventured in a
friendly tone. "That was worth something. I'll bet it made
those smug bastards take notice, right?"

Gretsky's hands dropped from his face, and he stared at
the floor. "Yeah, it did. They even let me into the club for
a few days. But they were scheming behind my back to
steal my client. I could tell. Thought they were better able
to handle the deal," he sneered.

"But you showed them, didn't you? You found the perfect piece of land," Burt offered.

"Oh, yeah," Gretsky said, staring at the bookshelves
now. "And just when I was about to lose the client." He
nodded, obviously remembering. "This letter comes from
the adoption researcher I'd hired the year before. And
would you believe my very own mother lived in the same
town? And even better, she sat on one of the choicest commercial parcels around."

"Wow, that was lucky," Burt said admiringly. Kelly watched his approach in fascination. Big, likeable, kind-faced Burt was a relentless interviewer. "So you got the landlord on this one to sell first, right?"

"Yeah, I needed that as the anchor. Once I got his commitment, I knew Big Box was in the bag." His face darkened. "But she refused to cooperate. After all those weeks of visits and phone calls and presents, she refused to sell. Even when I told her that I'd gone into debt to finance this deal with the developer. She still refused. I couldn't believe it. How could a mother refuse her only son?"

Kelly stared at Gretsky in growing disgust. It was obvious that he'd been so self-absorbed for so long he couldn't fathom any response other than his own.

"What'd you do then?" Burt prodded.

"I was desperate. I tried one last time. I came over late one night and told her she was ruining my career and my family's life. I mean, without that deal, I was going down the drain. The recession had wiped all my savings. I had nothing left and was in debt up to my ears trying to make this deal go through."

He stared at the windows for a long moment, saying nothing. Burt prodded once more. "Then what happened?"

Gretsky took a deep breath. "I'll never forget . . . she was sitting in that chair she liked, knitting. And she announces real calmlike that she was going to the lawyer and changing her will so the property would become gardens for the city if her niece didn't want it. She'd never sell it to me. Then, she pointed to an envelope on the desk and said there was twenty thousand dollars. That I should take it and leave. She never wanted to see me again. Claimed I didn't want a mother, just a meal ticket."

He closed his eyes, and his voice began to tremble. "Something inside snapped. Her rejection was one too many. My own mother . . ." His breath caught. "The next thing I knew, my hands were on her throat, choking her. I can't remember how long. I don't even remember her stabbing me. Just saw the blood on my hand . . ." His voice trailed off.

Kelly stared, appalled at the confession but feeling a huge weight lift off her shoulders in that same moment.

Burt leaned closer and whispered, "What about Martha, Helen's cousin in Landport? What happened there?"

Gretsky lifted his head slowly, as if it weighed a lot more than usual. "I was afraid Helen had talked to her about me. I couldn't take that chance . . ."

"How'd you find out about her? She kept to herself."

"I overheard them talking . . . I came to tell her about my clients." He pointed to Kelly.

Kelly's heart sank, as all those carefully hidden accusations and fears came creeping from the bushes where they'd been lying in wait. Ready to pounce. She knew it. She *was* responsible for Martha's death.

"And this big woman," Gretsky's hands jerked out in an attempt to gesture. "Was talking at the top of her voice. Hell, I didn't even have to eavesdrop. I could hear her all the way to the door . . . talking about Helen's cousin."

Kelly's breath caught. Hilda. It was Hilda talking that day in the shop. Gretsky'd overheard and was waiting in his car for Kelly that afternoon when she left. He talked about his clients' offer. Then he waited and followed her. Bastard.

"How'd you find her?" Burt probed softly.

He shrugged, shoulders drooping despite the expensive tailoring. "I kept an eye on her." Pointing to Kelly again, "Figured she'd pay a visit sometime."

"Smart."

"Yeah, I thought so." Then his toned, tanned face started to sag just like his shoulders, as if the realization of what he'd done was working its way through his body. He closed his eyes and whispered, "God help me . . ."

Burt slipped his arm under Gretsky's once again and

helped him to his feet this time. "Let's get you downtown, Mr. Gretsky. You'll want to call your lawyer. A squad car is outside now."

Gretsky looked up, perplexed. "So soon?"

"Yes sir. Don't worry, I'll go with you," Burt promised and led him to the foyer and out the door.

Kelly stood watching, amazed at what they'd witnessed. Lisa and Megan and Jennifer gathered around. "That was unbelievable, wasn't it?" Kelly said.

"Thank God, it's over," breathed Megan. Jennifer and Lisa nodded, not saying a word.

Kelly stared out the windows. The morning sunlight shimmered on the dew-glistened greens. "I . . . I need some time to think. Let all of this sink in." Glancing toward the sunlight slicing through the skylights, she suddenly pictured Helen sitting on the patio, knitting. Sunshine. She wanted sunshine. Now. "I'm going to sit out on the patio for a while."

"We understand, Kelly," Lisa said and squeezed Kelly's arm. "We'll be inside."

Kelly turned to her friends. "Actually, I'd love to have you join me, if you want to."

"You bet we will," Jennifer said. "Let me go tell Pete."

"Don't forget Mimi," Kelly added with a grin. "She's still in her office waiting for the all-clear."

With that, Kelly headed outside into the Colorado sunshine, her friends following after.

Kelly's First Scarf

Use two skeins or balls of colorful chunky wool yarn (like Rowan Biggy Print, for example), which gives 5½ stitches to 10 cm/4 inches with US size 35 or 36 needles (19–20mm).

Cast on 10 stitches and knit entire scarf in garter stitch using both balls of yarn. Bind off and tuck ends.

Lambspun's Whodunnit Shell
Very Easy Knit with Bulky Yarn

Sizes:	Small	Medium	Large	XLarge	XXLarge
Bust:	40	44	46	50	52
Length:	17	18	18.5	19	19.5

GAUGE: 2 sts/in

MATERIALS: US size 15 needles (or size to obtain gauge), 14-inch straight
Very bulky yarn with gauge of 2 sts per inch

INSTRUCTIONS:

BACK: With yarn required for gauge, CO 40, 44, 46, 50, 52 sts. Work in garter stitch, (knit every row) or if you like an edge that rolls, work in stockinette (knit one row, purl one row) throughout garment. Continue in garter or stockinette until piece measures 8, 8.5, 9, 9, 9

inches or desired length to armhole At armhole edges
BO 3 sts once, 2 sts once, 1st once. Work on remaining
28, 32, 34, 38, 40 sts until piece measures 14.5, 15,
15.5, 16, 16.5 inches.

NECK SHAPING: Work 11, 12, 12, 14, 15 sts. Join second ball
of yarn and bind off center 6, 8, 10, 10, 10 sts. Work remaining sts, turn. Working both sides at once, bind off
1 sts from the neck edge 3 times. Continue working on
reaming sts until piece measures 17, 18, 18.5, 19, 19.5
inches. Place remaining 8, 9, 9, 11, 12 sts on holders.

FRONT: CO 39, 43, 45, 49, 51 sts. Work in garter stitch, (knit
every row) or if you like an edge that rolls, work in
stockinette (knit one row, purl one row) throughout
garment. Continue in garter or stockinette until piece
measures 8, 8.5, 9, 9, 9 inches or desired length to armhole. At armhole edges BO 3 sts once, 2 sts once, 1st
once. Work on remaining 28, 32, 34, 38, 40 sts until
piece measures 14.5, 15, 15.5, 16, 16.5 inches.

NECK SHAPING: Same as for back.

FINISHING: Join shoulders with three-needle bind off. Single
crochet around every edge. Hand seam sides together.

Pattern courtesy of Lambspun of Colorado, Fort Collins, Colorado.

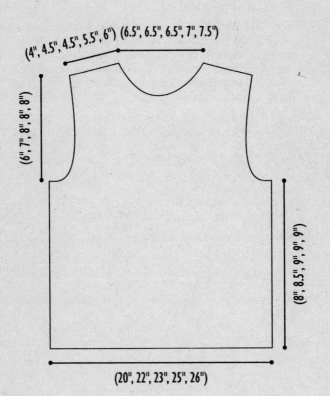

(4", 4.5", 4.5", 5.5", 6") (6.5", 6.5", 6.5", 7", 7.5")

(6", 7", 8", 8", 8")

(8", 8.5", 9", 9", 9")

(20", 22", 23", 25", 26")

Maggie's Cinnamon Rolls

DOUGH:
  3½–4 cups of all-purpose flour
  1 package active dry yeast
  1 cup whole milk
  1/3 cup butter
  1/3 cup sugar
  1/2 teaspoon salt
  1 egg, beaten

FILLING:
  2 tablespoons melted butter
  1 cup packed dark brown sugar
  3 teaspoons ground cinnamon

LEMON CREAM CHEESE FROSTING:
  4 ounces cream cheese, softened
  2 tablespoons butter, softened
  1 tablespoon lemon juice
  2 cups confectioners' sugar

OPTIONAL:
  1/2 cup walnuts, pecans, or raisins

Stir together the yeast and 1½ cups of flour in large mixing bowl and set aside. In a saucepan over medium-low heat, combine milk, butter, and sugar. Add salt and beat till warm and butter is melted. Slowly add to flour mixture with beaten egg, stirring until well blended. Beat batter for 2 minutes, then stir in as much remaining flour as possible. Place dough on lightly floured surface and knead until smooth and elastic (5 minutes). Shape dough into a ball and place in a lightly greased bowl, turning once.

Then cover and let rise in a warm place until doubled (about 1½ hours).

Make frosting. Combine softened cream cheese and butter. Stir until light and fluffy. Add lemon juice. Beat in confectioners' sugar gradually until well blended and smooth. If needed, add half-and-half until desired consistency. Set aside.

After dough has doubled, punch down the dough and turn onto a lightly floured surface. Cover and let rest 10 minutes. Grease a cookie sheet or large baking pan(s) and set aside. Roll dough into a 10 x 18 inch rectangle. Spread with melted butter. Stir together dark brown sugar and cinnamon and sprinkle over dough. Add nuts or raisins if desired. Tightly roll up dough from the long side. Pinch and seal ends. Cut dough into 1-inch sections and place on prepared baking sheet or pan. Cover and let rise until doubled (40–60 minutes). Brush rolls with melted butter. Bake in 350° oven for 25 to 30 minutes* until golden brown. Remove rolls to wire rack and frost while still warm. Makes approximately 12 rolls.

*Baking tip: For best results, please adjust baking time and temperature accordingly.

Now Available in Hardcover

Dyer Consequences

A KNITTING MYSTERY

by Maggie Sefton

Kelly Flynn is eager to renovate the alpaca ranch she's just bought, but someone else has different ideas for keeping her busy. As disturbing incidents continue to pile up, Kelly knows she must try to pick up the stitches of these crimes before a killer strikes again.

Praise for
the Knitting Mysteries:

"Cozy up with a great new author."
—Laura Childs, author of *The Silver Needle Murder*

"A darn good series with vivid, breathing characters."
—*Mystery Scene*

"A terrific series with a heroine who grows more and more likable with each investigation."
—*The Mystery Reader*

penguin.com

From acclaimed author

PIERS ANTHONY

"Piers Anthony is always entertaining."
—*Rave Reviews*

Virtual Mode

Fractal Mode

Chaos Mode

The Apprentice Adept series:

Phaze Doubt

Unicorn Point

Robot Adept

Out of Phaze

M23AS0907